A Quandry at Knowles Corner

By

Randall Probert

A Quandry at Knowles Corner

by Randall Probert

www.randallprobertbooks.net

email: randentr@megalink.net

Cover Illustration by
Ed Palmer
Rumford, Maine

Second Edition

ISBN: 978-0-9852872-6-9

Printed in the United States of America

Published by
Randall Enterprises
P.O. Box 862
Bethel, Maine 04217

A Quandry at Knowles Corner

INTRODUCTION

1808

"Damn it, Bill, I told you we would be pushing our luck! We're out here a month too early. We should have waited until June!" Gus was angry and scared. Another bolt of lightning just ahead of them, spraying sea water over the deck.

"I know it's early, Gus." Bill was having a difficult time trying to keep their fishing schooner (The Judi Ann, named after his wife) heading into the wind. "I know we're a month early. But if we get to the fishing grounds in Passamaquoddy Bay before the other fisherman discover the sea trout are already running, we'll fill our holds and be on our way home and we'll still be able to return for a second hauling before the run stops. One load will pay all expenses for this year. Then everything else we catch will be pure profit."

"Yeah, damn you! We may never make the trip through Manan Channel, let alone get to the fishing grounds! The wind has picked up and the waves are bigger and coming at us with a faster rhythm! I'm glad you agreed to bring along a larger life boat. We may need it." Just then Bill's face turned ashen. The rain was coming in harder, as was the wind. Bill could see a huge wave coming at them about three-hundred yards ahead.

"Gus!" Bill hollered. "We had better take in the mainsail and ride this wind out! If we don't, the wind will snap the mast."

Bill tied the wheel off so the schooner would stay into the wind, while he and Gus pulled the mainsail in and secured it.

"You might as well go below Gus. No sense in both of us drowning. I'll hold the wheel into the wind."

"What if the wind, or a rogue wave blows you overboard? No, I'll stay."

They both watched in horrified wonder as that huge wave picked the bow of the schooner up. They were now on a thirty degree incline on the leading edge of an angry wave. Just as both Bill and Gus thought they were about to go over backwards, they crested the wave and were pitched sharply into the trough, as the bow plunged through the next wave. The two brothers looked at each other with worried expressions, fully realizing now the predicament they were in.

Below decks were filling with water. The hatch covers had rattled loose and were blown overboard. Bill and Gus stood posed at the wheel…knowing what their future was about to dole out. They stood motionless in silence, waiting for the next rogue wave that would in all likelihood capsize them. They didn't have long to wait. Another huge rogue wave was just ahead. "We'll probably go over when this one hits us, Gus. Hang onto the ship at all costs!" The water was still too cold to survive for more than a couple of hours, but unless they held onto something, life would be over in a heartbeat.

The wave was now only fifty feet away, "Gus, get in the lifeboat!" Bill said this with such sternness Gus didn't hesitate or argue. Bill was behind him. "Cut the ropes!" Bill hollered over the roar of the wind. Just then the bow started to rise even higher than before. This time when the schooner crested the wave and pitched forward into the trough, the bow didn't regain its buoyancy. The bow plunged down towards the ocean floor and the two brothers were set adrift in their life boat. They huddled together in the bottom of the boat to keep the center of gravity as low as possible. Perhaps, just perhaps, they'd be able to ride out the storm. But where would they be when it was finally over?

An hour had passed, which in reality seemed more like an entire day, but Bill noticed that the wind was beginning to change directions, as they were being buffeted more in circular motions. "The wind is coming from the West now," Bill said. "Hopefully it'll blow us close to Grand Manan Island."

"What's on the island?" Gus asked.

"Nothing, only it is a better place to be than here. The only approach available with bigger boats is from the east side of the island. Not many stop there. No reason too, actually."

"Were you there once?" Gus asked.

"Yes, two years ago, when I was fishing with Dave Henry. We had to stop and make repairs to the sails before continuing on to the Bay of Fundy. The island is mainly rock."

An hour and a half after being set adrift in the life boat, the storm had passed and there was now only a gentle breeze from the west.

"Look!" Gus said excitedly. "There's the island. Maybe we don't die today, brother." They both began to laugh. They were not out of trouble yet, far from it actually, but they had endured the storm and soon they would be standing on solid ground.

"It'll be good to get a fire kindled and dry out before the cold settles in tonight."

The boat finally ran aground about fifty yards off shore in amongst a field of submerged boulders. Bill and Gus stepped into the cold water, slipped and fell. Finally they were able to drag the boat ashore and they lay exhausted in the sand. "Come on, Gus, we have to drag this above high tide and get a fire going before we freeze to death."

Once the boat was secured, they quickly found enough dry material to start a fire. Gus had stored away sulfur matches in one of the survival kits in the boat. Soon, they were sitting with their backs against a rock warming themselves and drying their clothing. The wind had changed directions again. It was now blowing from the East, not strong, but enough to make Bill and Gus feel fortunate that they had made it to the island. The smoke from the fire was being blown out to sea.

"Are you hungry, Bill?" Gus asked, still leaning back against the rock.

"Yeah, but I'm too tired to eat right now. Maybe in the morning. I'm just too exhausted now to do anything except lie here."

If they were going to stay warm, then they would need more wood. Lots of it. There was plenty of driftwood all along the shore line and soon there was enough piled in front of the fire to last for several nights. Gus put several pieces of wood on the fire and then sat back down, leaning against the rock. Bill was almost asleep already. Neither wanted to think about how they were going to get home. No one there would be expecting them for three weeks. How long could they survive on this rocky island? Surely there weren't enough animals for food for very long. Again, neither of them wanted to worry about that right now. So they were silent and slowly drifted off to sleep.

* * * *

They awoke the next day before the break of dawn. The fire had burned out and they were now cold. Gus stirred the ashes and awakened some hot coals. Bill already had some dry kindling ready. The flames were soon blazing high and the two leaned back against a rock, but neither were very interested in sleep. They were in a dilemma and they knew it. Gus opened his mouth to say something and then thought better of it. There was no sense in blaming his brother for wanting to get ahead of the other fishermen. Instead of finding blame, they had to find some how to get home. Bill was thinking similar thoughts, except he was blaming himself for the situation they were in.

When dawn came over the Eastern horizon the sun rose with all its splendid brilliance. The ocean was calm—not like a mirror—only a little chop with easy rolling swells. "This would be a nice day to fish," Bill said and then they both laughed. "Come on let's see what we have in the survival kit."

The only food was hard tack filled with bacon fat and sugar. Enough for four days and water enough for several days. There was an axe, a few square yards of canvas cloth, a few sulfur matches, a compass, some rope and some fish line, for hand-lining. There was one tea kettle for boiling water, but no tea or coffee. "I guess we drink hot water with our hard tack," Gus said.

When breakfast was finished Bill banked the coals in the fire with burned ashes and any wood still burning he threw into the water. "Let's see if we can find any fresh water and what this island has to offer for food."

Inland, away from the shore, the vegetation was not as sparse. Here, tall jackpine trees grew, alder and scrawny white birch and a maze of low growing bushes. They found an abundance of rabbits, fox and woodchucks. No larger animals at all, not even tracks. Gus found a cool bubbling spring. "Well, we have fresh water and if we can snare some of these rabbits we'll have meat with our hard tack and for the trip home."

"Just how do you propose we get home?" Gus asked.

"We find a straight tree for a mast and we fashion a sail from the canvas cloth in the boat. Of course, it'll be a small sail."

"And what do we use for a boat? Not the life boat! A mild wind will topple it. Then we'll be worse off than we are now."

"Then we make out-riggers for it. One on either side. That should keep the boat upright," Bill said.

From the spring they started making their way through tangles of alders and bushes to the height of land. The sun was hot and they had to stop several times to rest before reaching the summit. Once at the top, they stopped and looked behind them. Hoping they would see the faint outline of the coast of the territory of Maine. But the coast was too, too far away.

"It's a long way across there, brother," Gus wasn't as sure as Bill was about getting home. "I hope you know what you're doing."

Bill turned to look out across the Atlantic Ocean. He shielded his eyes from the sun's glare with his hand. "Gus! Gus, holy shit Gus, there's a sail on the horizon. A mighty big sail, too."

Gus was looking now, "It's getting bigger. It must be coming this way. It looks like a big four-master ship." They stood there in silence watching the massive sails approach.

"We don't have any sulfur matches with us, do we?"

"No, I put them back in the kit box where they'll be dry. And no rifle. Those went down with the fishing boat."

"Well, all we can do now is wait. Remember we do have the life boat, so we aren't marooned here indefinitely," Bill added.

"She's flying a flag but I can't make it out yet. She sure is a big'n."

"Looks like a British man-of-war. But what is it doing here patrolling this close to the American coast?"

"You thinking that ship shouldn't be this close to the United States?" Gus asked.

"Yeah, a ship like that shouldn't be here. I mean the Brits were very upset about losing the Revolutionary War. I have to ask, why she is patrolling this close? You know this island, Grand Manan, is in British control. I'm not so sure now, Gus, whether we want to be rescued by that ship or not."

"Well, what do you propose we do? Sit here?" Gus asked.

"I think maybe we should sit tight and wait. See what happens."

They were both silent then. Their attention riveted on the British man-of-war. It was coming directly towards the island. "What do you suppose she is up to?"

"I don't know, Gus. But I'm glad now our little boat is on the other side of this island. I don't think we will want to be seen by them."

The crew were beginning to furl some of the sails. But the ship was still on a direct course for this part of the island. They were not making much noise. Maybe they didn't want to be observed by any unnecessary individuals. But what were they doing?

There was only one sail left now. Probably the mainsail. But little by little, the ship kept coming closer. Then when the ship was about one thousand feet from shore, the last sail was furled and the man-of-war drifted silently, ever so slowly towards the island. Almost as if some body onboard knew the two brothers were marooned there and were coming to offer their assistance. Still there was no noise coming from this great war ship. The men were all mute. The only sound was the sea gulls flying overhead.

The ship finally laid anchor about four hundred feet out. Bill nudged Gus and said softly, "Let's work our way down to that rise above the sandy shore. That's probably where they'll come ashore if that is their intention."

"Why do you want to get that close to them, if you are afraid to be rescued by them?" Gus asked.

"I want to know what they are doing." And he began to crawl on his stomach through the bushes. "You can stay here if you'd rather."

"I'm coming with you, brother," Gus said and began to follow Bill through the bushes.

The ship was just sitting there in dead silence. There was no movement on board. Only the gentle rolling of the swells, making an occasional squeak of some rigging.

"Look at that. Here they come, four of them," Bill said as they watched four men lower a shore boat to the water and then get in. Two men were rowing while one stood guard at the bow and the fourth manned the tiller. "Something of great importance is in that chest. I think we should lay right here and see what they are going to do," Bill said as he tried to lay flat on the ground. Gus was already trying to burrow like a woodchuck.

"The one in the bow is the captain. The one in the stern with the tiller is a mate, and I'm not sure about the two who are rowing, probably crew by the way they are dressed. The other two have distinguishing uniforms. Limeys sure and sure. Look at that pure arrogance of the captain. Whatever they are doing, it is no good."

The boat ran aground before reaching shore and instead of the captain stepping out and pulling the boat up to the shore line, he arrogantly stood in the bow while the two rowers got out and pulled the boat up to the sandy shore. Then he stepped out onto dry sand, and then the mate.

"Don't just stand there you bloody fools! Pull that boat up and heave to on that chest. Now get to it," the captain ordered.

"You sure about this, Captain?" the mate asked.

"Bos'n, you and Pete dig a hole at the base of that ledge, ten meters from that green tree there," and the Captain pointed to a jackpine tree. The Captain ignored the mate's question.

"Captain, aren't we taking a great risk leaving this here… for who knows how long? You aren't sure when the Ministry of the Royal Navy will start this fight to subdue the Colonist Navy and their pathetic merchant fleet. It could be years, Captain."

Captain Holigard looked sternly at his first mate, Brian Jolly. His chin was set like iron. "No matter how long it takes, the fight will be worth it. His Royal Majesty was thoroughly embarrassed having to surrender to George Washington and his pitiful army. If it had not been for France's intervention, England would still have our flag flying over the colonies. This time we'll take the fight to the seas where we already outnumber their pitiful man-of-war ships. This time we'll show these criminals how true gentlemen fight. Or my name is not Captain Horace Holigard. During their uprising they call the Revolutionary War, instead of fighting like gentlemen out in the open, they hid behind trees and stone walls and sniped at our men. There was nothing at all honorable, fighting like that; fighting like savages, they were.

"I lost two brothers; one fighting on a battleship and the other was wounded early in Massachusetts and died in prison from infection from his wound. No sir, Mate, this time we'll make them pay and in the end, England will once and for all times control the seas and with these pious colonies back under our control, England will be the greatest country in the world.

"If I had my way I would start the attack today, before they have a chance to reinforce their navy.

"And when we do defeat these criminals, then and only then will we come back to this island and retrieve this chest. I intend to set myself up as Governor in the south, where it is warm. There's enough gold and gems here to allow us both to live comfortably."

"Captain, you realize, I'm sure you do, that what we are doing is robbery. We liberated this fortune from that Spanish Galleon and rightfully this belongs to His Majesty. If anyone was to know, we would be strung up by the yard-arm." The First Mate was nervous.

"I am aware of these details, Mr. Jolly, and without witnesses?" Captain Holigard looked at the two who were digging. The meaning was obvious.

Bill and Gus looked at each other. What Captain Holigard had said was alarming. Could this be true? Was England planning to engage the United States in another war? Bill chewed on the idea. He hated to think about it. He hated the English for all of their pompousness and beguiling arrogance. He wouldn't be at all surprised that after the two finished burying the chest that the Captain would shoot the two and leave their bodies to rot.

"If I had a rifle I'd shoot those two bastards right here," Bill said.

The Bos'n stopped digging and said, "Captain, Captain Holigard, we have dug as far as we can. There is ledge all about down here. What do you want for us to do Captain?"

"That'll have to be deep enough. Set the chest in the hole, then pile rocks on top of it before covering everything with sand."

"Aye, aye, Captain."

The Captain watched as the Bos'n and Pete lowered the chest into the hole and piled rocks on top and then covered everything with sand and then brushed the surface clean. When the two had finished, without warning, the Captain drew out his pistols and shot them both in the back of their heads. Bill and Gus watched all this and now were sick to their stomachs.

"Captain! Why did you do that? How are we going to explain this to the rest of the crew?" Jolly was thinking he would be shot next.

With a smirk on his face, the Captain replied, "Actually these two died two weeks ago of malaria and we buried them at sea. You can check the log book if you'd wish. It is all there. You see Mr. Jolly, by the time we return to Liverpool, everyone, excepting you and I, will have died of that terrible disease and all of them had to be buried at sea. You see, Mr. Jolly, no witnesses. Then after we defeat these colonies we'll be free to return to this dreaded little island and retrieve our spoils. Then we sail to Charleston Harbor in South Carolina and if I have to, I can afford to buy my way to the governorship; and you by my side as aide, of course, Mr. Jolly.

"Now, Mr. Jolly, drag these two decrepit chaps to the water's edge and let the crabs feed on them."

Jolly did as he was told; fearing a bullet in the back of his head.

Bill couldn't believe what he and his brother had discovered and witnessed. He knew he would have to get word of this to Washington somehow...the threat of England waging war, not about what was inside of that chest. That would be spoils for he and Gus.

The Captain and Mr. Jolly climbed back aboard their landing boat and they soon were on their way back to the ship. It was getting dark, but Bill and Gus lay quietly in the bushes, fearing their least movements be discovered by someone on board with a telescope glass. "Come on, Bill, what are we waiting for? Let's get back to our boat on the other side of this island."

"Not yet. I intend to have the gold and gems that are in that chest. If only to defy that bastard. And when we get back home, I intend to send a letter to President Jefferson about the Limeys intention of controlling the seas and retaking possession of America. With that treasure, brother, we won't have to fish any longer."

"Yeah, if'n we live to spend it."

"We'll sit tight right here, as long as that ship is anchored out there. When she's gone and out of sight we can haul that chest back to our boat and begin to build outriggers and a sail.

Once Captain Holigard is gone, it'll be a pretty safe bet he won't return here until after the fighting is over. By then, brother, we'll be long gone with his spoils. The arrogant bastard."

* * * *

It was long after dark before the ship pulled anchor and left. Probably waiting for the outgoing tide. "It looks as if they are finally leaving," Bill said.

"The Captain and Mr. Jolly probably killed the rest of the crew during this wait."

"No, I don't think the Captain will do that until they are much closer to home. He'll need the extra hands to sail her. I would like to have had stolen the Captain's log book and send it back to his Majesty with an explanation."

Bill and Gus could rest easy now and stretch their cramped bodies. It was dark, too dark to attempt to dig up the chest. They would have to wait until morning for daylight. They found the ledge and sat down on the sand and leaned back against it. They each were too excited to sleep; sitting on top a wealth of riches.

When daylight finally came Gus asked, "How are we going to dig this out Bill? We don't have any shovels."

"Let's look along the shore. There must be some flat wood we can use to dig with." They walked by the two dead bodies. Crabs were already eating away the faces. Bill and Gus both turned away in disgust.

They didn't have any trouble finding what they needed. Once they came to the rocks the rest was easy. Gus pulled the chest out of the hole and broke away the lock and lifted the top. In the early morning light, the sun made the gold come alive as it glittered on the gold coins. Gus ran his hands through the coins, letting them slide through his fingers. Bill picked one coin up and turned it over and over, examining it.

"It's gold alright. But we'll never be able to sell any of it as coin."

15

"What do you mean, Bill? Gold is gold in any shape or form."

"Yeah, but look what is stamped on each coin." Gus picked one up then, turning it over and over.

"I guess Captain Holigard wasn't lying about stealing from a Spanish galleon. Someone has stamped the word Spain into every piece. It wouldn't be long before the Captain discovered us, if we were to sell any of it like this."

"Then what do we do with it?" Gus asked.

"We smelt some. A little at a time as we need it. Pour it into sand and make our own nuggets and dust. It'll be more work that way, but safer for us."

The gems or uncut stones were on the bottom of the chest. There were several different gems. Bill was only sure of one; the diamond. There was another that he thought might be yellow sapphire but he wasn't sure. The uncut gems would have to be sold probably in New York. But they would worry about that later. "Close the lid, Gus. We have a long hike, carrying this chest back to the life boat and I'm hungry. Let's get started."

The chest had been made with handles on both sides so this made carrying it a little easier. "If we had something water tight, I'd like to leave Captain Holigard a thank you note," Gus said as they picked up the chest and began their hike back to the other side of the island.

When they reached the height of land they put the chest down for a rest. "Probably most of this gold and gems came from South America, wouldn't you say, Bill?"

"That would be my guess. And Holigard probably came across the Spanish galleon somewhere in the Caribbean. He probably killed all on board and sank the ship."

By the time they had gotten back to their lifeboat, it was in the middle of the afternoon. They were hungry, but first they needed a drink of water and rest. "While I get us some fish to eat tonight along with the hardtack, why don't you see about setting some rabbit snares."

Gus set six snares and the next morning he had four rabbits. Bill had had as equally good luck fishing. He found an abundance of clams and two small lobsters and he caught one mackerel, hand-lining. After eating that morning, the two went to work building two outriggers and a mast and sails. First though, they had to find some driftwood that had washed ashore. There was plenty of that around, but Bill was particular. He selected the best pieces he and Gus could find. By the end of that day, the outriggers were in place and secured to the boat.

The next day they worked on building the sails and mast. "We'll put a small foresail at the bow and a mainsail in the middle of the boat. We are going to need more of that pine root for lashings. I'll give you a hand with that Gus...'cause I'll need help with the sails and mast. Once the boat is finished, we'll have to try it out, of course, then we'll have to put together enough food for the trip home. That'll take us several days in this small boat I'm afraid. One good thing about it though."

"What is that brother?" Gus asked.

"We'll be riding low in the water." Gus just grunted.

*   *   *   *

They were two more days finishing the sails and mast. The two took the little sail boat out for a trial run and it was working perfectly. Although it looked cumbersome and awkward with the two outriggers and short sails, the little boat actually performed better than Bill had anticipated. If anything, it was a little slow, but they would have to endure. He was pleased.

While Gus snared rabbits and smoked the meat, Bill found some clay and made extra jugs for carrying water. These had to be baked in the fire to harden. He also searched the shoreline for more crabs, lobsters and clams. He also caught many fish hand-lining.

Ten days after the boat was finished, Bill and Gus agreed they had enough food and water cached onboard to make the trip. "I want to wait a few more days, Gus, until the full moon passes. I think we'll find better weather if we do."

* * * *

The full moon came and passed and Bill waited two more days before setting sail. It was early June. "We should be home before the middle of the month."

"I surely hope so," Gus replied.

The two brothers loaded everything they had into the boat. There wasn't much room. They each had just enough to sit down. They would have to nap sitting up and hope they wouldn't fall overboard. They pushed the boat through the shallow and then climbed in. Gus set the foresail and although there was only a slight breeze, the sail filled out and the boat was moving. Bill set the main sail and now they were moving even faster. Bill estimated about ten miles an hour. "With a stronger wind we might be home sooner than we thought."

"I just as soon not have the wind blow too hard. I'm not sure how much this little boat could handle without dumping us. This speed is just fine with me," Gus said.

Bill checked his compass. He wanted to navigate a course straight across the channel before turning south and following the coast line.

They had plenty of food, enough water if they rationed it every day. But what worried the two the most was a storm or a strong wind that could capsize them. Away from the island the sea became a little rougher. The swells were higher and in the small sail boat the effects were much more noticeable. But they stayed on course all day without any difficulty. The full moon was waning, but still bright enough for Bill to see his compass and know they were still on course.

Long after the sun had set and the wind had died down some, Gus could see a tree line ahead of them that had to be on a ridge above the shore. "Bill! Look at that, we made it across the channel. See that line of trees?" Bill could hear the excitement in his brother's voice. He changed his compass heading more southerly following the coast. If they should lose sight of the coast during the night, all they had to do was steer a little more west and Bill knew he would pick up the coast line again. If a storm did come in suddenly now, they were close enough to the shore, so they could hold up while the storm passed.

During the afternoon of the fourth day a storm did blow in and they had to turn towards shore and look for shelter. "I have been thinking, Gus, about Captain Holigard. When the Limeys start their war against the United States, they will ultimately lose. But that won't stop Holigard and Jolly from trying to find who took their treasure chest. We can no longer live anywhere near the coast. If rumors were to leak out that we had some gold, I'm sure the two would investigate."

"What have you in mind, brother?" Gus asked.

"We go inland and away from the coast and away from any settlement. There's new land opening up, up north. I think we should go to the Aroostook Country with our families. And I think we should go as soon as possible, so we can get settled in before winter. There is something else also, Gus."

"What is that?"

"That we do not under any circumstances tell anyone about this chest. Not even our wives or father. Because if Holigard and Jolly ever discovered who took their treasure, they would kill us all. The same as he did his own crew."

"Agreed. I was tired of fishing anyhow. We will become trappers and gentlemen prospectors," Gus laughed. "That's a big wilderness up there."

"That would be a good idea. That way we could sell off a little at a time, without raising any suspicions."

* * * *

The storm blew itself out over night, but the wind was still too strong for their light boat and it was blowing from the south which would have made sailing very difficult, particularly in this boat. So they waited another day for the wind to change.

On the third morning the sky was clear and the sea was calm and the wind coming from the north. It was a good wind and they made excellent time. Three days later they were at the mouth of Penobscot Bay. "One more day and we'll be home," Bill said, trying to cheer Gus up.

They kept sailing as long as there was enough light for Bill to see his compass. But by 10 p.m. they had to stop for the night. "It is too dark to try going any further tonight, Bill. We need to pull over to an island."

This close to home neither of them slept much at all. By first light they were back in the boat with the sails unfurled and set. That morning they met three other fishing boats heading out, probably for the sea trout run at the mouth of the St. John River. Bill steered a wide berth around them, not wanting anyone to recognize who they were, or see into the boat and ask questions about the chest.

About a mile below their home in Bucksport, they pulled the boat ashore on the eastern side of the Eastern Channel of the Penobscot River. They had made it home. "We bury this here, then tomorrow we come back and smelt a few of the coins so we can buy enough supplies to start our trip."

If their plans had gone as Bill had wanted, they would have been back by now with their first load of sea trout. Bill already had a story for his wife Judi Ann, to explain where he and Gus had come into so much money. The chest well buried and the ground swept clean and the little boat dismantled and tucked in under a thicket of fir trees, Bill and Gus walked home.

* * * *

Gus and Bill's families shared a two story home with their father, Ebenezer, on the Penobscot Riverbank in Bucksport. To

Judi Ann and Polly, Gus's wife, the men were not home unusually early. This was about the time in June when Bill said they should to be back with their first load of sea trout. Stay over two days, resupply and back to the sea trout runs.

"Did you have a good catch this trip?" Judi Ann asked Bill.

"We filled the holds and have already sold the catch and the boat. Gus and I are out of the fishing industry. No more smelling like stinking fish."

Both Judi Ann and Polly were taken by surprise. Fishing is all either Bill and Gus had ever done. Their father looked shocked as well.

"Well, what are you two going to do now?" Polly asked.

"Tomorrow, Gus and I are going to find a buyer for this house, which shouldn't be too difficult, and when we have enough supplies, all of us are going north. We have decided that we want to trap and prospect. We'll homestead and clear us enough land for a small farm. But no more fishing." Bill said.

"Where up north?" Judi Ann asked, "Do you have any idea?"

"In the Aroostook Country. After we see about a buyer for this house, we'll enquire at the land office on Main Street." Ebenezer looked long and hard at his two sons. *What could have put these ideas into their heads. The Hastings family had always been fishermen. What did either of them know about farming, trapping or prospecting.*

Bill's son, John, ten-years-old, was eager for the adventure. "Will there be any Indians up there?" he asked.

Gus's daughter, Mary, two years old, was too young to understand what was happening and Polly didn't care as long as they were all together.

*   *   *   *

The next morning, Bill and Gus were up early and out of the house. Their first order of business was to smelt some of the gold coin into nuggets. Gus also brought with him a couple of rasps, so he could file some flakes off the coins, so they would have some gold dust as well as nuggets to sell. It would be more convincing since gold is more commonly found as small flakes or dust. Bill picked up a cast iron ladle to smelt the coins in and then to pour the molten gold into small sand pockets to form the nuggets.

They soon had a fire going, using the remains of the boat. "Gus, you tend to the smelting and I'll go back into town and see about the house and the land office."

"How much of this do you think we should smelt?" Gus asked.

"Five should give us about a thousand dollars. Rasp off some filings from each of those five. Enough to fill this small cloth pouch. It'll hold maybe three ounces. I should be back before you're finished."

Bill went to see Mr. Hamilton at the hardware store. He knew Hamilton would purchase the house and had the money to pay for it. "How much are you asking Bill?"

"Six hundred dollars," a flat statement.

"You want that in coin or on the books?"

"Coin. We'll be moving down the coast some…warmer weather." Bill didn't want any one to know where they were really going. He was that concerned about Captain Holigard and Mr. Jolly.

Bill returned to help his brother and when he arrived, Gus had heard something coming through the dry leaves and bushes and he had stepped back away from the fire with his rifle to his shoulder and cocked. When he saw Bill step out from behind the bushes, he let out a sigh of relief. "Next time I'll whistle, to let you know it's only me."

"Well?" Gus asked.

"Mr. Hamilton bought the house, no questions and paid what we wanted. It was just like you said. How are you doing?"

"Almost done. Here is the gold dust. Neat little pouch. There must be two hundred dollars worth of gold in that. The nuggets are in that sack over there. I'm waiting for these last couple of coins to finish smelting and then I'll pour that into the sand molds. This is a neat little enterprise."

"Yeah, just pray Holigard and Jolly never learn of it." Bill hefted the pouch of gold dust and said, "There should be enough here to get us a freight wagon and a couple of horses and supplies. We'll say we were paid in gold dust for our boat and fish."

"What about these nuggets? Where do we sell them?" Gus asked.

"We'll wait until we get to Bangor. There should be an assay company there that'll buy the gold. And we'll need to know more information about where to best pick up more supplies."

"What did you find out at the land office?"

"In the Aroostook Country there's a place called Rockabema Plantation that sounds just what we need. There is land available for homesteading, on the northern border of the township. And isolated from other people. After this fighting is over, maybe it'll be safe to go some place else, where there are people. Probably the women would appreciate the move."

"So when do we leave?"

"Mr. Hamilton gave us one week from today to be out."

Polly and Judi Ann couldn't understand why they were moving so far away, but neither of them were about to question their husband. They would go and not complain. The father, Ebenezer, knew something had happened while his two sons were out fishing, but he didn't know what, nor would either of them explain.

* * * *

That night Bill wrote a letter to President Jefferson explaining what he and Gus had heard and witnessed while on Grand Manan Island.

Dear Mr. President,

This May my brother and I were marooned for a while on Grand Manan Island and we overheard a conversation between Captain Horace Holigard and his first mate Brian Jolly. Apparently they had pirated some valuable treasure from a Spanish galleon and then scuttled the ship after having killed her entire crew. They buried it there on the island and then shot the Bos'n mate and a crewman, and had plans to do the same to the rest of the crew before returning to Liverpool, England. We also witnessed a conversation whereby the Minister of War in England was planning to wage war again against the United States, in hopes of dominating the seas. I don't know when this is to happen. Only in the near future. I hope you will take appropriate actions. The treasure they buried is no longer there. Respectively, can't give you my name. I'm sure you must understand.

* * * *

Mr. Hamilton had a heavy freight wagon and two work horses, "That, I'll let you have for eighty dollars. Cash."

"Okay, that includes the harnesses, correct?" Bill asked.

Hamilton grunted a couple of times before agreeing.

"We'll also need canvas, smoked beef, salt pork, beans, coffee, sugar, flour, salt and rope. What does all that come to, including the horses and wagon?"

Hamilton did some figuring and then said "The total comes to one-hundred and fifty dollars."

Bill gave the pouch containing the gold dust to Mr. Hamilton, "Weigh out what you need and give the rest back to me."

"Where did you come by this dust?"

"That's how Gus and me were paid for our boat and fish. Down river a bit."

Mr. Hamilton weighed up what he would need and handed

the pouch back to Bill. Hamilton had taken a little more than half. Bill considered this a fair deal. Everything was loaded into the wagon and the horses hitched and Bill took them home.

He and Gus already had one freight wagon, a work horse and two saddle horses, a bull and a milking cow.

In five days everything was loaded into the two wagons and what they couldn't take with them, Mr. Hamilton bought, at a reduced price of course. At daylight on the morning of the sixth day they started on the road to Bangor. Bill was in the lead on one of the saddle horses, followed by Gus and his family in one of the wagons and Judi Ann, John and Ebenezer in the last wagon. The rest of the livestock were tied to their wagon. The chest of gold and gemstones were in the last wagon with Judi Ann, and Ebenezer; safely padlocked and covered over with other dunnage.

The road was narrow and rough and they were two days getting to Bangor; traveling from sunup to two hours before sunset. The canvas was large enough so the two wagons were parked close together and the canvas spread over both loads, which also gave shelter for the families.

When supper was over and everything picked up and cleaned, the adults sat around the fire, too excited to think about sleep. "Bangor used to be called something else, wasn't it, Pa?" Bill asked.

"Yeah, Sunbury. The settlers had decided to send Rev. Seth Noble to Wakefield, Massachusetts with a petition to incorporate in 1786. Being Maine was still part of Massachusetts. Rev. Noble had a favorite Welsh hymn that he particularly liked, called "Bangor." Well, when he got home the name of the town was now Bangor and not Sunbury.

"In 1772 the first sawmill started operating and today I think there are a dozen mills that provide sawn lumber all up and down the coast and even some is shipped over to England."

"How is your leg, Pa?" Gus asked.

"It is aching some. But then it always does some. I'm just

glad that ole Brit's musket ball missed the bone. It tore a hole through my leg, so's I could see the bone though."

In 1779 the British Navy had attacked Castine and took control of the fort. Commodore Dudley Saltonstall countered the attack. Saltonstall then ordered his fleet to flee up the Penobscot River. The ground troops led by Paul Revere left the ships near Bangor and fled into the woods and hiked back to Augusta to regroup. The British burned the American ships. "Those were good ships too. Too bad there wasn't a stronger willed Commander than Saltonstall. I made it to Augusta, but the fighting was over for me. Now I have this bad leg to show for it."

* * * *

In Bangor, it was agreed from the start that either Bill or Gus would remain with the chest whenever they were in or near a settlement, so Bill left the rest of the family hunkered down and he went in search of an assay office. Paul Huntly, the assayor was surprised with the purity of the gold. "Except for some sand, it is pure gold. If I didn't know better, I'd say someone has already smelted it." Bill didn't comment, he just stood there with his hands in his pockets. "I'll have to know where this came from. Where did you find it?"

"I didn't find it, my brother and I built some small schooners for an Englishman. He paid us with this gold. Anything wrong?" Bill inquired.

"No, no, nothing is wrong. A bit unusual that's all." Huntly did some weighing and figuring and said, "Sixteen hundred and fifty dollars. How do you want it?"

"Coin. My brother and our families are moving to Massachusetts."

Huntly put a sack full of gold coins on the counter, "You can count them if'n you like. I'm an honest man."

"I'll take your word for it." Bill picked up the sack to leave.

26

"Those boats you and your brother built? I hope they sink. With those no good Brits in them."

"I understand you dislike the English."

Huntly spit on the floor and replied, "Indeed I do."

"Yeah," that's all Bill would say. He picked up the sack of coins and left. The sack of coins was put in the chest along with the rest. "How much did we get for the nuggets?" Gus asked.

"Sixteen hundred and fifty. In coin."

"Wow! That's more than I thought we would get."

That night they all slept inside a boarding house, located on the outskirts of town. This would be the last time under a roof until they got to Mattanawcook (note) about thirty five miles up the Penobscot River.

"Bill–Gus," Ebenezer asked, "have either of you thought about how we are going to feed all this livestock come winter?"

"Yes, I have," Bill replied. "We'll have to find a swampy area or heath and cut swale grass. I think we may have to shoot two of the horses for food. We can't kill the bull and cow until we have one to replace it. We can do without two extra horses. This first winter will be difficult I know. But I think we can manage.

* * * *

From Bangor to Mattanowcook the road wasn't as smooth or wide, more like a twisty-winding trail. But they were doing just fine. They met absolutely no one along the way, which pleased Gus and Bill.

"Where exactly is this Rockabema Plantation?" Ebenezer asked. "I have never heard of it."

"It is about thirty miles west of Houlton and—well I'm not sure how far beyond Mattanawcook. From Mattanowcook we go next to Township No. 1 East Indian Purchase (note). There are a few settlers there on the bank of the Mattawamkeag River. We'll take a ferry across the river and from there, I'm told that there is only a trail that goes up through the woods. I think at the land office, he called it the Aroostook Trail (note). It is passable with a horse and wagon, but it'll be slow."

Sometimes the road would swing close to the river and then they would rest and water their animals for a while and let them feed along the river bank, while they fished for trout and picked fiddleheads and dandelion greens. These were a welcomed change from the smoked beef and salt pork.

The country had been flat so far. No steep hills or ravines to cross. They had been fortunate. The soil was dark too, good for crops. Too bad they had to go so far into the woods. This would have been a fine place to settle, along the Penobscot River. "Maybe in a few years, Judi," Bill assured his wife one evening.

Some days Bill figured they had traveled fifteen or twenty miles and some he knew were closer to only five. In four days, they camped that night just before the first settlement, at Mattanawcook. Bill was up early the next morning and told Gus, "Keep everyone here until I get back. I'm going to ride ahead and see what is available there. I should be back in a couple of hours."

Bill was truly surprised with what he found in the Mattanawcook Settlement. There was a land office, intergrated with an assay office, and a trading post from which almost anything could be purchased. Even women's clothing, and in the corner, glass panes caught his attention. He knew it would be difficult to carry the panes all the way to Rockabema Plantation, but he couldn't see building or living in a cabin without windows. He purchased four double hung windows. "I'll pick these up later if it is okay."

He bought planting seeds and tools he didn't already have. Two more double-bitted axes, rope, two bags of oats for the horses. Furniture they would have to make. He paid for these items and went to the land office to inquire about how to homestead in Rockabema. "Well, sonny, you stake off forty three acres and in seven years you show an improvement to the land and you file a deed with the land office in that county."

"That sounds easy enough."

"Where you going?"

"Rockabema Plantation, about three miles north of Rockabema Lake in The Aroostook Country."

"What on earth made you decide to go there? There ain't nobody up there in those woods. Well, I take that back, there is one settler by the name of Knowles. He came down here to file his deed…couldn't get to Houlton from where he was. I understand he now has a horse trail to Syrmna Mills, about eleven miles east. He calls his place Knowles Corner, as his trail intersects with the Aroostook Trail, on his property. The Aroostook Trail goes all the way to Masardis, about twenty one miles further north of the Corner.

"If you don't mind me asking, what are you going to do up there?"

"My brother and I are going to trap and prospect. I hear there is gold up in that country."

"Perhaps, but none of it has come down here."

"Well when we find some, I'll bring it here to have it assayed."

"Good luck to you, sonny," he laughed and went back to work.

* * * *

"I talked with the land agent there and bought a few more things. We'll have to stop at the trading post to load everything. I bought four windows for the cabin, and we'll have to be careful with them on the trail."

"Pa, while Gus and I load this stuff, you and the women walk around and see if there is anything else we need."

That night the two women and little Mary slept inside the trading post, but the men and John slept on the hay in the barn. That was still more comfortable than the ground. All of the animals were fed well, with molasses mixed with the oats. They had a welcomed rest also.

The next morning all were up early and on their way again shortly after sunrise. This was still pretty flat country and indeed, it would be a nice place to build a life, if it were not for the fear of what Holigard and Jolly might do, if they ever discovered who took their stolen booty. No, they would keep to their original plan. The trail was rough, but they were making good speed. After a day and a half, they came to the lone trading post at the ferry crossing at Mattawamkeag. All they needed here was a ferry ride across the Mattawamkeag Stream and directions to the Aroostook Trail.

"Mister, the crossing fee is 10¢ per person, 20¢ per animal and 25¢ per wagon. Let's see that's a total of $2.40. And you menfolk help pull the ropes." Oscar's eyes were glinting of riches. That was more money than he would make in a week.

"Before I pay you, I need directions to the Aroostook Trail," Bill inquired.

"You follow this trail until you come to a Y, take the left. If you stay on the right you will end up in Houlton. The turn off is about eight miles from here."

"How's the trail, rough?"

"Not bad at all to Benedicta. From there I don't know. You'll have some long grades to pull those wagons over. You better figure on four to five days travel to Benedicta. There is another trading post there that can give better directions from there up. Where you folks going, if I might'n ask?"

"We're not sure yet."

"Well good luck to you," Oscar bade them a farewell.

On the other side of the Mattawamkeag Stream, the soil became noticeably coarser and not as sandy or soft as what they had been traveling across. There were not as many low water or mud holes. But there were more rocks. The river was left behind them as they steadily climbed higher. As Oscar had said, a gradual grade up for many miles. At the junction to the Aroostook Trail it was agreed to rest there for two days. The animals surely needed a rest and there was grass in a nearby heath. John and his grandfather, Ebenezer, fished in the beaver pond and Gus went looking for fresh mushrooms in the hardwoods while Bill stayed with the gold.

While everyone was busy and away from the wagons, Bill watched a young moose ambling down the trail towards him. He pulled out his rifle from under the lead wagon's seat and took a fine bead at the base of the young moose's throat. He squeezed the trigger and the moose dropped in its tracks. "There, fresh meat and a nice tough hide for making leather." After he fired the rifle everyone came running back, wondering what had happened.

"I shot a young moose that was walking down the trail towards me. That'll be some nice fresh meat. The trout, we'll save for breakfast tomorrow."

*   *   *   *

With their stomachs full of fresh meat and mushrooms, they continued their trek to The Rockabema Plantation. The animals were refreshed and more energetic. It was very obvious with their gait and the alertness of the ears. Even the bull seemed to be more attuned to what was going on around him, particularly the scent of the cow ahead of him.

As they followed the grade up hill, they were leaving the softwood trees behind. Now there were great stands of rock maple, birch, ash and beechnut. "I hope there'll be some rock maple trees wherever it is, you plan for us to stop, so we can tap the trees for sap and make some maple syrup and sugar." Ebenezer said.

"Well let's hope," that's all Bill would say.

"Let's hope there are some cedar trees, so we can make some shakes for the roof," Gus added.

"Hey Bill, just a point of interest here."

"Yeah, what is it Gus?"

"Well, we're supposed to be going this far north and trapping and prospecting. But we do not have any traps."

"You know, you're right. Maybe the trading post at Benedicta will have some."

"You know Bill, when we decide to sell more of this gold, it might'n be a good idea to have some fur to sell also. It would help to create the image that we are actually trapping and prospecting."

They were three days before they got to the Benedicta Trading Post. Once there, they found quite a surprise. Green fields, some grass for hay and a few acres planted to wheat and oats. This was looking better and better to Bill. He was thinking that they would have to travel out to Mattanawcook each year for more supplies.

There was a farm there and hired hands. Oscar had never mentioned anything more than another trading post at Benedicta. Then again, Bill didn't ask. At the trading post, Mr. Gould, Vining Gould, came out to greet them. "Well I'll be to go to hell! Where you folks heading? There ain't much beyond here. The Aroostook Trail goes a might further though. Most wagons that come up the trail are only bringing in more supplies for the farm."

"Well, Mr. Gould, we're looking to homestead a piece north of here. My brother and I are going to trap and do a little prospecting. Do you have any traps?"

"Why sure, I have just what you're needing."

Bill and Gus looked the traps over and decided on a dozen beaver traps, a dozen wolf traps and two dozen #2 Blake and Lamb traps.

"Is that all boys?"

"Do you have any ground wheat and corn?"

"How much you needing?"

"Fifty pound sack of each."

"Anything else gents? No, okay. Let's see that'll be an even fifty dollars."

Bill paid him in coin and Vining Gould almost fell over backwards with surprise.

"If you don't mind me asking Mr. Gould. What's going on here? I mean, we expected to find a trading post and nothing else. But instead, we find a working farm," Bill asked.

"Well, someday, not right off, but some day, I have been told, that the federal government is going to build a road up through here, all the way to the tip of Maine. And back at the junction? That route will be built all the way to Houlton. This farm here is to supply food and shelter for both the men and animals. This country is opening up fast."

"Is there another such place as this, or trading post beyond here?"

"Not along this route. But over in Smyrna Mills, there's a similar trading post by the river there. Run by Myron Leavitt."

"Could I purchase, either from you or the farm, some molasses and oats for the animals? Sure would help them out along the trail," Bill asked.

"How much do you need? You can pay for it here and drive your team around to the big barn door and pick it up."

Bill looked at Gus, "Another two hundred pounds won't slow the team down will it?"

"Well, they'll eat some of it along the way."

"For two hundred pounds, that's another two dollars." Both bags of oats was put on the wagon with the double team.

"What is the Aroostook Trail like north of here?" Bill asked.

"Well for the next twenty miles, it ain't bad. Don't know where you're going, but beyond twenty, the country gets awful hilly. Oh, it's passable with a team alright. But those hills will slow you down considerably," Vining said. "How far are you going anyhow?"

"Oh, 'til we get tired of those hills I guess."

"I only been beyond twenty mile, just once. Don't look much like farming country to me. But you folks don't look like farmers either." Vining Gould rubbed the whiskers on his chin and added, "Could be, you come way up here running away from something."

33

Bill tried to sound as friendly as he could, so not to raise any suspicions with Mr. Gould. "No Mr. Gould, the only thing we're running away from is a back breaking job of hauling fish over the side of a boat. No, we left that behind to trap and prospect."

"Well good luck to you. You'll probably strike it richer trapping than farming beyond here anyhow. Don't know about the prospecting. Well good luck to you."

Bill had wanted to stay there two nights, so the horses could rest and eat some good feed, but Mr. Gould was asking too many questions.

All was loaded and tied securely and they left the trading post and Mr. Gould behind. The trail was easy traveling and they were making fast time. They stopped a little before dark and had almost traveled the twenty miles. The day had been a busy and a tiring one for everyone. Now after eating and making sure the animals were well taken care of, it was time for rest, as some had already gone to sleep.

When they started the next morning, they were on a long, rather steep decline and at the bottom, there was a rocky stream. Wagons could be pulled through, but there were several large rocks that had to be moved first. The next two miles or so, was easy going and then they came to another steeper hill and another stream crossing at the bottom. This stream had a sandy bottom and easy to cross. Then they went up hill again for a mile and decided to call it a day, even though there were still several hours left of daylight. The horses were tired.

"Bill, I'm going to ride ahead for a while and see what's up ahead," Gus said.

"That's a good idea."

Three hours later Gus returned, exhausted and so too was his horse. "We're in sort of a saddle here. About a mile ahead we go down a hill again then across flat ground for about a mile. Then it is all up and down hills. We'll be lucky to make five miles a day once we cross that flat section."

"Any more stream crossings?" Bill asked.

"Only one. It's a narrow stream but rocky. We'll have to move rocks again."

"Here, I'll take care of your horse. Get yourself something to eat and rest."

Ebenezer had been watching his two boys very closely ever since they started upon this journey. He didn't know what was driving them, but he knew it wasn't trapping or prospecting. Had they gotten themselves into some kind of trouble? He could only guess.

That night after supper Judi Ann asked, "Bill, how much further do we have to travel?"

"It shouldn't be much longer. I'd like to find the marker at Knowles Corner. Then we go just beyond that."

"Well, how many more days before we reach this marker? We are all tired, Bill."

"I can't say for sure, but I think we must be getting close, from what Mr. Gould said about the hills before we reach Knowles Corner. This has to be the hills he was speaking about."

Again the next morning they were on their way early. When they crested the steep grade prior to the flat stretch, they could see a tall mountain off to their left. The top was all ledge rock, clear of any tree growth. Ahead of them they could see several smaller mountains. One in particular had a very sharp pointed top.

"There must be some good hunting in these hills John," Ebenezer said. "I'm beginning to like this idea of coming up here."

"What about the winters Grandpa?" John asked.

"I don't know boy. But I guess we'll find out, won't we." They both laughed.

"Are there any Indians up here, Grandpa?"

"Can't say for sure; we have never heard of any troubles. But then again, there probably haven't been many settlers here abouts either."

By midday they had crossed the rocky stream and had made it as far as the top of the first hill beyond the stream. The horses were exhausted.

"Bill, this has been an awful work out for the teams this morning. I think we should stop here for the night," Gus said.

"No, there are too many good hours left. We'll rest the horses for two hours and give 'em a few oats and push on a little further."

"I didn't go beyond here yesterday," Gus said.

"Take John with you and ride up ahead a couple of miles and find us a nice place for the night. Mark it and then scout up ahead for tomorrow," Bill said.

* * * *

With each passing day they encountered more and steeper hills and the trail was becoming rougher. Entangled with tree roots. Then finally one day after they had started out after the noon break, Ebenezer pulled his horse and wagon to a stop and hollered up ahead, "Hey! Hey Gus, Bill, come see this!" As he and John stepped down from the wagon and walked over to a column of rocks that had been stacked up around a wooden yellow post with writing chiseled into the wood. "One of you boys will have to read what is on that post. My eyes aren't good enough to make out the words. Looks to me like a property corner post."

Gus was looking at the column of rocks and at the ground around them. "This post and rocks was put here recently. I'd say within the last two months."

"This post is the northeast corner of a lot owned by Henry Knowles from Corinna. It gives the lot's measurements and compass bearings from this corner. This lot has been staked out by Henry Knowles."

"Then this must be Knowles Corner," Gus said, and then hollered to everyone, "We have made it! This is Knowles Corner!" Judi Ann and Polly started to cry with relief. Bill and Gus looked at each other and smiled. Ebenezer noticed the exchange.

"Unhook the teams from the wagons, but don't remove the harnesses just yet. I'm going up ahead to scout. Make yourselves comfortable. John, saddle your horse and come with me." Ebenezer thought it a little peculiar that Bill hadn't asked Gus to go with him.

When Bill and John rode over the hill and started out over a flat area, Bill knew he had made the right decision to come this far north. He stopped and sat his horse taking in the beautiful landscape. There was a large beaver pond on the left and a tundra like swamp on the right with a narrow dry causeway in between. Ahead of them and mostly towards the east was a huge burned over area. He could look down across this to a long opening in the tree line, that had to be water. He could see acres of grass growing at the edge of the burnt land and on the burnt land, blueberries were growing everywhere. There was a sow bear with three cubs feeding on the berries, "Well, what do you think John?"

They rode on to the height of land, which was an easy grade. The Aroostook Trail continued on towards the north. "I think we make camp right here and look around for a place to build a large log house for all of us. Let's get back to the others."

"You two are back early. Did you forget something?" Judi Ann asked.

"Nope, hook the teams up. About a mile from here, we'll make a temporary camp until we find a permanent spot to build. Just beyond the bottom of this hill, there is a beaver pond on one side and the other, a tundra swamp and up ahead is burnt land full of blueberries, that stretches east to water with acres of grass. It's a real garden of eden."

A tremendous weight had been lifted from Bill's shoulders. He was actually smiling. The first smile since he and Gus had returned without their boat. Ebenezer knew his two sons were carrying some kind of load. More so with Bill than Gus. Perhaps, because he was four years older. Gus always looked up to his older brother.

Knowles Corner was behind them now, and now everyone began to appreciate the journey to this end of the territory a little more. This was indeed a garden of Eden. "It is so beautiful, Gus!" Polly exclaimed as she jumped down off the wagon and began picking blueberries.

"We need to build a log house now," Gus said.

"Yes, but not here," Bill replied.

"Why? Everything we'll need is right here."

Bill glanced towards the chest and Gus followed his glance. *Yes, the chest. Of course, always the chest,* Gus thought to himself. He looked at Bill and nodded his head. "We set up a temporary camp here. We'll put up the canvas to cover the wagons and give us shelter when it rains. In the morning, I'll do some scouting for a permanent location. Some place where there are some fine tall spruce trees for the house, so we won't have too far to twitch them with the horses. And water for the animals."

The camp was set up and the livestock taken care of and supper things put away and a nice dessert of fresh blueberries that Polly and John had picked earlier. All but Bill walked across the burnt land to the water beyond. Ebenezer looked back at Bill sitting with his back against a tree. *One of them was always on guard for something. But what. What were they up to. Or better yet, what had they done to warrant keeping such a close watch?*

Ebenezer couldn't walk as fast as the others, so they had to wait for him often, which gave them a chance to pick more berries. "Look at all this grass, Pa! There's enough here to feed all of the animals all winter without having to kill any. This isn't a pond, it is a wide stretch of deadwater. I think we should name this stream Hastings Stream, after the family. John, in your idle time, make a sign and put it up here—Hastings Stream."

"Okay Uncle Gus."

Just then two huge bull moose came out of the trees on the other shore heading towards the water. "Maybe we should leave," Judi Ann said as she led the way back.

The next day Bill and John left the camp on foot to explore to the west, looking for a place to build a home. Flat ground preferably, with water and good soil for crops and with a stand of spruce trees and hopefully some huge cedar trees nearby for making shakes for the roof. Bill took a compass reading of the trail; it was running pretty much north and south. He and John were traveling west, so no matter where they stopped, they would have to come east to get back to the trail.

The landscape was gentle rolling knolls, studded mostly with huge spruce. But there were some hardwood trees mixed in. The walking was easy amongst the tall trees. But this didn't look like good farming soil. The soil would be too acidic for most crops. Bill and John soon reached the height of the rolling knolls and started on a decline. And here also, the forest was mainly spruce with the exceptional hardwood.

As the landscape started to level off, Bill could hear running water in a brook. This drew his attention. He found a large beaver pond and water was spilling over the dam. They circled around the pond to find the inlet, and then began following it. They hadn't gone but a short distance and on the west side of the brook there was a flateau about five feet above the brook. It stretched back further than Bill or John could see through the trees.

"That flateau probably would have good soil for crops, John. The trees are mostly alder bushes and some hardwood. There won't be as much acid in the soil. We can tap those large rock maples for syrup and sugar."

They continued up the brook only a short distance and found a raised mound on the east side of the brook with many smaller spruce trees and fir. "This is where we'll build our house John, on the top of that mound. We'll clear the trees and use them for the house. The soil is sandy here as well. That'll be good." He was thinking about digging a hole to put the chest in.

They continued up the brook, and about two hundred yards beyond the sandy knoll, Bill found several huge cedar trees. Some were already dead, but still standing and dry.

"We have seen enough, John. Let's get back to camp and tell the others."

"But Bill, it is so beautiful right here. Why can't we build here?" Judi Ann pleaded.

"The soil isn't any good for crops here, Judi Ann. Too acidic and the trees we'll need for the house are too few here and too widely scattered. When you see this place, I'm sure you'll change your mind."

The next morning everything was once again loaded into the wagons and moved two miles west to the new location. "I have an idea. The other stream, why don't we call it East Hastings Brook and this one the West Hastings Brook," Gus said. No one objected. "I guess, John, you now have two signs to make."

The next day Bill and Gus were busy felling trees, while Ebenezer and John pulled the stumps out with the teams. At the end of the second day they had enough trees down and peeled to build their house. Everyone's hands were black with dirt and pitch from the sap of the spruce and fir trees. On the third day there was a gentle rain so they burned the slash and stumps. "We'll need clay and a lot of it, to pack for a floor and to chink the logs, and build a fireplace. The fire is burning good, John you come with me, I saw a vein of clay at East Hastings," Gus said.

While they went after clay, Bill and Ebenezer set the bed logs for the house and scaped the loam off exposing the sand. Once the roof was on, they would tamp the clay in for the floor. This was going to be a grand log house, a separate bedroom for Bill and his wife Judi Ann, one for Gus and his wife Polly, one for Ebenezer and John and one for little Mary. The remaining space would be kitchen and dining. Two bedrooms on either end, with the center of the house open. The overall dimensions were twenty-four feet by twenty-six. One story.

They didn't have many nails so the ends were notched in the corners and the bedroom walls were tied into the outer wall for strength. They were only a day and a half putting up the four walls with windows and two doors. The roof and gable ends took them another four days.

"Now we need the dry cedar trees I found up the brook." The cedar was cut into four foot lengths and painstakingly split into inch thick shakes. These had to be nailed into place. When they were finished with the house, Judi Ann and Polly stood back and began to cry with happiness. They could sleep inside now, and not on the ground. "I wouldn't have believed that the four of you could build this log house so fast. Now, we'll need beds and tables and chairs," Judi Ann and Polly both agreed.

The clay and sand mix had to dry for a week before a fire could be started in the fireplace, so for now, the cooking was still done over the outside fire. Ebenezer was a natural when it came to inside carpentry. He did most of the work. The beds were made first and then the chairs and table. Dry fir boughs and dry grass was used for sleeping mattresses. They didn't need a well. The water in the brook was cool and pristine.

While John helped his grandfather with the inside carpentry, Gus asked , "Bill, where are we going to hide this chest of gold and gemstones? Have you thought about that?"

"Well, if we put up a log shelter for the animals over there, behind the house a ways and put the chest in the ground under where the grass will be stored, that should be safe enough. Just remember, only you and I must ever know about what we have," Bill said.

After finishing supper one night Ebenezer said, "You know boys, we should clear a little land across the brook this fall and plant some winter wheat and grass. I'm thinking, come this time next year we'll need the wheat."

"That's a good idea Pa," Gus said. "And as soon as the barn is up, I think we should start getting grass for the winter."

There was a lot to do. The barn was finished and Gus and John had put up a lot of grass, but they would need more. When the barn was full, they piled it up outside and covered it with one of the canvases. Bill worked alone each day clearing the flateau across the brook. And he thought hauling fish nets up and over the side of his fishing boat was hard back-breaking work, but it didn't even compare to this. What he was clearing was mostly hardwood and that he chunked up for fire wood. The tops and slash he piled up around a cluster of stumps to burn. The soil was dark brown and rich. It smelled good—fresh soil.

He had cleared about an acre. There were some rocks and he piled those at the edge of the clearing. He didn't have a ground plow, so he harnessed the double team and walked them around and around in the clearing until he had broken up the ground. He then hand raked the acre trying to smooth things out the best he could. He scattered the wheat seed by hand and then dragged a spruce top around the acre to set the seed in the mineral soil. He finished about the same time that Gus and John had finished with the winter grass. Ebenezer was almost done with the inside finish-carpentry also. When he had finished, they all took a two day break to rest.

"We need some lard for baking," Polly said. "I understand bear fat ain't no real difference than pig."

"That'll be John's and my job," Ebenezer said. "I'll ride one of the saddle horses out to the burnt land and John can walk. There still should be an ole bear picking away at the few berries that are left.

"Judi Ann, I'd like you and Polly to make a list of whatever we might be needing for winter. I can think of a few things, and one of us will have to make a trip out to Benedicta before we get closed in with snow."

They would need more winter clothing for the extreme cold up here in the north. Snowshoes for everyone, a ground plow and more seed, flour, sugar, salt, coffee, quart canning jars, and extra cloth for making shirts and dresses. "We should have some squash, pumpkins, and turnips. They will store okay inside here. We need more laying hens also, Bill."

Bill decided to get only two pair of snowshoes. The others they would make during the cold days of winter.

"Why don't you take John with you Bill? He would be good company. I don't like the idea of you going off alone," Judi Ann said.

"I'll be okay. Besides, John is needed here to help his grandfather kill a bear, and there's more to do before cold weather. We'll need more fire wood, John. Get the bear first, then the fire wood. Pile the wood up against the barn walls to help insulate the barn. And I think we'll be needing more winter grass, too. It'll take more than we have to feed seven head all winter."

"How long will you be Bill?"

"A week down and a week back. Maybe faster, unless it storms."

"Are you taking the double team?" Gus asked.

"No, I don't think the load will be that heavy."

* * * *

Bill left for the trading post at the Benedicta farm and Gus, Ebenezer and John went to work on firewood. They started clearing more ground across the brook. By lunch time each day they would work up two wagon loads. In the afternoon until dusk, Ebenezer and John went hunting for a bear. Once the bear was shot and the hide stretched and the fat rendered to lard and canned, then the three would cut more grass and haul it home. But first they had to shoot the bear.

"This is a pretty good life out here, Pa. I was tired of smelling fish."

Ebenezer was still puzzled why they had packed up and left so suddenly. He didn't think the law was after his boys. *But what was it?* He was sure there was something a lot more drastic about the sudden decision to come up north than wanting to trap and prospect. But it was apparent that neither of his sons was going to confide in him.

On the third day of their quest for a bear they spotted a lone bear at the edge of the berry bushes, where the bushes met the heath grass. Ebenezer tapped John's arm and pointed. There was no talking. They had to get closer. They lay down on their stomachs and began crawling through the bushes towards East Hastings Brook, always keeping an eye on the bear. The wind was in their favor so the bear could not smell them. About one hundred and fifty yards away Ebenezer rested his rifle against a burned out stump and took a fine bead, high and just behind the front shoulder. He squeezed the trigger and the bear fell where it had been standing. "That was a good shot, Grandpa!" John was excited. Ebenezer was too, but he tried not to show it.

Ebenezer reloaded his rifle and said, "Let's sit right here and wait a minute. If we go charging down and that bear ain't dead yet, he might attack and maul one of us."

After ten minutes the bear hadn't moved so they went down, cautiously. "That's a pretty big bear, Grandpa."

"It sure is, Grandson; it sure is."

After the bear was dressed off, Ebenezer and John started for home to get one of the horses to drag the bear back. Before they got to the top of the burnt land, Ebenezer dropped to his knees and motioned for John to do also, and then he pointed to a string of animals going south on the Aroostook Trail. There were so many he couldn't see the end, in either direction. "What are they Grandpa? Moose?"

"No, John. Those have to be caribou migrating to their winter range. I have always heard of caribou in the northern territories, but I have never seen any. We'll get a little closer and shoot one towards the very end of the line."

They crawled up closer to the migrating caribou and the caribou never seemed to pay them the least bit of attention. "This is good here, John. Now pick out a comfortable spot where you can rest your rifle. I'll tell you when to shoot."

They waited another ten minutes and the last of the caribou were in view. "Okay John, pick out one and aim high just behind the front shoulder and squeeze the trigger—don't jerk it." Ebenezer had his rifle to his shoulder also and the sights on one of the animals, just in case John's shot missed.

John waited and waited and finally the rifle bucked and filled his lungs with black powder smoke. The caribou went down. "Now reload John and be quick about it. If it gets up, I'll shoot."

The caribou didn't get up. It was shot through the heart. "Okay Grandson, you watched me as I cleaned out the bear. This is your kill; you clean it. I'll hold the legs for you."

They had the horse and wagon tethered in the shade away from the trail and they walked back to it. "We are going to need your Uncle Gus's help, John. You take the horse and wagon back and bring him out here. I'll stay here."

It was after dark before they got back with the wagon load of fresh meat and lard for baking. The fat was stripped from the bear and the hindquarters put on the smoking racks. Most of the caribou meat was canned; some fresh meat was set aside, and would be used first before it could spoil. "We need a root cellar, Pa. Tomorrow we start digging one."

The hides were nailed and stretchcd out on the wall of the house to dry. *These will make grand rugs for the floor this winter.*

"I hope Bill brings back canning jars. We are all out, and there is still some caribou meat left," Polly said.

"Well, in a few days the root cellar will be done," Gus said.

"The meat will spoil before then, Gus. There is too much for us to eat it all," Polly said.

While Ebenezer scraped flesh and sinewy tissue from the two hides, Gus and John began digging for the root cellar in the sandy bank below the log house, next to the brook.

When the hole was dug, Gus and John went back to the cedar swamp with the horse and wagon and cut cedar logs and hauled them back to the hole.

Bill was up early each morning and on the trail by daylight. He stopped often to rest his horse and often times would walk beside it while going up hills. He didn't stop for the evening until there was just enough daylight left so he could see to take care of his horse and fix a fire for the night and warm up his meal. He was only four days travel to the trading post at the Benedicta farm.

The proprietor, Vining Gould—it was a company trading post—was surprised to see Bill. "What happened, mister, you change your mind about the north country?"

"No, not at all. We need more supplies if you have them and can part with them." Bill handed Mr. Gould the list.

"I think I can let you have everything on this list. If I don't have it here, the farm will surely have it. A freight wagon was here last week from Mattanawcook. The driver, Rusty, had some interesting news."

"Oh, what was that?" Bill inquired.

"Seems like those damned Redcoats we defeated are causing a hell of a ruckus on the open seas now. Spain has lost several of their merchant vessels to the Limeys. And two of the United States merchant vessels were attacked but managed to escape. If you ask me, we should have driven the bastards out of Canada, too. The French are good neighbors, but I don't like those Limey bastards."

So it is beginning already, Bill thought to himself.

"Is that all Mr. Hastings?" Mr. Gould asked.

"I'd like some oats with molasses for my horse for the trip back, if you can spare it."

"Sure thing, how much do you want."

"Oh, give me a hundred pound sack."

Bill could have stayed at the farm that night, in a comfortable bed, but after hearing the news about the British attacking merchant vessels, he wanted to be on his way home.

He drove the horse harder, even with the loaded wagon. The news was unsettling for him. Each noon he would rest the horse for an hour and give it some oats and molasses, and then again before putting the horse up for the night and before starting each morning. He expected more work from the horse, so he had to give it more food.

He still was four days getting home. But the wagon was loaded.

* * * *

The hides were cleaned and stretched and were now being tanned with the oil from hemlock bark. The root cellar was complete, all except for burying it and covering the top with sand. "This was a good idea, Gus. You sure have been busy. I want to see how the winter wheat is growing. Walk with me, Gus."

Gus knew there was something troubling his brother. Bill didn't say anything until they were across the brook and out of earshot.

"It is beginning to start already, Gus."

"What is Bill?"

"The damn Limeys." Bill told Gus everything that Mr. Gould had told him.

"Do you think they can beat us, Bill?"

"The Brits are so steeped in tradition, they no longer have an imaginative faculty. They have only one way of doing anything. They have more ships with heavy armament, but they lack the will to defeat us. Our Yankee ingenuity will prevail…I hope."

"I hope you're right, Bill. I'd hate to live under their domination after two wars."

"I think come spring we should build you and Polly another log house near enough to the Aroostook Trail so we know what and who is using it. More of a lookout post. I don't think there'll be any need to winter there.

"You did an excellent job building this root cellar. Do you think we have enough grass put away for winter?" Bill asked.

"To feed all seven head, probably not."

"Maybe we should work on it. It would be too bad to have to kill one of the horses if we could put up more feed now."

"I agree."

*　*　*　*

Life had a sudden turn for the better for the Hastings clan. They had a comfortable warm house, plenty of food, firewood and hopefully enough feed for the animals. The new laying hens Bill brought back from the trading post at Benedicta were laying now, and they had more eggs than they knew how to use them all. Since Ebenezer couldn't explore great distances from home, he was content with stripping out the moose hide for lacings for the snowshoes he was making. Bill and Gus started trapping, for fox and otter first, and then for beaver when the ponds froze over. They didn't travel together. One always remained back and kept a close watch on the chest. There were plenty of chores to do around the little farm. The livestock kept them busy, and then there was wood for the fireplace and snow to bank around the house.

Trapping was a new experience for both Bill and Gus. They lost almost as many animals as they caught. And they each in turn learned about thin ice on beaver ponds. They both came home more than once cold and wet. They only set traps for beaver on East and West Hastings Brooks. By the end of winter they had a dozen beaver, five otter and ten foxes. The beaver, they discovered, was excellent tasting meat, especially if baked.

By April, the feed for the animals was getting scarce. The snow was pretty much all melted, so they herded the animals in the woods, letting them strip bark from trees and eat it. They could also find a little dead grass around the beaver ponds and at the flowage on East Hastings. "Another winter, Bill, we'll have to put up a lot more grass or kill one of the work horses."

They wouldn't need the horse for meat. They had more meat than Bill had thought. No one had known anything about the caribou migrating through there.

While they waited for the ground to dry, the men cleared another two acres of trees and brush. And since the ground was still wet and soft, the workhorses were able to pull all of the stumps out of the ground.

Bill dragged a hardwood tree top behind a workhorse to break up the ground. It worked well. This new land was planted to grass for the livestock. They already had plenty of wheat.

"When the Aroostook Trail is dry, someone will have to take another trip out to Gould's trading post, until then we should get busy building that log house, Gus. Once the trail is dry, I expect others will be traveling through here."

This house was not nearly as large, and they would need four more windows brought up from Benedicta.

*   *   *   *

Three years had passed since the Hastings clan settled at West Hastings Brook. During the passing of each dry season Gus and Polly had observed folks heading north, deeper into the big woods, to get away from failed livelihoods, some looking for adventure and sadly to say, some fearing this new piracy being carried on by the Brits on the open seas. Where would it stop this time? People were beginning to move further inland away from busy coastal areas. One day while Gus was working around his house a small regiment of army regulars came up the Aroostook Trail. All had horses but they were leading them.

"My name is Captain Samuel Robertson and I have orders to proceed to the Aroostook River where canoes await us. Can you tell me, sir, how many days march is the River from here?"

"To be honest with you, Captain, none of us have ever been

49

beyond here. You're welcome to rest a spell, Captain. There's water for your horses out back and Polly can have coffee for you and your men in five minutes."

"That would be greatly appreciated, sir."

"I just made three blueberry pies, Captain. They would wash down real fine with coffee," Polly said.

"Thank you, ma'am."

"Why are you going to the Aroostook River, Captain?" Gus asked.

"There has been more activity of the Brits raiding merchant vessels and I have been ordered to take my men down the river, near the border with New Brunswick. The Aroostook River joins the St. John River and the defense department is afraid that England might send a patrol up the St. John and into the Aroostook and come in behind Bangor, while the Brits attack from the water. If any British troopers are spotted within our borders I have orders from the President to engage them in guerilla warfare and send out a messenger to Bangor. And another messenger to the large garrison in Houlton."

"So war has been declared, Captain?" Gus asked.

"No, not yet. These are only precautionary measures. President Madison is being very careful.

"Have you seen any Brits on this trail? Or those claiming to be from Canada?"

"We haven't seen any Limeys; as for Canadians, I wouldn't know. Each year, more and more people are traveling along this route." Gus replied. "All going north."

When Captain Robertson and his men left, Gus went immediately to tell Bill about the alarming news. "If we come under British rule, Captain Holigard will surely discover who took his treasure. This news ain't good, brother," Bill was exceptionally worried.

"When one of us makes the trip to Benedicta next week, I think we should have enough rifles here for everyone. Right now we have only the two. We'll need more shot and powder, too."

"How much money do we have now? Maybe we should sell some more gold," Gus said.

"That might be a good idea. If you don't mind, Gus, I'd like to make the trip. The caribou will be migrating north soon and I know how much you like to hunt." Every year they had shot caribou while they were migrating north for the summer and then two in the fall when they migrated south to the high Katahdin Range flateau.

* * * *

Bill left for Benedicta the following week. The Aroostook Trail was dry and he wanted to be home in case of an influx of people coming in to this country this year. He didn't meet anyone on the trail until a day out from Benedicta. There were two families looking for farming land somewhere north of Benedicta. Bill pulled his horse and wagon as far to one side of the trail as he could, to let them pass. He didn't waste any idle conversation with them; he wanted to talk with Mr. Gould and get the latest news.

"Good day to you, Mr. Hastings. I figured you'd be showing up soon. How was your winter?"

"It was cold and every winter we get more snow. But the trapping was good this year. We sold half of our catch to a French fur buyer out of Quebec. He wintered out in a place, I think he said, D'allagash. He didn't speak much English and he was very hard to understand. Anyhow, he bought half of our fur and paid us with gold that he had panned there at D'allagash."

"I'd like to sell you the rest of these furs and my brother and I panned a little gold too."

Mr. Gould sorted the furs and looked them over closely. "These are nice hides, Mr. Hastings. You take good care of the fur.

"You say you have some gold to sell along with these furs?"

51

Bill pulled out a small pouch from inside of his shirt. "Between the gold and the hides we had a pretty good season."

"Where did you find the gold?" Mr. Gould asked.

"In the brooks near our farm.

"As I said earlier, some of it we took in trade for our fur from the French buyer. Don't ask me his name. I couldn't tell you if I wanted to. He was that difficult to understand. But he did know his fur business."

Mr. Gould weighed out the nuggets and dust and then added the value of the hides and said, "Total, that comes to fourteen hundred and fifty-five dollars. I'll have to walk down to the farm, Mr. Hastings, to get that much money."

"Well, before you do that, here is a list of supplies, and I'll also be needing five rifles and two hundred rounds of shot and powder."

When everything was loaded into the wagon, Mr. Gould said, "Your supplies come to—I'll round it off for you—an even two hundred dollars. Take that out of what I owe you, Mr. Hastings?"

"Yes." While Mr. Gould was gone, Bill poured himself a cup of hot coffee from the stove and went outside and sat on the step, watching the crews at work clearing land for the farm. They had two hundred acres cleared now, some planted to wheat and oats and the rest to clover and grass. There were a few head of cattle, but most of the livestock was workhorses.

"That's a good amount of money, Mr. Hastings." As he counted out each coin.

"Yeah, it is. But you know, Mr. Gould, you eventually get it all back. Where else is there to spend money around here." They both laughed.

"Now, down to more serious matters. What is the latest news about those damned Limeys. Are they still causing problems?"

"Well, I heard they raided two French vessels this winter. Nothing reported on land yet. But our military troops are strengthening the garrisons along the coast and all along the borders with Canada." Bill told him about Captain Robertson.

"There is a large garrison at Houlton now. They went through Macwahoc last fall before the snow. They have been building a good size fort almost on the border there.

"Between you and me, Mr. Hastings, I'm not too confident with President Madison. I wish President Jefferson had stayed for another term. He wasn't afraid of those damned Redcoats. And we'd have gun ships equal to theirs too. No sir, I'm not impressed at all with Madison."

"If something does start, Mr. Gould, could you send someone from the farm to let us know. We are four days, maybe five, from here. We have one house in sight of the Aroostook Trail. We're not hard to find. I'd pay him for the trip, of course."

"What's all this trouble about anyhow, Mr. Hastings?"

"England was embarrassed when they lost the last war against the United States and now they think they are strong enough to defeat us and take control of all of North America. And to be supreme on the sea, and control all of the merchant shipping by having all shipping funnel through their ports in England. They have proclaimed themselves superior to any and all. They are afraid the newly risen United States will some day topple their traditions."

"It's too bad Napoleon failed in France's attempt against England. I could put up with the French coming through here a whole lot easier than I could the damned Brits."

"You know what is even sadder, Mr. Gould?"

"What's that?"

"That there are still people...even in the Maine Territory, that would like to go back under England's reign," Bill said as he climbed aboard his wagon. "Good day, Mr. Gould."

*   *   *   *

The return trip seemed to be much longer than the trip down. Bill was submersed in fears—if the British ever did land on their soil again, what would he do? Maybe he should have left the treasure there on Grand Manan Island. But he was too repulsed by Holigard's attitude not to take it.

When Bill would stop to rest his horse, all he could think about was the impending war with England. At night, he ate little and sat by the fire long into the morning hours before laying down to sleep.

At Knowles Corner, almost home, he met a detachment of soldiers who had just finished bushwacking a trail west from Smyrna and Houlton. Sergeant Williams said to his men, "Take a break men, while I talk with this traveler."

"Hi there," Williams said. "Where are you coming from?"

"Benedicta, Sergeant. I live up the Aroostook Trail about a mile beyond here."

"Oh, you must be Mr. Hastings. I'm Sergeant Williams from the garrison in Houlton."

"What are you, making a new road through here?"

"Maybe eventually. Right now just a short cut to the Aroostook Trail, so we don't have to go by way of Benedicta. This will save us three days traveling if we have to dispatch extra troops to the Aroostook River."

"Sergeant, why don't you and your men follow me home and I'm sure we could fix you a hot meal and a comfortable place to rest."

"Okay, you go on ahead. We don't want to hold you up. We'll be along shortly."

Gus saw Bill coming up the trail and went to greet him. "Any problems along the way?"

"No problems, but I have more news about what's happening with the Brits. There's a small detachment of soldiers that'll be here soon. I told them they could get a hot meal and rest."

"Are they going up to the Aroostook River too?"

"Actually, no. They just finished bushwacking a trail from Smyrna to Knowles Corner. They're from the garrison in Houlton."

"How much money did you get for the gold after the supplies were taken out?"

"We have all the supplies we wanted and twelve hundred and fifty dollars." Bill handed the sack of coins to Gus. "Better put this inside before the troops arrive."

While the men sat outside in the shade drinking coffee and telling each other the latest news as they each knew it, Polly cooked up a large kettle of caribou stew. "The caribou went through three days after you left, Bill. I'm surprised you didn't encounter them on the trail. John and I shot two big bulls; we canned what we could and there's a lot still hanging in the root cellar. The ice is keeping it fresh." Gus said.

Bill noticed the Sergeant looking around. He didn't want to tell him about the main farm two miles west at West Hastings Brook, unless he had to. The fewer people that knew, the better.

"You sure have a nice view out across that old burnt land. That must have been some forest fire. We ran into the same burn two miles east of the Corner. The burn went south as far as we could see. No blueberries there though."

* * * *

After Sergeant Williams and his men left, Bill and Gus sat outside in the evening twilight discussing the news of the impending war. "What do we do, Bill? Move further back into the woods than we are now?"

"I think the only way we could ever escape Holigard's wrath would be to go west. Way out west. But we would be taking an awful gamble moving that chest of treasure that distance without someone discovering what we had. I think the only solution is to stay here and see how things progress."

The wagon load of supplies were unloaded, most of it being stored at the farm. With the additional rifles, shot and powder, Judi Ann, Polly and John were taught how to shoot, load and clean the rifles. "This is in case we ever have to defend ourselves."

Up until now the Hastings families had lived a tranquil life there at West Hastings Brook. Of course the extra gold did allow them to live in relative comfort. Bill and Gus both knew that was going to change.

Ebenezer had noticed that ever since Bill's return from the trading post, he had seemed overly worried about something—distraught. He realized that Bill not only disliked the British and what they were attempting to do, but he sensed that Bill was a bit fearful also. He knew his two sons were hiding something from the rest of the family. *Could they be in trouble with the law? But that wouldn't explain Bill's fears about the British.*

Later that summer, Gus watched as another small detachment of soldiers headed north on the Aroostook Trail. This group was laden with supplies. They had come across the new trail from Houlton and Smyrna. "There are five hundred soldiers garrisoned in Houlton now," Captain Gough said. "There'll be more troopers coming to the Aroostook River before winter too. I'm afraid that war with England is inevitable now. British forces are increasing their numbers and strength in the Chesapeake Bay region, along the Gulf of Mexico and along the Canadian Border. It's quite possible the British will cross the New Brunswick border into Maine and attack Bangor and Castine and then work their way down the coast to Portsmouth and Boston."

"It isn't looking good, is it, Captain," Gus said rather than asked.

"No, it isn't. But we'll run those Limey bastards off our soil again, if it comes down to it. President Madison has taken President Jefferson's recommendations seriously and is strengthening our land and naval forces."

* * * *

"Gus, while Ebenezer and John are hunting caribou, I think you and I should make some more gold dust and nuggets. Just in case something happens, I think it would be prudent to have the money now, instead of waiting. And I want to see if Mr. Gould has any current news before the winter snow locks us away in here."

"That might not be such a bad idea. I think we ought to make more dust this time, in case Gould is getting suspicious. And maybe we should sell off more this time. It is anybody's guess what next year will bring."

Bill left for Benedicta two days later with a small sack full of gold dust and a few nuggets. Bill figured he had about two thousand dollars worth of gold. *That would take four years of fishing,* he mused. He laughed to himself. For there wasn't anyone else around for miles to laugh with.

While Bill was gone, Ebenezer and John hunted every day, looking for the caribou. "The migration is late this year, Grandpa."

"Maybe it means warm weather this winter, John. Let's stroll down to East Hastings Brook; maybe there'll be a nice fat moose we can shoot." There was. A huge bull was wading across the brook coming towards them.

"Wait until he is out of the water and then shoot him at the base of his throat. He should drop right there and not run off."

John waited with his rifle poised. When the bull stood on dry ground, John squeezed the trigger and the moose died in his tracks.

"While I clean this John, you hike back to the farm and bring a horse and wagon out here."

*   *   *   *

Bill met more soldiers heading north. They were in a hurry and didn't want to stop. "We have to be at the Aroostook River before it freezes. Sorry, we can't stop."

At the trading post, Mr. Gould had just come outside with an arm load of hides that were going south to Bangor. "Well, hello Mr. Hastings…sure wasn't expecting to see you again so soon. Not until after the spring mud season that is. You must be needing more supplies before freeze up."

"No, actually we have about everything we'll need, Mr. Gould. We had a pretty good year panning and I'd like to sell what I do have before this conflict escalates any more."

"Well, let me see what you have."

Bill removed the sack from inside of his shirt and handed it to Mr. Gould. "My, you did have a good year. With this much gold to sell, I'll have to know where you found it."

"Well, a little came from the brook that runs through our farm and some from two brooks to the west and some from the inlet to a lake, just north of us. I don't know the names of the two brooks to the west, or the lake."

"Finding this much gold dust, Mr. Hastings, you should file a claim, so you keep other people out of it."

"Where would I have to go to do that?" Bill had no intentions of filing a claim, but he would let Mr. Gould think he intended to.

"The closest place would be the land office in Mattanawcook. Do you know how much you have here?"

"Roughly."

"You have $2,132.00 in dust and nuggets. I assume you'll want that in real coin like the other sales?"

"Yes."

Vining Gould had to walk down to the farm to get the money. He never kept that much at the trading post. While he was gone, Bill sat on the front porch thinking about how ironic it was. He and Gus filed and smelted gold coin ingots, for gold coin currency.

Mr. Gould hurried back and gave Bill a sack of coins, almost equal in size and weight as he had given Mr. Gould. "Thank you."

"Any news about what the British are doing?"

"It seems that they have stopped strengthening their forces

in the north and are now concentrating more in the Gulf of Mexico and are preparing to blockade our merchant fleet. No one foresees any real action starting until spring. After the cold and snow is gone. Those Limeys don't like the snow and cold.

"There's been talk by some folks around Portsmouth and New Gloucester that we should go back under England's rule. But thank God those people are not in the majority. If you ask me, we should kick 'em out of here and send them back to England, if they love England so much."

Bill thanked Mr. Gould and started back up the Aroostook Trail and home. "See you in the Spring, Mr. Hastings," Bill waved good-bye.

*   *   *   *

"More folks have traveled through since you left two weeks ago, Bill," Gus said.

"These folks came over from Houlton on the Smyrna Trail. The traveling was too rough for wagons, so they were using pack mules. Said they were going to settle at a place called Masardis. Said there used to be some lumbering going on there before the 1780s, and these folks want to reopen the old mill.

"There's a smaller river there that joins the Aroostook River and makes up some fertile bottom land. Masardis is where the troops have been putting in to canoe down to the New Brunswick Border.

"There'll be more folks coming before freeze up along with another small detachment of troops," Gus said.

Two days later the people Gus had been talking about came through, escorted by eight soldiers. Bill sold the soldiers the old bull they had brought up from Bucksport and one milking cow for twenty-five dollars. "We have a bull calf, and we only need one milking cow. Those two would eat up a lot of feed and we don't need the extra meat," Bill said.

Gus, Polly and Mary moved back to the farm after the last

group of settlers and soldiers had gone through. The next night it snowed and left twelve inches of dry snow. The three men were sitting outside the house when Ebenezer said, "Have you boys thought about what you'll do if war is declared? Would you join up with the military or stay here in case the British come down through here on their way to Bangor?"

Bill said, "I have given that a lot of thought. I don't honestly know what I'll do."

Gus said, "My first thought would be to join up and drive those Limeys off this continent. But I'd hate to leave you and the women and two kids here alone."

"It is a load to think about." Then on a completely different note Ebenezer said, "Boys," he paused, "boys, four years ago something happened that changed both of you. Or you two were involved with something." He looked first at Bill and then Gus. Neither of their expressions or poise had changed. "Whatever it is, you have kept it to yourselves. I have not mentioned this to anyone else in the family. But I believe you two are purposely keeping something from me."

Still no change from either Bill or Gus. They continued staring into the darkness. "Is the law after you two? Is that why we came way up here from no where?"

"The law isn't after us, Pa. And no, we haven't done anything." It was a lie and Bill hated lying to his father. But he figured a lie, in this case was better than the truth.

Ebenezer knew it would be useless to pursue the topic any further. But he knew that there was a lot his sons were not telling him. And somehow, he didn't understand it, but he felt whatever it was that was going on with his two sons, had something to do with the threat of war, and more pointedly, whatever it was, was tied directly to the British.

Gus wanted to change the subject of conversation away from their troubles. "With these folks traveling to Masardis just before winter…well, there must be housing already there."

"Probably they'll be staying in the old crew camps that

were left when the mill there shut down. They shouldn't take much work to make them livable again for the winter." In the four years they had been there at West Hastings Brook, not one of the men had explored any further north along the Aroostook Trail. Bill and Gus had gone East and West, but never North. They knew nothing about the land that lay beyond them. Perhaps life there at the farm next to West Hastings Brook was simply too tranquil to explore any beyond home.

Bill and Gus trapped that winter and when they were not tending traps or stretching hides, Bill worked on next season's fire wood. They had plenty for the winter and next spring, but Bill wanted more, in case he and Gus left to fight against the British. Ebenezer was aware of what Bill was doing and expected that come spring, he would probably join the military. He didn't know about Gus. He didn't seem to be as obsessed as Bill about the British.

* * * *

The winter of 1812 was pretty much uneventful. Life for the Hastings families was normal since they had no outside contact of worldly events, locked away at their farm for five months. Bill and Gus had good luck trapping beaver, fox and bobcats.

It was Gus's turn this time to take the fur and only a little gold dust to the trading post in Benedicta.

"Hello Mr. Hastings," Mr. Gould greeted Gus as he stopped in front of the trading post. "I see it is your turn to make the trip out. I see you have some more hides," Mr. Gould said as he began to look them over.

"I'll give you two hundred dollars for the fur. Any dust this trip?"

Gus removed the small pouch from inside of his shirt and gave it to Mr. Gould. "We didn't find as much this time. Maybe next trip."

Mr. Gould weighed the dust and said, "Eight hundred dollars for the gold. Two hundred for the hides, total one thousand dollars."

"Sounds good to me," Gus said. "What do you hear about what the British are doing?"

"It ain't good, son. Congress is debating whether or not to give President Madison the authority to issue a declaration of war against England. There is a lot of opposition in Congress, but Madison is putting pressure on those. It is rumored that he'll get his request."

"When will that be?" Gus asked.

"Congress will adjourn for the summer in the middle of June. So we'll know by then."

Gus picked up a few supplies and thanked Mr. Gould, "Thanks, Mr. Gould."

"Okay, son, bring me some more of that dust. It's real pure stuff. My buyer really likes it."

* * * *

When Gus told his brother the news about President Madison requesting authorization from Congress for a declaration of war against England, Bill was beside himself with anxiety and worry. One day after Gus's return from Benedicta, Bill and Gus were by themselves in the wheat field across the brook. "Gus, I have made up my mind. I can't just sit here and worry about the British ruling over us again, or about Captain Holigard. I'm going to go to Bangor and join the military and help stop the British from moving into the territory of Maine. I have had all winter to think about this, and I have to do it."

They walked to the other end of the field without either of them saying anything. Finally it was Gus who broke the silence. "We sure have done a lot of work here in four awful short years. We have built us a nice farm out of the wilderness. I'm sure going to miss it." He turned to look at his brother. They were both smiling.

"Are you sure, Gus? Don't do this because that's what I'm doing."

"I have thought a lot about this also, Bill, and the only conclusion I could find…well is the same with you."

"The question…I guess there are actually two," Gus said. "When do we leave? And what do we do about the treasure chest? Do we not say anything to the rest of the family, or do we explain to them?"

Bill was quiet for a long moment, quietly thinking, weighing the two decisions against each other. "You know, if we tell them about it, we only put everyone in jeopardy. What if one of them says something to another, who tells another. Or what if they can't lie as fluently as you and I have, about where we get the dust and nuggets? Or perhaps one of them decides to sell one of the sapphire stones? No one is going to believe that it was found around here. In all honesty, I think everyone would be better off if no one knew about the chest except the two of us."

"You're right of course. But how much real money have we got?" Gus asked.

"A little more than thirty seven hundred dollars in coin," Bill replied.

"Wow, I didn't know we had that much. That should last, until we come home. The next question, when do we leave?" Gus asked.

"Let's get the spring planting in and work up more firewood. At least enough to see them through this coming winter." Bill was scratching his head.

"Pa and John should be able to look after things until we get back. John is what? Fourteen now? Mary is helping Polly and Judi Ann around the house." Gus said.

"By the time the planting is finished, Congress should have made a decision about President Madison's request. When that is done, then we leave, if war is declared. Okay?"

"Okay," Gus agreed.

The families were anything but pleased, but deep in their

subconsciousness they knew Bill and Gus were doing the right thing. No one wanted to return to British occupation. This also dispelled Ebenezer's worry that his two sons might have been wanted by the law. Now, he understood it was the Brits they were concerned about, and he reckoned there was more to it than occupation.

"I want to go along also," John blurted out. "I'm old enough to fight."

"Yes you are son. But you are needed more right here. You and your Grandfather are going to have to take care of the farm, until we get home. Your responsibilities here, John, are going to require a lot more of you than if you were going off to war."

John knew his father was correct, but all in all, he still would have liked to go along and fight the Limeys side-by-each with his father and uncle. "What about the other house? Does Polly and Mary live there in the summer?"

"I think that would be wise. If only so you'd know who was using the trail and maybe pick up news about the war and what is happening. Pa, it might be well if you stayed with Polly and Mary while they are at the other house."

No one liked the family being torn apart like this, but they each knew that it had to be. Gus was beginning to wish that they had left the chest of gold and gemstones there on Grand Manan Island.

*   *   *   *

There was no one traveling along the Aroostook Trail, not even soldiers. May had passed and now the end of June was nearing. Still there was no word about the resolution or a declaration of war. "I can't sit here and not know. I thought there'd be troops on the trail before now that could tell us. It is almost the end of June. Surely Congress would have passed or not, on President Madison's request. They were to adjourn by the middle of the month. I'm going to take one of the saddle horses and ride over to Smyrna. Maybe some one there can tell me."

The Smyrna Trail was rough and he could ride only slightly faster than he could walk. Once he was east of East Hastings Brook, he left the softwood forest behind and he could make better time through the open hardwood.

About two miles out from town he caught up with a couple who were going to Smyrna also. "We're going to Leavitt's Trading Post. Maybe someone there will know if war has been declared."

Just as Bill stopped at Leavitt's Trading Post a military messenger from the Houlton Garrison came to a running stop. People were gathering around him to hear the news.

"People! Ten days ago President Madison declared war on England. Mr. Leavitt, if you have a fresh horse I would appreciate it. I must get through to the detachment on the Aroostook River as soon as possible."

"Sergeant," Bill offered, "if you are traveling through to Knowles Corner today, my family has a cabin one mile north on the Aroostook Trail. You can stay the night, feed and rest your horse. I'm heading back now, but you'll travel faster than I."

"Thank you; and you are?"

"Bill, Bill Hastings."

* * * *

Bill didn't arrive home until well after dark. Gus met him on the porch. "Judi Ann doesn't know yet Bill. I thought it best coming from you.

"When do we leave?" Gus asked, his voice hoarse.

"Tomorrow, after breakfast. There's no sense in putting this off any longer. Every one has already said what needs to be said."

"Where do we go Bill?"

"Castine. We know the country there and we know ships."

1812

CHAPTER 1

"Aroostook Sheriff's Dispatch, calling Ian Randall. Come on Ian, you haven't had time to get home yet." Ian's radio shocked him awake.

"This is Ian; go ahead, Dispatch."

"What is your 10-20, Ian?"

"I am almost home."

"There is a complainant waiting for you in Putt Gerow's store at Knowles Corner."

"This had better be good, Dispatch. I just drove by my home and my wife saw me."

"I know you just brought Parnell to jail and that you have been out in the woods for five days, but there is a four year old girl missing in T7-R5, about one and a half miles north of Knowles Corner, before the Cold Spring Picnic Area."

"Okay, Dispatch, but my wife is going to divorce me this time." There was laughter on the other end. Ian was serious, there was no way she was going to understand why he simply drove by, after being gone for five days. No sir, Ian knew this time his absence would be a divorce.

Ian stopped his car in Putts Store's driveway. There wasn't any other vehicle here except for Putt's. Ian knew he must look an awful sight. He had five days growth of whiskers, he needed a shower and he smelled of fly dope and wood smoke.

"Hello, Ian," Putt said. "She's in back sitting down with Audrey. Her husband left her to telephone for help and he went back to look for his daughter."

"Where exactly were they when the little girl came up

missing?" Ian queried.

"Do you know where the old Hastings house used to be on the west side of Route 11?" Ian nodded his head that he did. "About half way between there and Cold Spring Picnic Area. The family had stopped to pick strawberries that were growing beside the road. The little girl, Haley, wandered off into the woods when the parents weren't watching. The girl's mother, Lydia, said there was probably twenty minutes between when they last saw Haley and when someone realized she was missing. The father, Everett, and three sons are up there now, still looking."

"I'm going to leave Lydia here with Audrey, if that's okay. She will be more of a nuisance there than anything." As soon as he had said it, he figured maybe that wasn't the right comment to make, but he was tired and dirty and he didn't want to spend another night outside in the woods.

Putt knew Ian must be exhausted, by his appearance alone. So he wasn't offended with his last comment. "You go on, Ian, Lydia will be fine right here."

"Thanks Putt."

Ian was real proficient at finding lost people, but he did not enjoy looking for young children. The parents quite often are looking for someone else to blame and can be very irrational and refuse to listen to good common sense. Up ahead, Ian saw vehicles pulled over to the roadside. A throng of people had gathered, willing to help look for the lost child.

Haley's father had just come out of the woods and walked over to Ian. He looked at Ian's unkempt uniform and the growth of whiskers he was wearing. "Hi, I'm Haley's father, Clarence Buller."

"Mr. Buller, I'm Ian Randall. Is there any one in the woods right now?"

"No, we all just came out."

"Good; this is what I want you to do. Can you use a compass?"

"Yes."

"Good. Here is a roll of flagging ribbon. I want you to take two of these young boys with you and go down to the picnic area and string a line of ribbon west until you come to a stand of thick fir and spruce trees. Tie off a ribbon every fifty feet. Leave one boy on the line about one hundred and fifty yards in from the road and the second another hundred yards. Every five minutes you and the boys holler for Haley and then listen. But stay on the line and at the edge of the thicket. I'll take some folks with me and drop down some and string a line of ribbon down to the same thicket and then we'll start searching, and working our way up to you. Do not move until one of us comes through to you."

"Okay."

"How was your daughter dressed?"

"She had blue pants and a lighter blue top and sneakers. PF Flyers, I think."

"I want to take your oldest son with me Mr. Buller. I want him to tell me about Haley.

"I need five people to go with me, who know how to get around in the woods. I don't have any more compasses for you, so those of you who want to come with me must feel comfortable about being in the woods." Seven people stepped forward.

"Now I want two of you women to walk back and forth along this road to the picnic area and back, in case Haley comes back to the road. If she comes out, someone sound a car horn until everyone is out of the woods."

Ian led his party of searchers down the road to a thick clump of fir trees and then left the road and circled behind the clump of fir trees to an old, old, well-used trail. "There was a log house here a long time ago and this trail goes back to the thicket I told your father about. I don't know where it goes from the thicket, I have not been able to follow it from there," he told the oldest Buller boy, Fred.

"I want one person to follow the road contour as we search, so that person will have to stay in sight of the road. The others spread out about fifty yards apart. It's open hardwood up through here, but look in brush and under blow-downs she may have crawled under to rest. I'll work my way along the thicket of fir and spruce trees back to Mr. Buller. If you find her holler out, make sure the person next to you knows, so the word can get passed along to everyone."

Ian began following the old well-worn trail through the woods. Periodically people would drop off at the correct distance from the previous searcher. In places the old trail looked as if it might have been a wagon road at some time, and in other places it was just a foot trail. Whatever had made the trail had used it frequently for a long time.

Ian reached the edge of the thicket. It was as if God had drawn a line through the woods. The hardwood trees stopped and were taken over by fir and spruce. He followed the line, trying not to go too fast, and listening, always listening for the slightest sound.

Oh, he was tired. He needed two days of undisturbed sleep. But he didn't know if he could get that once he was home. He knew that the minute he walked through the door, his wife, Paulette, would start in on him for being away from home for so many days.

After about a half an hour, Ian stopped to quench his thirst from a small spring stream that was running crystalline towards the road. When he bent down to drink, he noticed a little kid's track in the black mud. Only one track and it was pointing parallel with the thicket line of trees; the same direction as he was going. He hollered and waited. No answer. He hollered again. Still no answer. He didn't believe Haley would enter the thick fir and spruce trees and leave the open hardwoods, but Ian kept watching for signs, any indication that the girl decided to try walking through that thick tangled mess. He was looking for tracks, disturbed moss, broken branches anything that would indicate she had left the open hardwoods.

He stopped to wipe the sweat from his forehead and neck and saw a flicker of light blue in a little hollow in the ground, covered with dry leaves. The warm sun was shining on her, as Haley lay asleep, unaware that her rescue was only feet away. Not wanting to freighten the little girl, Ian didn't walk right over and jump her. He stopped about six feet away and began saying her name, "Haley," softly, "Haley," a little louder each time until she rolled over and looked at Ian with a big grin on her face.

"Boy! Am I glad to see you!" she exclaimed and jumped to her feet and ran to him. "Are you lost also, mister? I am. My name is Haley."

Ian sat down on the ground and began to laugh and then he had to wipe the tears away from his eyes. "I think we had better go see your father."

"Okay." She took Ian's hand in hers as they walked together following the line of fir and spruce trees to Haley's awaiting father.

Ian breathed a sigh of relief. That was taken care of, now he could go home. Yeah, and face his wife, Paulette. He would almost rather take a beating.

*　*　*　*

Ian shut the engine off to his car and picked up his notebook of field notes and reports that he would have to write up. Well, Paulette didn't meet him in the driveway. He opened the kitchen door and walked in. She was watching the television in the living room.

"Hello Paulette." No answer, she continued staring at the television. "Sorry I couldn't stop earlier. There was a lost four -year-old girl I had to locate." Still no comment.

As Ian turned to wash up at the kitchen sink, Paulette followed him into the kitchen and said, "What blonde were you with this time?"

"I was working in the St. Croix area. I told you that when I left...."

She interrupted him, "Yeah, that was six days ago!"

"Well, I got delayed with some one new...."

Again Paulette interrupted, "What was her name?"

"I arrested Parnell Purchase and had to walk him out of St. Croix."

"You always have a reason for staying away, Ian. I go visit friends and family alone. I have no close friends because everyone is afraid of you. I don't have a life, Ian. You start working night hunters in July and you don't stop until December. You say you're working some night hunter or other, but how many do you arrest. Night after night you go out and you don't catch anyone. Why? What are you doing! You say hunters can't hunt on Sunday; so instead of spending time with me on Sunday, you go out to work Sunday hunters, when you know damn well hunters can't hunt on Sunday! So what am I to think? How many girlfriends are there, Ian?

"Do you even know what color our bed sheets are?"

"White?" only logical guess.

"They're pink, Ian! And I have had them on OUR bed for three months. You spend more time sleeping in the woods than you do in MY bed!"

She was right of course. The pink bed sheets though, he shook his head, that didn't go over so well. He was too tired to argue with her. "I don't want you sleeping with me tonight! Go sleep in the woods somewhere."

Ian didn't answer, he walked back outside and got into his car and drove off. "Damn it! Parnell wasn't this much trouble. He drove to the upper McManus farm on Route 11, in T8-R5 and spread his sleeping bag out under a spruce tree, on top of the knoll in an old field and he was soon sound asleep.

*   *   *   *

Ian didn't wake up until the next day after the sun was on a downward tilt towards the west. "Well...better go home and try it again. Maybe she has cooled off some."

Her car wasn't in the driveway. Ian swallowed in relief. "Maybe she's gone shopping." He needed to get to Grand Lake Sebois. Millworkers at the pine saw mill on Snowshoe Lake have reported hearing rifle shots in the evenings, north towards the fire tower on Spoon Mountain. Ian had suspected the fire watchman, Fred Smith of shooting deer and moose each summer. There was one big problem though. From the watch tower on Spoon Mountain, Fred had a 360° view. He could see anyone coming up the lake in a canoe and there were no roads real close. Ian had planned to canoe down the Wadleigh Deadwater from Walker's lumber camp during the night so he wouldn't be seen from Spoon Mountain.

That would have to wait now. He probably should sleep with his wife tonight, to appease her.

The kitchen door wasn't locked, so she was probably coming right back. This would give him time to shower and shave.

Taped to the counter was a note to Ian:

Ian,

I can't take being married to you any longer. You're more intimate with people you arrest than you are with me. You keep the house. I have the car and your savings account and checking.

Paulette

"Well, that settles that…guess I can't blame her none. Don't think I would want to be married to a game warden either."

He ate a large meal of bacon and eggs, shaved, showered and went back to bed…between pink sheets. *I hate the color pink.*

CHAPTER 2

Ian glided his canoe down Wadleigh Deadwater in the light of the full moon without making a sound, nor a ripple in the water. He had brought with him food and water, a sleeping bag and cigars to ward off blackflies. He was intending to stay for awhile if he had to.

There was more wilderness on this side of Route 11 than around St. Croix Lake, and he enjoyed the wilderness. But the people around St. Croix were different than those west of Route 11. They were friendlier and more fun to work.

The night air was cool and no humidity; stars overhead shone bright in the cloudless sky. The full moon was just peaking above the eastern horizon, behind him. Ian was truly in his natural element in the wild. There was just a wisp of air, enough to keep the bugs away, but not enough to make a ripple on the water. Crickets and frogs chirped along the shore and deer and moose would come to the water's edge to see what was passing by on the water, so quietly.

For a brief moment Ian thought of his wife Paulette and hoped she was happy. He certainly was.

As Ian canoed silently to the mouth at Grand Lake Sebois, he stopped paddling. A flock of black ducks were startled and took flight. A covey of loons were also startled and all at once they began to call out in alarm, as they swam towards the middle of the lake. Ian looked through his binoculars at the fire warden's camp on the opposite shore. The lights were out and the boat and canoe were tied up at the wharf.

Ian sat there watching the camp and poured himself a cup

of hot coffee from his thermos. He didn't know when he would have anything hot to eat or drink again; not until he was through here. He couldn't make a fire, that was for sure. Not with ole Fred sitting on top of Spoon Mountain looking for wisps of smoke. He sat there quietly in the night air sipping hot coffee, until he had finished the contents of the thermos. Then he picked up his paddle and began working his way over to the far righthand shore, without ever taking his paddle out of the water. He made slow circular strokes and the canoe floated on top of the water like a piece of dry driftwood.

Through the years, ice working along the shoreline had pushed up a berm of rocks and gravel about three feet high. Behind this wall, the ground was flat and grown in with large pine, fir, spruce and cedar trees. Ian very carefully pulled his canoe ashore and over the wall. On the other side he would be out of sight of the camp and the tower, even if Fred was using his binoculars. Ian turned his canoe over and if it should rain he could crawl in under it and stay dry. He made himself a rather comfortable bed from fir boughs and lay down and was soon asleep, in spite of the quart of black coffee.

Ian woke up at daylight when he heard the screen door on the camp porch slam closed. He peered over the wall of rocks with his binoculars and watched Fred as he walked out to the end of the wharf and picked up a fish pole that had been lying on the wharf. "I guess he is going to do some early morning fishing," Ian whispered to himself.

Just then Fred gave a quick snap to the pole like he had just set the hook. Ian was particularly interested now. And he watched as Fred pulled in a huge salmon, "Why that old bugger had that line set out there all night." That was illegal also, but Ian wasn't there for some petty fishing regulation. He wanted Fred for shooting a moose or a deer.

The sky was clear, promising a picture perfect day. This would mean that Fred would be in the watch tower all day. On rainy and cloudy days, when visibility from the tower would be poor, that's when Ian figured Fred would do his poaching—'cause he wouldn't have to be in the tower then.

Ian lay back on his fir-bough bed and went back to sleep. He was awakened soon after when the screen door slammed again. He figured this would be Fred going to work, so he closed his eyes. But this time he couldn't go back to sleep. Instead, he was thinking about Parnell Purchase and how he was going to be more of a challenge than John Corriveau. John's wife Stormy had held him in check most of the time, but there wasn't anyone to hold Parnell in check. Ian began laughing to himself as he thought about the walk out, he and Parnell had taken. "Oh, you're going to be a challenge alright, Parnell," and he laughed some more.

* * * *

Ian lay behind the rocky rampart all day, seldom moving from his fir-bough bed. He was still catching up on some well deserved rest from his last venture at St. Croix, and looking for little Haley when he was already exhausted. He lay there all day; not once for a moment did he think about losing his wife. He was happy there under the tree tops, doing what he was extremely good at doing. And enjoying every blessed moment.

At six in the evening, he heard the screen door slam shut again and this time he looked through his binoculars. Fred was walking up the trail to camp and his wife Lucille had come out to greet him. There was a brief conversation and then Lucille went back inside and Fred went down to the wharf. It appeared as though Fred was readying the canoe to go somewhere. Just then Lucille came out carrying a rifle. Ian's appetite was whetted, and more so when Fred and Lucille, both got into the canoe. They paddled close to shore heading towards Boody Cove.

Ian was excited and adrenaline was running so fast through his system he had to put his binoculars down and pee. This always seemed to happen to him when he got excited about his work. He often wondered if the excitement affected other game wardens the same.

The canoe was still visible through the binoculars, but Ian couldn't see very clearly what they were doing. He was looking into the setting sun. And now Fred and his wife were about three to four miles away. The sun was setting lower with every passing minute, and further blinding Ian.

He put the binoculars aside to rest his eyes…and then the whole Sebois watershed exploded with a thunderous roar from a rifle, the noise echoing back and forth across the lake. Ian knew that had to have come from Fred's rifle, the one Lucille had brought out from camp. And if he wasn't mistaken, the roar sounded just like his own .38-55 Winchester rifle. He wanted to launch his own canoe and paddle across the lake and be waiting for them at the wharf when they got back. But he knew from experience that patience would prevail. So he waited, and peed three more times.

The sun had set low enough, so Ian could use his binoculars again without being blinded. Fred and Lucille were just sitting there, like they were waiting for something. They certainly were not taking care of a freshly killed deer or moose. They were simply sitting there. Ian's curiosity had more than peaked. How he wished he could have been on that opposite shore.

The sun was down behind the trees on the western horizon and the sky line was a bright fiery orange and red color. The canoe started to move, back towards camp. They were not paddling as if they were trolling a fish line and then again not as if they were in any particular hurry. Ian sat and watched and nervously waited. He knew they had not gone ashore to take care of a dead animal or to load one into the canoe. They had stayed away from the shore.

Fred and Lucille paddled back to their wharf and got out and went into the camp and turned the kerosene lamps on. Fred had his rifle with him also. After a normal length of time that would take to eat something and wash up, the lights went out.

The moon was up and Ian kept a watchful vigilance on the camp.

The covey of loons gathered off shore in front of Ian, an owl landed in an old dead tree top behind him. Other than that, there were no other sounds. Ian watched the camp all night, waiting for the screen door to open. It didn't. He watched all night, to see if Fred would leave during the night.

At six the next morning the screen door slammed shut again. Ian was already watching. Fred walked out to the trail that led to Spoon Mountain. Ian laid back on his bed and fell asleep. During the day, Lucille would occasionally go outside and the screen door would slam shut and Ian would jump back to conscious awareness. But she would either be hanging out clothes to dry, work in the garden or after water. When Lucille wasn't outside, Ian would sleep.

Fred returned back to the camp at six in the evening. A repeat of the previous day. But today, he didn't leave the inside of the camp and at nine o'clock the lights went out. Again that night Ian watched vigilantly, but nothing happened all night.

By daylight, clouds had moved in with a light drizzle that lasted all day. Fred never left the camp all day. Sometimes he and Lucille would sit on the porch drinking coffee. Sometimes he'd split a little firewood for a few minutes, he'd fish, clean the canoe. He kept busy all day working at little odd jobs. He was not—as Ian had hoped—cutting up a fresh kill and taking care of it.

Ian stayed fairly dry, under the huge tree top canopy. His clothes and sleeping bag were wet from the humidity and smelling of mildew. His face was black with whiskers and he desperately wanted something hot to drink and eat. But he would not risk Fred seeing smoke from his fire.

At 9 o'clock the lights went out for the night and again Ian kept a watchful eye on the camp. If it had not been for the other night when Fred had fired a shot from Boody Cove, he would have picked up that night and canoed back up Wadleigh Deadwater and then home. But something wasn't right. He decided to wait a little longer.

* * * *

Fred Smith rolled over in bed; again. He couldn't relax enough to fall asleep beside his wife Lucille, who had fallen asleep almost as soon as the kerosene lantern was turned off. She hadn't moved. Not wanting to disturb her sleep, Fred quietly slid out of bed and walked out to the main part of the camp. It was easy to see without lighting a lantern; the full moon was shinning through the front window. Fred eased the door open and closed it behind him as he stood on the porch. He found his favorite chair and sat down. This would be a good place to spend a sleepless night. The lake surface was calm, like a mirror. What a life this was. He was doing exactly what he wanted for work. It wasn't that difficult or tiring. He and Lucille had a wonderful place to live during the summer and early fall, paid for by the state.

A flock of black ducks just took flight from the shadows across the lake where Wadleigh Deadwater puts into the lake. That's strange they would fly at night if not spooked by something. *Probably a moose had wandered too close to them while feeding,* he thought to himself.

Then he heard the ruckus that the loons were making. They had been quiet all night. Something besides a moose had disturbed them. With a keen eye Fred stared at the shadows across the lake. It was almost a mile across. Too far for the naked eye to discern anything at night, even under the full moon. He needed his binoculars. His good set was in the tower. Lucille always kept a pair here at camp though. He didn't want to awaken her, but he needed to know what was in the shadows across the lake.

The door squeaked as he opened it. Her binoculars were sitting on the table. "Fred is that you?" Lucille asked.

"Go back to sleep Lucille. I can't go to sleep tonight, so I thought I'd sit out on the porch for a while."

Fred picked up the binoculars and closed the door quietly, so not to spook whatever was across the way. He sat back in his favorite chair and rested his elbows on his knees as he steadied the binoculars. He scanned and rescanned the opposite shore. There was a definite line in the water that the shadows were making. And whatever was out there was astute enough about what he was doing, not to be caught in the open moonlight, outside the shadows. He still couldn't see or hear anything, but he knew something (someone) was out there. And there could only be one person, Ian Randall. But he wasn't a hundred percent sure that anyone at all was there. But he stayed on the porch until just before dawn the next morning.

Fred had an uneasy feeling as he left the camp yard to start his hike to the tower on Spoon Mountain. He kept stopping and to look behind him. He had an awful nagging feeling that he was being watched. *Had that been Ian last night across the way in the shadows? Or only my own imagination?* he kept asking himself.

All that day he kept watch at the cove where Wadleigh puts into the lake. Where the flock of ducks had been spooked, the loons crying a disturbing call of warning. Something had been there. But what? Nothing moved at all the entire day from the east shore. Or anywhere on the lake for that matter. Everything was quiet. He thought sure that if Ian had been there during the night in a canoe, then sooner or later he would kindle a fire to make a pot of coffee or tea and warm up some food. But there had not been any smoke at all.

When Fred was through work that day, and before eating supper he said to Lucille, "Come on Lucille, lets go catch us a bass, a big one for supper tomorrow." He took his rifle, just in case, a .38-55 Winchester.

"Why are you taking your rifle Fred? Thought you wanted a big bass."

"Oh, we might see a bear. The bounty would come in handy, you know, Lucille. One bear's tail is worth as much as I make all week." But Fred wasn't after a bear, and he didn't want to say anything about what he was expecting either. He didn't want to worry Lucille none.

They paddled up towards Boody Cove. A nice place in the evening for large smallmouth bass. Fred set the anchor and as Lucille was baiting her hook, Fred pulled his rifle to his shoulder and fired a shot into the woods.

"Jesus, Fred! Why did you do that for? You scared the living hell out of me! Damn you, why didn't you say something before you fired. What did you shoot at anyhow?"

Fred waited until she was done caterwauling and then he said, "Oh, I thought I saw me a bear. Guess it weren't...probably just a shadow."

Lucille knew better than that. Fred didn't go around shooting at shadows. But she had said enough. She finished baiting her hook and threw her line over the side of the canoe.

Fred was in no particular hurry to bait his own hook. Hell, he didn't care if he fished or not. He was there and fired that shot to see if he could bring Ian in, if he were on the lake, to investigate that shot. As Lucille fished, Fred kept turning the canoe around with his paddle so he could see all angles of the lake, to see if Ian was coming.

It was almost dark and Lucille had one two-pound bass. Not large, but it would fry up right nice. And no sign of Ian. They paddled home and after eating and lights were out, Fred stayed out on the porch for a long time with his binoculars, that he had brought down from the tower. There was nothing on the lake at all, so he went to bed and slept fitfully.

The next day, clouds ringed the area that Fred could normally observe from the watch tower and it drizzled rain all day. So this meant Fred did not have to work. He was glad of that. Now he could watch around his camp more closely, to see if and when Ian would try to sneak in. He split firewood and stacked it in the wood shed, he worked in the garden pulling weeds, he sat on the porch and fished from the wharf. Still Ian didn't show. Fred was beginning to wonder if he hadn't made a mistake and only imagined that Ian had come across the lake that night in the moonlight.

Fred and Lucille sat out on the porch until 9 o'clock that night. Then they both retired for the night and turned the kerosene lantern out.

The rain had stopped some time during the night and morning came forth with all its summer brilliance. Fred lived by a routine. He was up at the break of dawn and at 6 o'clock, he was on his way to the top of Spoon Mountain. This new, bright day was no different. At 6:30 a.m. that morning, as usual, he climbed the ladder to the watch tower.

By noon clouds had blown in blocking the sun, but Fred could still see out over the horizon. At about 1 o'clock there was a loud rifle shot that sounded like it had come from the direction of the camp. At first Fred was nervous, but soon decided Lucille had probably fired the rifle to scare off some animal getting too close to her garden.

Ian heard the shot also, and he was already watching Lucille through his binoculars when she came out of the camp carrying a rifle. He watched as she inched her way across the grass and pulled the rifle to her shoulder, pointing it towards the trail that goes to Spoon Mountain. Then she pulled the trigger and the roar echoed back and forth across the lake a dozen times before finally subsiding. *I hope she didn't shoot Fred. That'll be a lot more paperwork than if she shot a deer.*

Now he had to figure out how to get to that side of the lake without being seen by Fred in the watch tower, or by Lucille at the camp. There was only one way. He would have to wait for darkness and hope the clouds held.

Like clock work, at about 6 p.m. Fred was back at camp. But before he reached the opening in the Spoon Mountain Trail, about two hundred feet from the garden, he almost tripped over a nice plump spike horn deer. This was the shot he had heard. Lucille had shot the deer in the base of the throat, killing it instantly. *Guess that was no warning shot.*

He dressed the deer out, cleaned his knife on the inside of this pants cuff and walked to camp. Lucille was fixing supper.

"Did you see what I shot, Fred?" She was excited.

"Nice piece of meat, Lucille." He still had not said anything about his earlier suspicions, that Ian Randall might be watching the camp.

Ian had forgotten about leaving the lake and going home. He had forgotten how hungry he was. He was too busy watching what would happen next across the lake. At around 7 o'clock, Fred walked out to the trail and dragged the deer back to the wood shed and hung it up and then skun it, so the night air would cool the meat. He would take care of the deer tomorrow morning, once the meat had a chance to cool. He left the woodshed door open and went inside the camp. At 9 o'clock the kerosene light went out.

It had started to rain again, a little more than a drizzle this time. Ian waited until 10 o'clock and then as quietly as he could, he pulled the canoe over the rock wall into the water. When all of his gear was loaded, he pushed off and paddled north towards the upper end of the lake before turning to the west. He wanted to make a wide circle around the camp and put ashore about a quarter of a mile up from the camp, so there would be no possible way of Fred or Lucille hearing him.

There he waited until about 2 a.m. and then he began to work his way through the wet trees to just behind the camp, where he could observe the woodshed.

At daybreak that morning, Fred and Lucille were out of bed. When breakfast was finished, Lucille said, "Before you leave, Fred, why don't you bring that little buck in and I'll take care of the meat today."

"Do you have enough canning jars, Lucille?"

"If I don't, you can hang the rest up in the root cellar. We'll use that up first before it spoils."

Fred pulled his boots on and tied the lacings and said, "Where do you want the deer, Lucille?"

"Right on the counter is a good place," she replied.

Fred walked out to the woodshed. The meat was cool. He

used his meat saw and cut off the legs by the knee joints and threw the pieces in the corner of the shed. Then he cut the head off and threw that with the leg bones.

While Fred was busy trimming the deer, Ian sneaked closer to the woodshed. His heart was pounding with the excitement and he was sure Fred could hear him breathing and his heart pounding. He laid flat on the wet ground behind a small fir tree about six feet behind the shed.

Fred was a big man and he didn't have any trouble carrying the deer into the camp by himself. When the screen door slammed closed, Ian got to his feet and casually walked up the steps and opened the screen door and he let it slam shut, just like Fred had done. He was already through the main camp door to the kitchen.

Both Fred and Lucille looked up at the same time. Lucille's eyes kept getting larger and larger. She screamed, which stopped Ian in his tracks, and Fred stood there with blood on his hands and his mouth wide open. He was speechless.

"Good morning folks, I just stopped by for a cup of coffee. By the looks of things, I'd say I arrived in the nick of time."

Fred looked at Ian's dirty and rumpled uniform; his unkempt hair and several days growth of whiskers and smelling like he hadn't had a bath in a month. "Lucille, might as well make some more coffee. I think Ian could use a fresh cup. I know I could.

"It would appear, Ian, that you have caught me red handed with possession of a deer in closed season. You know, if you walk me out of here, there's nobody to man the tower. I'd hate to think, and I know you would hate to think also, that a big fire might get started because I wasn't up in that tower watching," he went over to the sink to wash the blood off his hands.

"You could leave Lucille here to watch, but Lucille can't climb the ladder and she's terribly afraid of heights. Never has been up in that tower. No, I suppose you could take Lucille in my place. That way I could stay here and watch for forest fires.

But she ain't got no blood on her hands. You'd have to lie to the judge just a little, Ian." Fred didn't think for a minute that Ian would arrest Lucille instead of him, least of all walk her out of there. But he needed to keep Ian talking until he could think of something.

Ian sipped his coffee and glanced at Lucille. She was furious about what Fred had said about taking her instead. She would fix him later. 'Maybe he'd like sleeping in the tower for awhile. See how he likes that.' She was determined to even the score.

The longer Ian sat there drinking his coffee the more nervous Fred and Lucille both were becoming.

Finally, Ian set his cup down and said, "I'm awful glad you wouldn't want me lying to the judge. That shows you really have character."

"So you're going to arrest me and walk me out of here, is that it?"

"No Fred, I'm not going to take you for possession. What I want is the person who shot this deer," and Ian looked squarely at Lucille. She began to cry.

"Well, I shot that deer. I guess you're still going to have to take me out of here," Fred said.

"Now Fred, you wouldn't want me lying to the judge. You already said that. Especially now, since I saw Lucille shoot that deer." There was total silence in the kitchen for several minutes.

Lucille broke the silence and asked, "Ian, are you going to make me walk all the way out of here?" She pleaded.

"No, I wouldn't do that. Besides, if I took you out of here, Lucille, who would cook Fred's meals and wash his clothes?"

"He may start doing all that by himself now regardless," Lucille added.

"I'll just give you a summons for killing a deer in closed season and I'll set the court date ahead. Now, when do you think you'll be making your next trip out of here?" Ian looked at Fred.

"Probably not until early October."

"Okay then, I'll set the court date for the seventh of October."

"How much is the fine, Ian?" Lucille asked.

"Twenty five dollars."

"Wow, that's as much as I make in a week," Fred said.

"Oh yeah, I forgot, I'll have to take the deer with me too."

Fred helped Ian carry the deer down to the wharf. "I'll leave it here and go get my canoe."

"Yeah, I have to get up to the tower," Fred said.

When Ian left, Lucille was still crying, as he walked back to his canoe, he was musing about the whole set of events. He wondered now who was the bigger poacher; Fred or his wife Lucille.

He picked the deer off the wharf and loaded it into his canoe and looked for Lucille to say good-day to. But she was no where to be seen. He paddled across the lake, up Wadleigh Deadwater and to his car. He sure wished he had a four wheel drive pickup and not a car.

CHAPTER 3

Roscoe Patch lost his job as forester for the Great Northern Paper Company and that was only the beginning of his bad luck. His wife of six years had been having an affair with an old boyfriend. Roscoe's job required him to be gone for days at a time, living out of lumber camps; this made it very convenient for his wife, Jill, to carry on an affair.

But when Roscoe lost his job, he was depressed and started drinking and this affected his chances of ever getting another forestry job. He was home too much for his wife to continue her affair, so one night when he came home from drinking with buddies, all of his clothes were packed in boxes sitting in the garage.

After the divorce and the house was sold, Roscoe had a few dollars in his pocket. By now he had stopped drinking, but he was broken hearted. He had a '56 Studabaker pickup, steel leg traps given to him by his grandfather, tools, clothes and half the proceeds from the sale of his house. He knew that if he didn't stay away from the booze, he would soon lose all of his money and probably end up in jail.

He bought an old log cabin on the outlet of Umcolcus Lake in T8-R5, from Frank McMannus—just a little north of the T7-R5 Town line. He figured that if he could lock himself away from bars, friends and beer stores, he could dry himself out.

The log cabin needed repairs and there was winter fire wood to work up. He planned to trap bear, for the state bounty, beaver, fall trapping and bobcats for the bounty also. He had done his home work. The cabin cost him a thousand dollars with another two hundred in repairs; he could live very well at the cabin for a thousand dollars a year. And that, he would earn from trapping.

That was a year ago. Now he was off the booze, the cabin was tight and clean. His depression was gone and he was making more money trapping than he would have believed possible. He was finally comfortable with his life and he could see no earthly reason why he should leave Umcolcus Lake.

From Route 11, just north of Tracey Brook in T7-R5, there was an old narrow gravel road which stopped right at the lake shore at the opposite end near the inlet. He left his pickup there and canoed up the lake to his cabin and during the winter, he snowshoed everywhere he wanted to go.

When Ian learned that Roscoe Patch was living permanently at Umcolcus Lake, he figured he would have to spend a lot of his time watching him. Particularly if he lived up to his reputation in the settlement.

* * * *

Roscoe had been in his log cabin for a year. Because of deep snow during the winter and the extreme cold, freezing the ice to new depths, he trapped few beaver. But his fall trapping offset the poor winter. He loaded his canoe with four bear traps, chains and wire to secure the traps, his axe, coffee and a lunch. He canoed up the inlet, to the middle tributary of Wadleigh Stream. He paddled as far up the stream as he could go and then he pulled his canoe ashore. The softwoods were now replaced with towering hardwoods. He shouldered his packbasket and checked his compass.

At the top of the ridge, he set one trap to the left and another on the right part way over the top of the knoll. Then he headed west towards the main branch of Wadleigh Stream. There, where the hardwoods met the softwood, on flat ground, he set another trap. Then he headed west again across the stream to a fir-studded and mossy knoll. There he set his last trap and then headed east, back to his canoe. This was June, when bear mate, and he figured both the male and female would be moving over a lot of country, looking for a mate. He'd wait three days before checking his traps. Until then, he would work on tightening the windows in his cabin. When the wind blew in off the lake, snow was blown in around the cracks. He also had firewood to work up. He wanted more than last year, though he doubted if temperatures could get any colder. Many mornings he'd wake up with frozen water in his water bucket and sink.

* * * *

Two days later Ian Randall had been on the Umcolcus Deadwater; downstream from the lake, there were three springs there that were widely known for large brooktrout and as many as you could catch. There was a twenty-five fish limit, however, and that is why Ian was there. He had received information that two potato farmers from Houlton would be flying in the next day. Ian wanted to be there a day early and already be set up to catch them. He knew where the spring holes would be and he knew these two would probably fill the plane with trout, if they felt they had half a chance.

Roscoe was busy on a front window when Ian walked around from behind. "Getting ready for winter already, Roscoe?"

"When the wind blows in off the lake, I have to shovel snow out in the morning to get to the woodstove."

Roscoe put the window repair aside, "...want something cold or hot?"

"Coffee would be fine." While Roscoe was brewing a new pot, Ian asked, "How was beaver trapping last winter?"

"Actually, the deep snow and cold temperatures paid off. No one could do a lot of trapping; therefore the fur buyers were willing to pay more for good fur. I held onto my fall fur, until spring and sold them at the same time as the beaver. Did pretty good actually.

Enough to grubstake me for another year. I'm trapping bear now for the bounty. If I can trap three or four a month, well, that'll go a long way in here. Not much here to waste my money on."

Roscoe knew Ian was just setting out on another mission. He was clean shaven and his uniform was too clean. *What would it be this time?*

Ian swallowed the last of his coffee, thanked Roscoe and left as quietly as he had come.

*   *   *   *

Ian crossed to the east side of the deadwater where Smith Pond joins the deadwater. He got wet too. And he set up camp in the woods, away from the water. The plane wasn't due to arrive until tomorrow morning, so Ian had time to catch a couple of nice brookies for supper.

He was ready in case it rained, but the skies were clear all night. At six the next morning he heard the faint drone of an airplane engine. He waited under his thicket of fir trees. He was hoping that the two would fish the spring hole in Smith Pond first and then come down to him. The best spring hole was where Smith Pond joined the deadwater. Fishermen usually tied off, whether canoe or plane, to the point of land on the east side.

The plane came in and circled the deadwater and then the lake. Probably looking for him. He remained concealed under the fir trees and waited. He had to pee.

The plane came in from the north and touched water out in front of Ian and taxied to the middle of the pond before coming to a stop; then it motored slowly towards the west side and stopped. Ian watched with his binoculars as the two got out and stood on the floats. *They must have all of their potatoes planted, to have time to fish,* he mused. He recognized them both: Carmichael and Hodges.

The fishing was good. They kept everything they caught and put them into an igloo cooler inside of the plane. Ian was keeping count. They had more than their limits now. He sat back and waited.

Hodges pulled the anchor at eleven and they taxied to the point right in front of Ian. Ian already knew they each had too many fish and to let them continue catching fish without trying to stop them—only so he could get a big case—then he would be just as guilty as these two. But he would try to work his way out to the plane without being observed, even if that meant they would catch a few more trout. The last few yards Ian was crawling on his hands and knees through the low bushes, trying to stay concealed.

Carmichael and Hodges were both facing away from him, so Ian stood up slowly, not making any noise. He had one hand on the wing strut and said, "Good morning boys. How's the fishing?" He knew this would scare the hell out of 'em. Ian knew it would take them off their guard and he'd have a little fun with them.

Hodges threw his pole and fell into the water. Carmichael hollered, "Holy Shit! What the hell!" Then he realized who he was looking at. He knew he was in real trouble now.

Hodges was still floundering in the water. He couldn't touch bottom without going under. He was trying to pull himself up on the float, but he kept slipping back into the water. Ian stepped onto the float and offered his hand to Hodges and pulled him onto the float.

"What do you say boys, let's take this cooler ashore so we can get an accurate count. I'd hate awfully if any slipped back into the water."

"Sure you would, Ian," Carmichael said.

The cooler was almost full. Once safely on solid ground Ian said, "Okay boys count out your twenty-five fish each. What's left will cost you two dollars a fish plus twenty-five."

When Ian had finished counting, there were seventy three fish too many. "Let's see, one of you will have to assume one more than the other. Thirty six fish for one, thirty seven for the other."

"I'll take the extra trout," Carmichael offered. "Gee, Ian, can't you give us a break? We only come fishing once a year. We probably don't take home any more than someone who fishes every weekend."

"Twenty-five brooktrout apiece, is plenty of fish. Anything beyond that is being a pig." Ian detested fish hogs more than he did night hunters. Besides, it was a whole lot more fun catching a night hunt. And he didn't have to fight the blackflies.

Ian stayed under the fir trees until the plane was off the water and out of sight. Then he loaded his pack with the seventy three trout and headed east, to find his car.

*   *   *   *

Roscoe was enjoying his last cup of coffee before going to check his bear traps when the float plane circled overhead. "This must have something to do with Ian being in here. Glad he isn't on my trail."

Instead of following the same route when he had set out the traps, he worked in reverse. The blackflies were particularly bad today, and to make things worse, it was unseasonably warm. At the first set he had a small female bear. She was subdued and tangled in the trees the trap had been secured to. After shooting her behind the head, Roscoe cut off the tail for the twenty five dollar bounty. He put the trap and chain in his pack and set off towards the next trap.

As he was approaching this set, something was different. The ground was all dug up and no bear. After closer examination, Roscoe discovered that the bear had chewed through the trees that the chain had been secured to; now the bear was dragging the trap along with five feet of steel chain. He guessed that the bear had caught its hind leg in the trap.

He wasn't having any problems following the bear. Not with dragging a trap behind it. He decided that this was probably quite a brute of a bear, to chew through those trees like that.

Every now and then Roscoe found where the trap had snagged on some bushes and the bear had chewed through those also.

Up ahead, he thought he could see the bear entangled in more trees and lying stretched out on the ground. He inched forward with his rifle ready. He didn't want to be mauled by his brute. Something here was wrong also. He stopped to watch the bear. It hadn't moved since he first saw it. *Perhaps it was dead already. Not likely, but why wasn't it moving?* He came a little closer, to get a better view. There, he saw the chest moving. The bear was simply exhausted. The trap was lodged between two hardwood trees. The bear had tried to chew through these also, but found he couldn't. Then he had started clawing at the ground with its front paws and dug a hole that he was now lying in.

The breeze suddenly changed direction and the bear winded Roscoe. The bear managed enough strength to stand, while slashing out towards Roscoe with its front feet. Growling and snapping his jaws together. He had been chewing at the trap also; his mouth was all bloody and spurting blood into the air. The gruesome sight made Roscoe take a step back before regaining his composure. Then he shot the bear in the base of the throat and the bear dropped and stopped fighting.

Roscoe set his rifle down and took his pack off. He was thirsty; it was only by chance that there was a cool stream near by. Before cutting the tail off, Roscoe sat down to rest after quenching his thirst and for the first time, started to look around him. He got up and walked over to a fir thicket. "There used to be a building here," he could still see charred remains. He looked across the brook to a flat area and then walked over. "This was a field at some time, long ago."

Standing there looking at the old ruins, he suddenly shuddered, as if an electric shock had passed through his body. He could feel the vibrations of the past here. And oddly enough these were not discomforting; in fact what he was experiencing was uniquely familiar. He shook himself, to clear his mind and then he walked over to the bear.

CHAPTER 4

Ian Randall had not been back to the Umcolcus Lake area since he caught the two farmers from Houlton in Umcolcus Deadwater with too many brooktrout. He had been too busy working on the east side of Route 11 in the St. Croix Lake area. He liked Roscoe Patch; he was very much like Parnell Purchase. They were very similar in some respects and then very different also. They both had chosen the hermetic lifestyle because of a woman. Ian knew Roscoe was an educated man, but he didn't know about Parnell. He really didn't know much about Parnell, other than what had brought him to Howe Brook. He wasn't stupid by any stretch of the imagination. He seemed to be well educated by his demeanor. He was certainly cunning and no doubt that under John Corriveau's tutelage, he could also be very devious. But he had learned from a master; Mr. Patch was self taught and equally as cunning, but not devious. Ian always knew where he stood with Parnell, but not with Roscoe, although he always seemed to be friendly. And what Ian found most strikingly about Parnell, he played the game very well.

After the close of the annual deer season Ian had had a meeting in Ashland with his supervisor and that morning as he drove by the turn-off to the Umcolcus Lake road in T7-R5, he noticed that a pickup had stopped at the mouth of the road and was waiting for him to go by. Ian recognized the vehicle and the driver, Geraldine Mitchell from Dyer Brook.

"Gerald must be snowshoeing in to his trapping camp on Batch Pond," Gerald was Geraldine's husband.

They owned and operated a small dairy farm on the Moro

Townline Road in Dyer Brook. While Geraldine looked after the milking and feeding during the winter, Gerald would spend a lot of the time trapping beaver and hunting bobcats. Geraldine would drop him off and Gerald would snowshoe about eight miles west to Batch Pond. Then in four or five days he would snowshoe back and Geraldine would pick him up at a predetermined time.

There was a red flag that went off this morning though, when he saw Geraldine. Although beaver trapping opened this day, December first in Aroostook County, the law had changed for Penobscot County to the fifteenth. This change had been mailed to all licensed trappers. He knew what Gerald was up to. There was a snow storm coming in day after tomorrow that would erase his snowshoe tracks.

The meeting in Ashland was cut short and Ian went right home to pack his gear into his packbasket and put on warmer winter clothes and boots. Then out the door.

Freil was lumbering just beyond the old caribou slaughter camp on the Umcolcus Lake road. He left his car there, out of the way and donned his snowshoes. He thought he would first pay Roscoe a surprise visit, seeing how the county line crossed the lake about one hundred yards in front. Gerald had left a good snowshoe trail and Ian followed it to Umcolcus Lake and then turned right up along the shore. He would pick up Gerald's trail later and follow it to Batch Pond.

From the sharp point halfway up the lake Ian stopped and looked at a new log cabin up ahead. Where Roscoe Patch's old log cabin used to be. Ian couldn't believe what he was seeing. He had no idea another cabin was going up. There was smoke coming out of the chimney, too. This was puzzling to Ian. He had no idea who this newcomer could be. Had Roscoe sold and the new owner built this new and larger cabin? There was only one way to find out. Ian continued on right to the screened-in front porch. There was a new wood and tool shed plus an outhouse. A lot of changes had been made since his last trip in here in June.

Roscoe came out of the woodshed carrying an arm load of

firewood; he spotted Ian. "Hello, Ian; come in."

Ian still hadn't spoken a word. He was so amazed with the new buildings. *How could Roscoe have afforded to do all this?* "Take your coat off and have come hot venison stew and coffee. You must be following Gerald. I saw him crossing the lake earlier with a full pack."

"When did you do all this Roscoe?"

"This summer, shortly after you were here. I was tired of living in that dirty cramped little cabin."

This cabin was huge and because of so many windows, the inside was almost like daylight. The logs had been bleached, so they were a light color, not chocolate brown like the old cabin.

Ian wanted to ask how he could afford all this, but that would be impolite. He doubted very much if Roscoe was making enough money trapping, and he had had to split fifty-fifty with his ex-wife when their house was sold. That, along with what he had made from trapping, would not have paid for all this.

"I made a deal with Freil's wood boss to twitch in some tall straight spruce logs. Then I hired me three fellas from the Jarvis McMannus farm on Route 11. Things have been real slow there and Jarvis didn't mind me taking the three boys for the summer. I still have some work to do, but that'll have to wait until next summer now."

"I didn't see your pickup out where you usually leave it for the winter."

"I don't have the old Studabaker anymore. I bought me a brand new Chevy 4x4 last summer, while I was in Woodstock, New Brunswick. If snow gets too deep this winter, like it did last, I just might take me a trip somewhere, where the weather is warmer."

Now Ian was sure Roscoe was into something that he should not ought to be. *But what was he doing, to be able to afford all this?*

"Thank you for the stew and coffee, Roscoe, but I think I'd better get going or I won't make it over the ridge before dark."

Ian cut diagonally across the lake and picked up Gerald's tracks. The snow was fluffy and about knee-deep and breaking trail wasn't that tiring. But Gerald, in the eight miles, never stopped to rest or broke stride. Every snowshoe track was just the same as the previous. Gerald was twenty-five-years or more older than Ian and Ian was beginning to tire once he hit the inlet to Cut Lake. There, he had to stop and rest. Gerald's tracks kept going.

Ian followed the track across the inlet brook and over a knoll and suddenly Gerald's track had turned hard to the left, back towards the brook. Ian stood there for a moment thinking and then he saw where there was another snowshoe track coming away from the brook and back onto the original course.

Ian didn't follow Gerald's track. Instead, he back tracked and circled around from the other side of the brook. He was sure that Gerald had probably set up a beaver colony. This was Penobscot County and the season wouldn't open for another two weeks. In short order Ian came back to a nice little flowage about fifty yards above where Gerald had crossed the brook. He didn't want to make any tracks, so he stayed on that side, or the east side of the flowage. He could see that the dam had been broken out a little—just a trough, to let some water through. A trapper would do this knowing that a beaver would realize water was escaping and would come to investigate and there'd be a leg-hold trap in the trough. A sure-fired way to catch beaver. Except it was illegal to set on a beaver dam or break away the dam like Gerald had done.

Ian looked around for signs of other traps. He saw a stake between the house and feedbed and another in the inlet channel. He decided he would spend the night right there. With a storm coming in, he knew Gerald would be back at about daylight and would probably pull all of the traps and would probably have a beaver in each set. Then he'd let the snowstorm cover his dastardly deed and he would be home free with three beaver.

Ian built himself a shelter using fir boughs and kicked

snow up and around it, to make it as warm and comfortable as possible. As much as he would have like to have built a small fire, he decided against it. Fearing that if Gerald ever smelled wood smoke he would never come back to his traps. So he would have to endure the cold and wait. He was prepared for it.

As he lay there on his fir-bough bed, he couldn't help but think of Gerald Mitchell and his remarkable endurance. He had snowshoed seven miles without stopping, only then to set three beaver traps after cutting ice for two of them. He had on occasions run into Gerald, but he had never had any reason to spend any time watching him. That is until today.

The wind had stopped blowing and as Ian lay there, he could hear snowflakes falling through the trees. It was a peaceful, heavenly sound and he was soon sound asleep.

At daylight Ian was awakened by Gerald chopping ice at one of his sets. Ian turned around inside of his fir bough enclosure so he could observe him. At the first set, Gerald pulled out a super-large beaver. Then at the second set; he pulled through the ice a much smaller beaver and at the third set, the one on the dam, he had the large mate to the first beaver. Gerald put all three beaver in his packbasket. He would skin them back at camp.

After he had strapped on his snowshoes and shouldered his packbasket, Ian quietly crawled out of his hidey-hole and started to cross the flowage towards Gerald. It was still snowing and all the old tracks had been snowed in and covered over. Gerald noticed movement out of the corner of his eye and turned to see what it was.

He was totally surprised to see Ian walking towards him. The only thing he could think of to say was, "Well, it's obvious one of us shouldn't be here."

That stopped Ian in his tracks. He had to choke back from laughing. Here was a true gentleman. He was going to hate himself for what he had to do. "That's a pretty nice catch, for so early in the morning."

"Well, while I'm out here at Batch Pond, I don't pack me in any meat. Too far to snowshoe with extra weight. I live on beaver meat while I'm out here. I didn't want the meat to spoil sitting under the ice or have some rascal of an otter eat it.

"You look a bit peaked, why don't you follow me back to the cabin and have some fried beaver with me and a hot cup of tea."

Gerald was talking as if he didn't know beaver trapping in Penobscot County didn't start until the fifteenth. But Ian knew all licensed trappers had been sent a notice.

Even with a full pack of beaver, Gerald never broke stride. The snow had already filled in his earlier snowshoe tracks. Ian was thinking about the eight miles back; new snow and he would be breaking trail.

"I almost had this one, Ian. In another hour there'd be no sign of my tracks on that flowage. How was it you happened to be here this morning? You must have come in yesterday and spent the night here." Gerald sniffed the air. "You didn't have a fire did you? You'd know I'd smell it and not come near. You're pretty crafty—damned determined too. Glad I don't do this often. I'd hate to have to be watching over my shoulder, every time I came into the woods."

There, it was settled, Gerald knew the county was still closed and his own admission of guilt. *This was going too easy.* It was still snowing.

They crossed Batch Pond, which wasn't much of a pond at all. It was completely enclosed with cedar trees. "Why did you build a cabin here Gerald? There's no beaver. There's no feed for them, only cedar."

"Well, you must know beaver will eat cedar if there is no hardwood, but me and Hazen built here for bobcat hunting. There are as many cats in these woods as there are beaver. But we don't do much cat hunting until later, after the snow settles; makes it easier for the dogs to run. While we're setting for beaver, we also set a few cat traps. But running them with dogs is more fun.

"Hang your snowshoes on those nails there," and Gerald pointed to one wall of the cabin. The log cabin was small, real small. The logs were cedar and the biggest one may have been five inches round. The roof was boards, and the floor was bare ground and only enough room to stand, as long as you were not too tall. There were two small bunks, a sheetmetal stove and one window on the pond side. The cabin was so well concealed in the cedar thicket, that it would be impossible to see from the air. The cabin was a true trappers cabin and only big enough to accommodate two people.

"You build the fire up, while I skin this big beaver. The bigger they are, the better eating. I've eaten a lot of beaver and have never found a tough one."

Gerald skun that beaver and one other, before Ian had a good hot fire blazing. Gerald cut off the hind legs and the tender meat along the back and put them in a fry pan with a slice of saltpork.

When they had finished eating, there was no beaver meat left, the salt pork was gone and they soaked up the last of the gravy with pan biscuits. And then they drank the pot of tea. It was still snowing.

"How much of an income can an average trapper expect, from fall trapping and winter? A few bear for bounty too?" Ian asked, still trying to figure out Roscoe Patch.

"Oh, if he worked real hard and took good care of his fur, you could make two thousand, maybe twenty five hundred. But then you have to take out expenses." That's about what Ian was thinking too. *You surely couldn't go out and buy a new 4x4 pickup and build a new log house.* Ian had decided he'd have to spend more time watching Roscoe Patch.

"You know what I have to do?—right? But, I'll go easy on you. I could take you for trapping in closed season, and breaking a beaver dam. If I take you for trapping in closed season, I'll overlook the other. But I take the three hides out with me. With one condition. You finish skinning all three. And, I'll take the hind legs and back straps of one beaver with me. I might get hungry on the way back."

"I hate to give up all three hides. You going to take my license too?"

"Not if you give up all three hides."

There was no question then. Gerald needed his trapping license to help supplement his farming income. Ian had him over a barrel and they both knew it.

"Have you always lived in Dyer Brook, Gerald?"

"Yes, I was born and raised right there at the farm. Geraldine and I took it over when my folks were too old to work it any longer." Gerald had the last beaver almost skun already.

"The Moro Townline Road was a pretty good place to grow up as a kid. As soon as I was old enough, I had chores to do seven days a week. But when the chores were done, I'd fish, hunt, or trap. When I was a kid, some of the best fishing around was in the west branch of the Mattawamkeag River. There was always a few beaver and otter on the river too. Occasionally, Dad would let me go up East Hastings Brook, as far as the meadows. But I had to stay on the main brook.

"We always had deer around the farm too. We had a big work horse, Blacky; if we had a big deer down in the woods, we would take Blacky down and throw the deer on his back and tie it on, and Blacky would go home on his own, right to the barn." Gerald started laughing then. "I tried that once, once mind you, with a little she bear. Blacky didn't like bear, let alone one on his back. He bucked and threw the bear off and ran home. Dad had to help me drag it back to the farm. After that I couldn't shoot any more bear off his property.

"Up the river from the bridge, we used to have a nice swimming hole. Every Saturday afternoon, all the kids in the neighborhood would get together there." Gerald stopped talking to light up a Pall Mall cigarette. Soon the inside of the small cabin was filled with blue smoke.

"There was always something to do, growing up as a kid.

Not to say that we never got into any trouble…'cause sometimes we did.

"I have another log cabin, perhaps you already know of it. It's on Mud Lake in Moro, down near the dam. I use that one to trap out of also. Geraldine drops me off at the mouth of the Pleasant Lake Road on Route 11; I tend traps on the way in, spend two nights and then she meets me at the mouth of the Rockabema Road. I tend traps coming out also. I don't do much cat hunting in there, though. The country is too rough for dogs. And no deer in those hardwoods in the winter and bobcat like deer meat. To get cats in the winter you need to be close to deer yards."

Ian hadn't said much since writing out the summons. He was enjoying listening to Gerald and Gerald was enjoying his company, as much as Ian was. Still snowing.

"I don't mean to say that we were all angels, all the time. We had our moments. I'll tell you a good story. This all happened before I was born. It is a story handed down through the family." Gerald put out the Pall Mall and made a pot of real rugged coffee. "Sorry, no milk for the coffee."

"That's okay," Ian thanked him.

"The big farm on top of the hill? West of the river? You know which one I'm talking about? The Bates Farm. There were two Bates brothers that kept company some with the devil. My great-grandmother, Sarah Burcklbank Darling, she was from England; married my Great Grandfather Bill Darling. They lived in the old Darling farmhouse next to Tilly Palmer. Well, she was, some say, a witch. She was mean, and couldn't get along with anyone. Nobody liked her. She put my great-grandfather in his grave at an early age. Well, the town of Moro wanted a new cemetery between Bear Mountain Camps and Secret Pond Camps on Route 11. The state said that there were two other cemeteries in Moro and said that was enough. But some in the town kept after the state, that they wanted another cemetery. So the state finally agreed, with one condition. That some one had to be planted in the cemetery by a certain date or the deal was off.

"Time was getting close and still no one was planted in the cemetery. My grandfather said that two of the Bates brothers decided they would take care of that. Sarah liked to ride her bicycle a lot. One day the brothers loosened the nuts on the front fork of her bicycle, when Sarah decided she would ride up where Bill and Carey Palmer live now. She was coasting pretty good down Mill Brook Hill when she hit a rough stretch. The bicycle got to chattering and the front fork came loose and fell off the axle and dug into the gravel. Sarah..." Gerald was roaring with laughter, "...Sarah, she came over the handlebars and when her feet hit the road she was running. And then she ran the rest of the way to the farm.

"The deadline was close and the town was afraid they would lose the cemetery. So another day, Sarah wanted to go horseback riding. So the same two brothers saddles her horse for her and they put two tacks under the saddle, so when Sarah sat down, they would prick the horse and the horse would buck and throw Sarah off. Well, she got into that saddle and the horse bucked alright, but Sarah rode the horse out and climbed down from the saddle." Both Ian and Gerald were laughing now.

"Deer season started and the deadline is almost up and no one was planted in the cemetery. The two brothers took her hunting across the road, down towards Emerson's old lumber camp, no one there any longer. Well, old Sarah is filled with buckshot and planted in the cemetery and the town named it, the Darling Cemetery." Again, the two roared with laughter.

"That's a good story, Gerald."

"Well, everyone in the family swears it's true." Still snowing.

"You know the corner just above the Millbrook Crossing going towards Bill Palmer's?"

"Yeah, I know where you're talking."

"If you go off the corner with your compass at about 75°, you'll come to another old Darling homestead. The ground was so rocky, they didn't stay long, but old Darling found an outcropping of almost pure limestone. They built a kiln there to burn the limestone to make wall plaster. All the farms around Moro and Hersey, the houses are plastered with lime that came from that deposit. There is still one large outcropping left and there is a bowl shape depression in one side where the caribou used to lick it for the calcium. It's just west of Jackson Sluice on the river. There are still old appletrees in there and it's good bear and deer hunting."

Gerald lit another Pall Mall cigarette and soon the inside was filled with blue smoke. Ian looked at his watch 10:40 a.m. If he left now he still probably wouldn't be back to his car before dark. Not snowshoeing through this new snow. He looked outside. "Still snowing."

Gerald smiled and took a long deep drag from the cigarette before putting it out. "No sense in leaving before the storm is over, young fella. You might get lost," Gerald chuckled.

"Do you know what I mean by Harris Bog? That boggy area on the east side of eleven just north of Knowles Corner?"

"Yeah, I know what you mean."

"My grandfather told me that when he was just a kid, maybe six or eight, his father brought the whole family up there to pick blueberries. A long time ago a terrible forest fire had burned through that country. From the spring at the picnic area, down along both sides of the East Branch of Hastings and it crossed Route 212...'course there was no road there then. But it burned down along the brook all the way to the meadows. Walking anywhere through those woods you can still see old charred tree stumps. The fire was so hot, my grandfather said, that for decades after, nothing would grow on the burnt land except blueberries. The woods along the brook have never been cut in my life. The trees, they grow so slow there, because the fire burnt away all the goodness from the soil. In those days it was awful good bear country."

"Do you know how Knowles Corner got its name?" Ian asked.

"I suppose because old man Henry Knowles settled there," Gerald replied.

"Maybe; I'm not sure. I was picking strawberries there last year and I had my malamute dog, Sheba, with me. There was an old boar bear there and Sheba put the runs to it. Only she didn't come right back. Not for a couple of hours. She must have run that bear into the next county. I knew she would come back there to find me. She'd follow her own scent back. While I waited, I started looking around where the old buildings and such had been. I found an old corner post, partially buried in leaves. I dug it out and on one side I could still make out some writing that had been chiseled into the wood. It said 'something' 'Knowle,' no "s," then NE, probably northeast "Corner." I figured that had to have been Mr. Knowles northeast corner of his lot."

"Knowles Corner," Gerald said, "that's logical."

The two sat there waiting out the snowstorm long into the afternoon. Telling stories. Mostly it was Gerald telling Ian about his childhood years and what it was like growing up along the Moro Townline Road. The only thing Ian couldn't get straight in his mind was the story about Sarah Burcklbank Darling. Some day when he didn't have much to do, he'd stop at the Darling Cemetery and look at her headstone.

"Sun is setting early today, because of the storm." Gerald opened the door and stepped out. "Hey Ian! Snow stopped." There was two feet of new dry fluffy snow on top of what they already had. "No sense in you trying to find your way out in the dark. You might as well stay here tonight and get an early start. One condition though."

"What's that?" Ian asked.

"We eat the beaver you were figuring on taking along with you to eat on the trail. I only brought enough food for me, until I hike out of here. Besides, with you leaving at daybreak you won't have to worry about staying out. Unless you can't read a compass."

"I don't think I'll get lost."

"I don't quite understand you, Ian."

"Oh, how's that?"

"Well, what made you snowshoe eight miles in here, sleep out burrowed in a snow bank like a hibernating bear and now tomorrow morning, you'll have to snowshoe eight miles back to your car through an additional two feet of new snow. For what! A twenty five dollar fine! I'm in here to supplement my income. You could as well be home sitting beside your own stove. What drove you to make the trip? I'm not that notorious.

"I'm not mad at you. You caught me red handed, and gave me a break."

"The truth of the matter, Gerald. I enjoy it. It's a great game."

* * * *

During the night the temperature had dropped off to -10°. Even with the woodstove heating a small space, neither of the two slept much. It was cold and one of them had to keep stoking the fire. So they both sat up. At daylight Gerald said goodbye to Ian. "Remember, young fella, to follow your compass East all the way." They both laughed and Ian strapped on his snowshoes for the arduous trip ahead of him.

Gerald watched as Ian disappeared. He had kept Ian there all the previous day and the night for a special reason. Now Gerald would have a packed trail to follow out when he left, instead of him having to break trail through two feet of new snow. "Make a good trail, young fella!" Gerald hollered after him. And then he began to laugh until tears clouded his vision. He had used Ian, and no doubt Ian knew full well that he was being used, to break trail. Gerald truly admired Ian though, in spite of the charge. It could have been worse.

* * * *

105

Ian made it back to his car before dark. He knew he would have to pace himself, to keep from tiring too soon. The snow was deep, but because of the cold temperature, it was dry and fluffy. As long as he stayed to the old trail, he would not have any problems. It most cases, he could see a channel ahead of him in the snow where the old trail lay. Once in a while he would misgauge and step off and then the snow was really deep.

At the height of land, east of Cut Lake, he stopped and built a fire and ate what was left of his supplies that he had brought in with him. He melted snow for water and quenched his thirst. After he was well rested, he started out again. *From here it is all downhill to Umcolcus Lake, then two miles more to my car.*

As he was crossing Umcolcus Lake, Ian stopped thinking about Gerald and the stories he had told him, particularly the one about his Great Grandmother Sarah Darling. He put thoughts and stories of Gerald aside and began thinking about Roscoe Patch and where he had come across enough money to build a new, grand, log cabin and buy a new 4x4 pickup. He surely wasn't making that kind of money trapping. Maybe he was selling deer to non-resident sports? But still, that would take a lot of deer to account for Roscoe's new expenses. No, he was up to something else. Maybe he was involved in something more sinister like robbery. Whatever it was, Ian was determined to find out.

When he reached the western shore of Umcolcus Lake he paused to rest. He thought about sitting on Roscoe's cabin to see what he was up to. Whether or not he'd be out trapping. But he was tired after this ordeal and all he wanted now was a hot shower and his own bed.

CHAPTER 5

The rest of the winter passed and Ian didn't see Gerald Mitchell again. He had snowshoed in around the inlet and outlet of Umcolcus Lake and didn't find any of Roscoe's beaver traps. There were plenty of beaver also and an easy opportunity to set traps. The rest of the winter, Ian spent in the St. Croix area watching Parnell Purchase.

Spring came with rumors that the Camp Violette Road was going to be extended so that it would run southerly on the east side of Cut Lake down to Weeks Brook and Lane Brook. And then the following year it would continue from Lane Brook east, crossing the west branch of Hastings and back to Route 11, across from the Harris Bog.

This would open up a lot of the woods for sportsmen and increase pressure on fish and wildlife, but it would also save a lot of walking and snowshoeing for Ian.

Before the fishing season got off to a good start, Ian put several days worth of supplies and water and a piece of mill canvass in his pack. He was going to spend some time across the outlet from Roscoe's log cabin. He wanted to know what exactly Roscoe was doing and how he was coming up with all of this sudden wealth. He would have the warden pilot drop him off at the Umcolcus Deadwater.

"I'll be back here at five in the afternoon, Ian, five days from now. You be here," Jack said.

"I'll be here," Ian got out and pushed the float plane away from the shore.

He had to stay back away from the brook. Just in case

Roscoe might be out fishing or trapping muskrats in the spring season. He doubted if Roscoe would be rat trapping, but he'd have to be cautious.

There was still quite a bit of snow in places where the fir trees grew so thick that sunshine couldn't get at the snow. The nights would be cool, or maybe even cold, but he wouldn't have to endure the hordes of blackflies and mosquitoes.

He set up camp back away from the lake, so if the wind was from the right direction he could have a small cook fire. He built a fir-bough lean-to and draped the piece of canvass over it and a four foot section as an overhang in front of the lean-to. This would keep him and his gear dry. As he was building the lean-to, he, for whatever reason, thought of his ex-wife, Paulette. It was no wonder she had left. She had been correct. She wasn't even part of Ian's memories, because he was always in the woods. They never did anything together to have any memories.

The truth of the matter was, he enjoyed just what he was doing right at the moment. This was more important to him than family life.

The lean-to finished and his gear stored away, he took his binoculars and found a secluded spot from which he could watch Roscoe's cabin (mansion). There was no smoke in the chimney, but that wasn't too unusual. He could be fishing, out exploring, or doing whatever it was that was netting him some money.

There had been no movement at all around the cabin. No noise, no smoke, nothing. In the late afternoon there was a canoe with two fishermen in it, working their way slowly up along the shore towards the outlet. For nothing better to do, Ian started watching these two. He recognized them both from town, but he didn't know their names. They were real intent on fishing. There was very little conversation and no beer. That was unusual.

Their luck was good, but Ian doubted if they would come close to exceeding their limit of twenty five. They left just at dusk. Still nothing at Roscoe's. Ian could see the front and the north side of the cabin. There were no lights on and no smoke.

Maybe he is out for the night.

Ian went back to his lean-to and kindled a small fire, since the wind was blowing from the west and Roscoe wasn't home. He warmed up something to eat and had a cup of hot coffee and then went to bed. It was cold, but he slept well.

At daylight several loons had gathered at the outlet and were singing him a chorus, it seemed to him, since they were directly in front of where he was camped. Ian got up and the loons swam off. Before he started a breakfast fire, he checked first to see if Roscoe had come back during the night. No smoke, no sound and the light conditions were just right, so Ian could look through the cabin windows with his binoculars and no one was moving around on the inside. He built a small fire of dried pine limbs and boiled a pot of coffee and warmed his breakfast of a hard wheat roll, saltpork and raspberry jam. When the coffee was boiling, he let the fire go out.

He watched the house all day and still no sounds or any kind of movement. *Had Roscoe gone somewhere during spring break-up?* Maybe he should have found out for sure if he was indeed at home, before starting this vigil.

At dusk he took his flashlight and crossed the dri-ki dam where the brook actually begins and worked his way quietly up to Roscoe's cabin. He waited behind the woodshed for complete darkness. If Roscoe was inside he would probably light a kerosene lantern. But no light came on. Ian was satisfied that he was not home. He stepped up onto the porch and peered through the windows. Everything was very orderly inside. Ian noticed there was new furniture, a new gas cooking stove, hardwood flooring and a new braided rug. All the signs of someone with money. Not a trapper. Ian also noticed that Roscoe had cemented in rocks underneath the cabin outer walls, sealing the crawl space underneath. There was an access door and that was padlocked. Ian stood back scratching his head. Maybe he was simply too suspicious. *Maybe Roscoe had come by the extra money legally. Maybe he had received an inheritance. It could happen.*

He thought about packing up his gear and in the morning walking out of there, but he didn't have anything else requiring his immediate attention, so he decided to stay until Jack would pick him up at the deadwater in a few days. It would be a long few days.

Roscoe didn't return and no other fishermen appeared on the lake. To break the boredom, Ian fished from shore. Always keeping his attention on Roscoe's cabin. Most of what he caught he threw back. He kept only enough for his next meal.

On his last day there, as he was packing up, he paused. He thought he had heard a motor. He finished packing his gear into his pack and then sat in the shadows, waiting to see if the strange noise would return. The wind was blowing down the lake and away from him, making the noise less audible. He saw two fishermen in a canoe come around the peninsula, but they were not paddling. Then he heard the noise again. They had attached a small outboard motor to their canoe and the operator was having a difficult time trying to keep the motor running.

"I told you we should have brought two paddles," the one in the bow said.

"I'll turn us around and paddle back close to shore and you can fish." Their luck ended before it got started. Ian was just as happy. It was time he left, to meet Jack at the deadwater.

* * * *

Ian spent a couple of days at home. He wanted to plant his garden and take care of a few other jobs. The story Gerald had told him about his Great Grandmother Sarah Burcklbank Darling intrigued him. Gerald had said she had met her misfortune before he was born in 1912, but didn't know exactly what year she had met her demise.

The next evening after returning home, he visited the Darling Cemetery in Moro Plt. He found the Darling monument easily enough—William, Sarah's husband who died at the age of fifty-eight in 1886. And below that was inscribed wife Sarah V. But no statistics. No date of her death. Behind the monument was a square plot all rocked in nice and neat. On the left side of the plot was William Darling's headstone. And next to that on the right where Sarah's headstone should have been, there was nothing at all. Ian looked closer and it appeared as though there had never been a headstone set there. But Gerald was very adamant about Sarah being planted in the Darling Cemetery.

Could there have been some truth to the story Gerald told? Ian questioned himself. *Or perhaps maybe she had gone back to England.* The answer would always remain a mystery.

*   *   *   *

Freil Lumber Company was making a new road across the Dudley Deadwater in T7-R4 just north of Route 212. Dudley Brook had always been a favorite for brook fishermen, and now they would have easy access to it. T7-R4 was also excellent country and habitat for moose. One day while Ian was mowing his lawn, Keith stopped to see him, "Hello Ian. I'm surprised to find you home during the fishing season."

"Well, I had to take a break to finish some chores around here. What can I do for you?"

"There are two brothers working for me from Linneus, Paul and Larry Jacobs. They are carrying a British .303 rifle in their pickup and there's been a cow and calf moose hanging round the deadwater on Dudley. Just thought you might want to know. I don't hold none to any tom-foolery while working for me."

"What time in the morning do these two usually arrive at work?" Ian asked.

"They're usually in a little before daylight and are one of the last crews to leave in the afternoon. The cow and calf were still there when I drove out to find you."

"Thanks Keith, I'll see what I can do. If they should shoot one, would you like some of the meat?"

"I'd appreciate it, but I wouldn't want any of the crew to find out I've been talking with you."

* * * *

Ian was up and on his way to Dudley Deadwater at 2 A.M. He knew he was probably a lot early, but he wanted to find a hidey-hole for his brand new state issued Chevy 4x4 pickup. The only spot he knew of was about a half of a mile the other side of the deadwater.

He hid his new green 4x4 pickup and brushed out the tire tracks where he had turned off the main gravel road. The walk back to the deadwater was refreshing. The stars were still out bright and the air temperature was still cool. The only sounds were an owl sitting atop an old dead tree out in the deadwater and a loon calling at the far end. Before nearing the crossing at the deadwater, he watched as a lone coyote crossed the road.

He set his pack out of sight of the road and with his binoculars he crept silently down to the two huge four foot culverts under the road. The water in the deadwater flowed through these two culverts. Actually they were sections to an old iron smoke stack. The cow and calf were above the road, feeding on aquatic plants. Ian sat down on a stump just off the road right of way to wait.

Off in the distance, he could hear a big log truck coming off Route 212 and beginning its run up the Dudley Deadwater road. For an inconspicuous place to hide, Ian decided on the inside of one of the huge culverts. That way, if the truck stopped, he would be concealed and still be able to see what was happening. The big truck never even slowed as it approached the crossing. As the truck passed overhead, the weight of the truck squashed the top of the culvert, but it sprang back into place once the weight had passed on.

Just as Ian was getting out of the culvert, a loaded truck was coming out. This one was traveling just as fast as the previous empty truck. He ducked back inside of the culvert and waited for the truck to pass. When the full weight of the truck was directly on top of the culvert, it squashed it a good twelve inches. Ian held his breath as he was sure the culvert would crumble. Perhaps this wasn't such a good place to hide after all.

He went back into the thicket of trees to wait. The cow was still feeding, but Ian couldn't see the calf. Perhaps it had had enough and had gone back to shore.

Ian lit a cigar to ward off the mosquitoes. They were really bad this morning. He had only taken a few puffs when he heard another vehicle coming. Ian's sixth sense had kicked into gear and he knew this would be the Jacob brothers. He crushed out his cigar and waited. Adrenaline was beginning to flow and he had to pee. He was excited and he began to shake with anticipation.

Sure enough, the pickup came to a full stop on the crossing. Ian could see the moose. She lifted her head to look at the commotion on the crossing. The driver had his rifle out of the side window and fired. The noise caught Ian off guard and he flinched. Ian waited to see what the two brothers would do then, as his heart began to beat again.

The driver pulled the rifle back inside and then sped off. Ian figured they would probably stay late, until the other crews had gone, and then come back and take care of the moose. When the Jacob pickup was out of sight, Ian picked up his pack, crossed the road and circled through the woods to the moose laying dead in the tall grass.

Ian waded through the grass to the moose. She had fallen onto solid ground, out of the water. Ian was already wet. *Neat kill though. One shot to the throat.* He knew the meat would spoil if he didn't open her up and pull the guts out. His knife was sharp and he soon had the moose slit open to her brisket. Just as he was about to pull the guts out, another vehicle came along and stopped on the crossing. Ian lay flat in the grass next to the moose. He knew he could not be seen from the road. He began to wonder if the calf moose had wandered back out into the deadwater and was about to be shot.

Ian raised his head just enough to peer through the grass. There were two people, probably wood workers by their dress, standing on the road, fishing. Ian mopped the sweat from his face with his handkerchief and then laid flat in the grass. He hoped these two would move along soon. The mosquitoes were getting worse. And out here in the open deadwater, he couldn't light a cigar. He would have to endure.

He had to keep concealed so other workers would not tell the Jacob brothers that a game warden was hot on their trail and spook them.

By the excitement in the voices coming from the crossing, Ian assumed the two were having quite good fishing. Apparently these two were not serious workers. When they had stopped fishing, they did take the time to clean the fish before the flesh softened and the trout spoiled.

Eventually the two drove off, leaving Ian to finish his job. When he had the moose opened and cleaned, he reached way up into the chest area and cut out the heart and pulled it free. That he washed out in the brook and then wrapped it in plastic and put it in his pack. Now he was ready to find the two brothers.

As he walked back to his pickup, he looked at himself and laughed. He was covered with blood, hair, and black mud. He didn't care, he had the Jacob brothers dead-to-right. He could clean up later at home.

Ian stopped at the first crew he found. "Hello, Jeff, I'm looking for the Jacob brothers. Can you tell me where they are working?"

"Sure, what did they do, shoot that moose that's been showing up on the deadwater?"

"I need to talk with them."

"Go right to the end of this road. They will be the last crew you come to."

"Thanks, Jeff."

Ian saw Keith on this way to see the brothers. He paid no attention to his passing at all.

Paul was sharpening his chainsaw when Ian drove up and parked his pickup out of the way.

"Hello, Warden. Nice day ain't it?" Paul said.

"Yeah, it is at that. I think maybe this evening, I'll come back and fish the deadwater. There must be some nice brooktrout in that dark cold water." Ian walked around the yard waiting for Larry to come out with the next twitch of wood.

Paul was getting nervous. "Do you want something, Warden?"

"No, just stretching my legs. This is nice wood. There must be a lot of moose in these woods."

Paul got nervous and the file slipped off the chain tooth and he cut his hand badly on the chain. While he was bandaging his hand, Ian walked around the yard looking through the trees. He knew he was worrying Paul, but he didn't want to say anything until Larry came back. He walked by the pickup and noticed the rifle still lying on the seat.

Paul was getting so nervous he put his chainsaw in the body of the pickup and forgot about sharpening it.

"Have you and your brother been working in here long?" Ian asked, as he watched Paul's reactions.

Paul tried to light a cigarette and it slipped out of his mouth into the mud. "Want me to walk down and get Larry?"

"Oh, no, that won't be necessary. Are you two going to work in here this winter?"

"Huh, oh, I don't know. Larry owns the skidder. I just work on the yard."

"The wood is nice in here. Good hunting, too." Ian was playing with him now.

After another agonizing few minutes, Ian could hear the skidder bellowing under the strain of a heavy load. The old Detroit engine was working hard and screaming its anguish into the air.

"It sounds like a Franklin skidder," Ian said.

Paul didn't say anything. By now, he knew the warden was there for a reason. He knew—he and Larry were going to jail.

As the Franklin came through the last mud hole before the yard, Larry had to drop the twitch and drive ahead while spooling the cable out. Larry hooked the blade of the skidder behind a piss-maple tree and engaged the winch and began twitching the load through the mud. The Detroit engine really began to groan and bellow now. Ian wondered how much more of that noise before Larry lost his hearing.

Larry finally brought the twitch into the yard and dropped the load and dismounted from the skidder. "What can I do for you, Warden?" Larry asked.

"I was just telling Paul, here, you sure have nice wood to cut," Ian wanted to see if Larry would get as nervous as Paul.

"Yeah, it is nice wood. We should do alright too, if we are left alone."

Ian could see Larry was a tougher nut to crack than his brother. "Well, I suppose you know, I'm not here just out of the blue." Ian paused to see what their reaction would be. Larry remained stone faced, while Paul was almost ready to cry.

He still had blood and mud on his uniform, so there shouldn't have been any doubt why he was there. "I had to take care of a moose this morning."

"Someone shot a moose in here?" Larry asked.

"Yeah, that's right."

"I hope you catch the son-of-a-bitch," Larry said.

"Well, if it would make you feel any better, there's a good chance I'll catch up with the two."

"There were two?" Larry asked.

"Yeah. They sat right on the crossing at the deadwater and shot a cow moose that was feeding upstream. Shot her right in the throat. That fellow is a good shot with that old British .303. I found the empty shell lying in the road."

Everyone was silent then. Paul knew he was going to jail and Larry also knew the jig was over. "You son-of-a-bitch. Where were you?" Larry asked.

"Standing right beside you." Ian walked over to Larry's

pickup and looked inside. He opened the passenger door and said, "You mind if I have a look at this old rifle? You don't see too many old British .303's anymore. Most people prefer the .30 06 or .270. Anything American made."

"Would it matter, if I didn't want you to look at it?" Larry asked.

"At this point, Larry, no." Ian took the rifle out of the window rack and opened the bolt action. There was a live round in the chamber. He put the shell in his pocket and the rifle, he secured in his new 4x4 pickup.

"So, what now?"

"Well, you both are under arrest for killing a moose in closed season. And I'll have to take you out to jail in Houlton."

While Larry and Paul took care of the last load, Ian inspected their pickup again.

"I guess we're ready, Warden," Larry said.

"I tell you what, you won't be in jail for long and you'll be needing a ride back out here. I'll take Paul with me and you follow us in your pickup."

On the way out Ian stopped at Jeff's yard to talk with Keith. "Keith, I'm taking these two to Houlton. They should be back before the end of the day. There's a dead cow moose upstream from the crossing, if you and Jeff want to walk his skidder out and get it, you and the boys can have it."

"Thanks, we'll go right out and take care of it."

*   *   *   *

When Ian walked into the jail in Houlton with Paul and Larry, the deputy looked at Ian and the disheveled condition of his uniform; at first the deputy thought that there must have been some kind of a fight to subdue these two. Ian still had blood on his uniform and hands. The deputy drew his revolver out thinking these two were real hard cases. "No need for that. This is moose blood. These two didn't give me any trouble at all," Ian said.

* * * *

On his way home Ian met Roscoe Patch. He was towing a new boat and motor. A pleasure boat and not a fishing boat. *He is spending more money, but where does he get it?* Ian thought as he drove home.

With nothing better to do, Ian decided to take a trip into Roscoe's camp and have a look around again, since he would be out pleasure boating.

Freil had extended the Umcolcus Road to the north and had stopped about a quarter of a mile from the Umcolcus Deadwater. It was getting easier and easier to get around in the woods with each passing year. The new roads also opened the wilderness to heavier and heavier pressures being put on the fish and wildlife resources. The limit on brooktrout had recently been reduced to twelve fish now in Aroostook County and eight fish in all the other counties.

Ian found where the T8-R5 yellow townline crossed the gravel road and pulled off to the side. He didn't even take his binoculars with him. This was going to be a quick reconnaissance trip.

It was a short hike to Umcolcus Lake. Roscoe's cabin was just up the shoreline from the yellow townline marker. Ian peered through the window on the front porch. Things looked pretty much the same as they had a while back. Except on the coffee table were travel brochures from New Brunswick and on the sideboard in the kitchen was a coffee cup with fancy lettering from New Brunswick. *So he is spending some time across the boarder. Is that where he is getting his money? But what is he up to?* Ian took his cap off and wiped the sweat with a handkerchief. There was no law against having money, only whether it was obtained legally or not.

There was nothing else there to indicate what Roscoe had been doing. Only that he had been traveling to New Brunswick. Ian found one peculiarity though. For someone who lived here and not just used for hunting or fishing, Roscoe always kept everything secured with padlocks. Even the crawl space under the cabin. The woodshed even had a lock on it. This was peculiar.

* * * *

Ian tried to forget about Roscoe Patch. But every time he met him on the road, more questions arose. *Where was he going now? What was he doing?*

One morning Ian was on his way to his headquarters in Ashland and he met Roscoe on Dunbar Hill traveling south. This was the beginning of the fall trapping season, and if Roscoe was making his fortune trapping, then he should be hard at it. Ian waved and Roscoe returned the hello. *Some day, Patch, I'll discover your secret.*

At the upper McMannus farm in T8-R5, Ian noticed wet tire tracks coming out of the field on the west side of Route 11 and it had turned to the north. Ian drove his pickup out of sight of the road and went to investigate the tire tracks. Whoever had been here had just left. He followed the tire tracks back to the west end of the old field where there were several apple trees growing along the tree line.

Could have been only a fox trapper, but Ian had a gut feeling he'd find more than a fox trap set. And he was correct. The tire tracks led to the largest of the apple trees and there lay a hot deer paunch. They had left the heart and liver. *Guess I have my supper.* He put the heart and liver on a crotched stick and continued his inquiry of the scene.

He found an empty wine bottle that had been thrown into the bushes. A brand he had never heard of before and the label indicated that it had been bottled in Italy and sold in Boston. Well, he now knew this wasn't the job of any local poacher or a trapper. He then found a cigar butt that had one of those white tips, so the smoker wouldn't have to soil his lips on the wrapped tobacco leaves. This too pointed to someone from the outside.

Wish I had been five minutes sooner. He had forgotten about Mr. Patch.

I guess I'll have to start spending some time here. He continued on to his meeting in Ashland. During the meeting his attention was focused on the illegal hunting that was happening at the Jarvis McMannus old farm. He doubted very much if this had been the first illegal deer to die there.

* * * *

When the meeting was over, Ian and Game Warden Dan Glidden had supper at Lil's Diner on Main Street. "What has Parnell Purchase been up to lately Ian?"

"Well, actually he has been pretty quiet. You know the warden service took over the old forestry camp there at Howe Brook Village. Feel free to use it any time you want. It'll keep Parnell on his toes if he sees a new face using the camp," Ian said.

When supper was over Ian said good-bye and drove south on Route 11 towards the upper McMannus place. He hid his pickup and grabbed his pack and was prepared to spend all night there if he had to. His stomach was full and he was restless.

He found a convenient vantage spot where he could watch the traffic on the road as well as the entrance to the back field. He wasn't much for sitting inside of his pickup while working night hunters. Even with the windows down, if a shot is fired, it is terribly difficult to tell where it had come from. With his wool blanket, thermos of coffee, binoculars and cigars, Ian found a perfect perch where he could watch both the road and the field without being seen by vehicles using the road, or if one should turn into the field.

He wrapped the wool blanket around his shoulders and leaned back against a rock. He poured a cup of hot coffee and lit a cigar. There was only a little traffic on the road that night and no one was showing too much of an interest in seeing what was in the fields.

At around eight that evening, he could just make out the sound of the B&A Train as it rolled through Howe Brook. Thoughts of Parnell came to mind and he began wondering what deviltry he was up to now.

At four in the morning loaded log trucks were on their way north to Levesque's Mill in Masardis. An animal resembling a German Shepard Dog stepped onto the road after the last truck had gone by; walking up the middle of the road. Ian thought, *There wouldn't be any dogs way out here from nowhere.* Then it occurred to him that this had to be a coyote.

The coyote stopped directly in front of Ian and sniffed the air and then turned its head into the wind. Just then Ian hollered, "Hey!" and the coyote ran off. When it got up to the Levesque Road, about a half of a mile away, it stopped and pointed its nose into the night air and howled a warning at Ian.

If they ever get a hold in this state the deer won't stand a chance, he thought to himself.

That was the end of the excitement for that night. Ian stayed tucked in his cubby until 8 a.m. Then a hasty trip home and to bed.

*   *   *   *

The next three nights were more or less repeats of the first night. Since all poachers poach on a fairly routine schedule, Ian wasn't truly expecting the same two to return until the following Sunday night. But just in case there was an odd-ball out here, he decided to make his own routine; every night until he had those he wanted.

Then on the fourth night, Friday, just before midnight, a pickup driving south slowed to a crawl when it came to the fields. It didn't stop, but Ian could walk faster than they were traveling. It had Massachusetts plates. A red and white Ford pickup, two wheel drive. He etched this vehicle into his mind. They hadn't yet put out a flashlight or spotlight into the fields, but they sure were interested.

The Massachusetts pickup drove out of sight, very slowly. *They're looking for a ditch deer.* Ian wanted to run back to his pickup and without lights, follow them. But he was sure that when they came back by, they would turn into the back field. The lighting law had gone into affect several years ago, so now between September 1st and December 15th, he could legally stop any vehicle that was using a spotlight to illuminate game. Before, he had to wait, almost until the poacher had blood on his hands, before he could legally stop a vehicle.

An hour later, the same Massachusetts vehicle came back. Still driving very slow. It stopped in the road where the vehicle had come out of the field on Monday morning. Ian was sure that some one would drop off, hunt and then get picked up later.

But the two occupants just sat there. *Probably drinking more of that Italian wine.* If a deer had crossed the road in front of them, Ian knew they would not hesitate about shooting it. How he wished he had a pet deer. "You come back another night and I'll show you a deer," Ian whispered.

As the Massachusetts vehicle drove out of sight, Ian was hoping that it would return and this time turn off the road into the field.

Being as cautious as they were, probably a deer had crossed the road in front of them that night and they had turned into the field. Whether or not it was the same deer they shot or not, it took a live deer to induce them to turn into the old field.

The rest of the night was calm. At four, the log trucks started rolling north and at daylight Ian recognized a few trappers heading out for the day. Figuring the party that he was after had already been there and wouldn't be back until another night, Ian left earlier this morning.

He ate breakfast first, but didn't go to bed yet. He had to build a set of deer eyes first for those Massachusetts ditch hunters. Years ago he had found, discarded along the B&A Railroad tracks, an old crossing sign with glass reflectors that when illuminated at night, looked just like deer eyes. He found a piece of pine, an inch square and six inches long. He painted the wood black and drilled holes to set the glass reflectors into, about four inches apart. He could hold the eyes in his hand, give the oncoming vehicle a blink with the eyes and then duck for cover. The eyes were small enough to fit in his back pocket. *This should get their attention.*

*   *   *   *

Ian hid his pickup in the same place and brushed out the tire tracks where he had left the road. As he was settling in, a pickup came out of the field. It was already there when he had arrived. From Ian's position he could look down into the pickup. This was a trapper and not a hunter. There was a strange aroma of skunk urine as the pickup drove by.

He would wait until after ten before using the eyes.

For a Friday night there wasn't much traffic on the road. He was getting tired of sitting still. So he started looking for an ideal spot to use the eyes. There was an excellent place just across the road on the east side. The field was small and it dropped off away from the road. Within the range of the headlights, there was a clump of short fir trees. He could hide behind these and give the eyes a blink and then lay down flat on the ground behind the small trees. If a spotlight was put out or the vehicle turned so the headlights could illuminate the field, the lights would be over the top of him. He hoped. He had no intentions of arresting anyone for simply lighting (illumination of game). He hoped that if a true night hunter saw the eyes and was interested, he might be curious enough to check out the back field, where there would surely be a deer near the apple trees.

He waited for more than an hour before a vehicle came along. It was going south. At the right moment Ian held the eyes out so the vehicle's headlights would illuminate them and then he gave them a blink and pulled back and flattened out on the ground. The vehicle slowed, but it didn't stop. Ian knew now he had chosen a good spot to use the eyes. They were being seen.

Another vehicle didn't come along until well after midnight. Ian blinked the eyes and the vehicle came to a full stop directly in front of him. Ian waited for the spotlight or the vehicle to turn. Adrenaline was flowing and he had to pee. But not this time; he couldn't move. The driver's window was down and Ian could hear them talking. One of the two wanted to check out the back field, presumably the one on the west side with the apple trees. The other was being more cautious.

After what seemed a lifetime, but actually was only a few minutes, the two drove on, very slowly. Ian's heart was racing and beating so loud, he was surprised the two couldn't hear him. He watched through his binoculars as the two drove south, just crawling. Brakelights came on and the vehicle started to do a 'J' turn in the road and come back. Ian ran to the other side and waited. They were still driving slow and neither of them had put out a spotlight. Ian knew that if they were serious about shooting a deer, then they would check out the back field.

The vehicle drove by slowly and didn't stop. As it drove out of sight, Ian's adrenaline stopped flowing with disappointment. "They'll be back, maybe not tonight, but they'll be back."

There was no more activity for the rest of that night. Just as Ian was finishing breakfast a local trapper arrived and wanted Ian to tag his raccoons and foxes. The coons were greasy and not very well taken care of. The foxes looked better. "You're tagging early this year aren't you Greg?"

"I need the money and a fur buyer from Belgrade will be here tomorrow."

Before Greg left, two more trappers and coon hunters arrived. It was the same story. They left and Ian pulled the shades closed...then the telephone rang. The complainant was hysterical. "Mr. Warden, he was only gone for a few minutes. We saw a partridge run across the road and Ben went in after it. He never came back, Mr. Warden, and I don't know what to do! I'm afraid something has happened to him. Maybe another hunter shot him!"

"Now Miss Bonny, calm down. Did Ben shoot at the partridge?"

"I didn't hear any shooting."

"Where were you hunting?"

"South Oakfield Road."

"He is probably just turned around. Where are you now?"

"I'm at Whitey's Market in Oakfield."

"Okay, you stay there and I'll be right there."

Ian pulled on a clean uniform and splashed water in his face to wake up. Miss Bonny was waiting for Ian outside, nervously walking back and forth in the yard. "Miss Bonny, hi, I'm Ian Randall. I'll follow you back where you lost your boyfriend. But first I need a cup of coffee. I'll only be a minute."

"You're going to take the time to drink coffee while poor Ben is lost and maybe hurt?" She was almost hysterical.

"I need a cup to wake up Miss Bonny. If I'm going to tramp through the woods looking for Ben, I am going to have a cup of black coffee first. I'll take it with me."

Ian got his coffee and followed Miss Bonny to the South Oakfield Road and then East until they came to the old Barrows farm just before Townline Brook. "We were coming this way." She indicated from Linneus. "And a partridge crossed the road about here and Ben got out and followed it into the woods. That's the last I saw of him," she was almost crying now.

"You wait right here. I'm going to go see if I can find any tracks." Ian disappeared in the bushes and thought Ben had probably followed the partridge down the embankment and then had gotten turned around. Instead of walking back up the embankment he had probably followed the lay of the land and stayed in the low land. If he did, he would eventually come out to another road that ran perpendicular to the South Oakfield Road. All he needed to do was find Ben's track heading in that direction. Ian had come about fifty yards from the road and doubted if Ben would have been able to follow the partridge any further without the partridge taking to wing. There was black mud in the low land and Ian circled it trying to pick up a track. It wasn't too too difficult; from the looks it appeared as if Ben had fallen in the mud. Then after picking himself up he had headed towards the other road. And at a fast pace according to the distance between his tracks. He was probably panicking now.

Ian returned to the road and told Miss Bonny. "I think I know where I'll find him. But just in case, you stay here." Ian drove down to the other road. There had been a lot of big truck traffic on the road. A half of a mile and Ian came to a woods crew. Ben was sitting in the pickup talking with the skidder driver's wife.

"Come on Ben. You come with me. Your girlfriend is pretty upset with you. What happened anyhow?"

"I followed a partridge into the woods at the old Barrows farm and when I turned around to come back to the road, I went off in the wrong direction. After a while I could hear this skidder working, so I followed the noise. I was only out here about five minutes when you showed up."

"Come on, I'll give you a ride back." Ian was too exhausted to carry on a conversation, but he had something fitting planned for Ben. Ben didn't feel like talking either.

Miss Bonny was pacing back and forth in the road when they pulled up beside Ben's vehicle. She came running over when she saw Ben. "I've been so worried about you, Ben!

"Where did you find him, Mr. Warden?"

"He was talking to a pretty blonde. Good day, folks." That was a dirty trick to play, but it was the truth.

On his way home Ian stopped for another cup of coffee at Whitey's Market. "You back so soon Ian? Did you find Ben?" Linda asked.

"Ben is out and okay. But I don't think his girlfriend is going to let him out of her sight for awhile."

"What have you been up to Ian?"

"Ask Miss Bonny when you see her. You'll appreciate it more, hearing it from her."

"You look awful Ian. When was the last time you had any sleep?"

"I don't know, maybe thirty hours ago."

* * * *

Ian tried to sleep when he returned home, but it was useless. In a couple of hours he would have to go back to the Upper McMannus place, so he took the phone off the receiver and laid on the couch to watch the television. He kept drifting in and out of consciousness (cat-napping). It is surprising sometimes how little sleep the human body needs at times. Sometimes it is just as beneficial to lay back and relax.

He was up in time to eat a hardy supper and put up a lunch and a thermos of strong coffee. He made sure he had his set of deer eyes in his pocket before leaving. He had a gut feeling tonight would be the night.

A month ago he had dragged a road-killed deer into the woods behind his house. He went out back and found one of the legs with the hoof still intact. It was a large hoof, and would leave a nice track.

He parked his pickup in the same hidey hole and brushed out his tracks. Tonight, he would use the eyes on the west side of the road and to create the illusion that a deer had just crossed the road, he took the deer hoof and made deep tracks in the sandy shoulder on both sides of the road to create the illusion that a deer had recently crossed the road. He sprinkled some sand on the road with a clump of grass, as if it had come off the deer's feet. Now he was ready. He actually had a better spot to run the eyes on this side of the road. It would look more natural. The only problem, the passenger would be the shooter. He would have to duck for cover in a hurry after blinking the eyes. This wasn't the first time he had used the hand-held set of eyes.

It was still early, so he poured himself a cup of hot coffee and lit a cigar. The cigar was for something to do more than he needed a smoke. He couldn't inhale.

Up until ten o'clock there was more traffic on the road than the previous nights. He hadn't used the eyes yet. All of the vehicles were traveling too fast to be hunting. When his Massachusetts hunters showed up, they would be moving slow, checking the ditch, looking for eyes.

Some time after eleven a car traveling south slowed and stopped just below Ian. His heart started racing. He thought maybe someone was going to get dropped off and hunt on foot. Then the door opened and a young woman got out and peed. Ian breathed a sigh of relief. He had never had to frisk a woman and he hoped he would never have to. She kept the door opened while she peed. Maybe because she was afraid of the dark, but all the while, she and her husband kept arguing about something. They drove off just as another vehicle traveling south also, came up behind them. Ian poured another cup of coffee.

He finished his coffee and laid back looking at the stars. They were out bright tonight. The Milky Way was shining like a neon light. Ian was watching the stars through his binoculars when he heard a slow moving vehicle coming south. He knew before he could see it that it would be the Massachusetts vehicle that he was waiting for. He had his eyes in his hand and tonight, he wore a black glove, just in case. Adrenaline was flowing already and he could not yet even see the on-coming vehicle. He couldn't pee now.

The headlights peaked over the knoll and Ian held the eyes out so the headlights would illuminate the reflectors. He turned them, blinking once, then held them steady. The vehicle was still coming slow. Ian blinked the eyes again and then pulled them back, as if the deer had pulled his head back. Then he crouched down below the bushes and waited.

The vehicle stopped right where they had seen the eyes. Ian recognized the passenger. Bourne Lincare from Masardis. He was known to be a pretty good shot. "That deer was right here, Vince. Here's his tracks. I thought I saw horns. He has a big track." Bourne said. "At least a six pointer." Ian wanted to laugh.

"There's tracks over here too, going that way," he pointed to the back field.

"Come on Vince, let's go. You know there'll be a deer at those apple trees. There has been every time we've been here," Bourne was saying.

"I know. But I have a feeling we're pushing our luck. I get arrested up here, my people in Fall River will punish me more than the law will here."

"Hey, Vince there ain't anybody here. There hasn't been all week."

"Maybe you're right. That last deer didn't last but two days," Vince said.

Vince turned the pickup off the road and into the back field. Ian started to run along behind it, but he was too tired to be able to run all the way to the back. So, he jumped on the back bumper and held onto the tailgate. He would ride with them.

When Vince had said something about Fall River, Ian knew what he was talking about. His people, punishing him. He was familiar with the camp in Oxbow where he was probably staying.

The vehicle stopped, but Ian didn't dare risk lifting his head above the tailgate to see. He was sure of being seen if he did. "There must be six deer there," Bourne said.

The pickup began to move forward again, even slower now, so they would not spook the deer under the apple trees. The deer turned in unison and looked into the headlights. Vince angled the pickup to the left, so Bourne would have a better shot from inside the cab without having to open the door.

Ian now could see the deer under the headlights. He also saw the large buck standing off to the side and figured this would be the deer they would shoot. "Make this shot count, Bourne, so we don't have to fire a second time," Vince whispered.

Ian saw the rifle barrel come out of the passenger side window. He thought about jumping out and grabbing the barrel, but just then Bourne pulled the trigger and the muzzle blast illuminated the pickup. Ian saw the buck drop and the other deer run off. Vince shut the ignition off and the two sat there quietly. Ian would have supposed that one or both, would have gotten out and run down to the fallen deer. He sniffed the air again and understood why. He could smell the acid aroma of gun cleaning oil. Bourne was cleaning his rifle. *He is smarter than I ever gave him credit for being,* Ian thought.

When Bourne had the rifle cleaned, he put it in the rifle rack in the back window. Both doors opened and the two walked towards the dead deer. Ian could easily see them now in the headlights. He waited until the two were busy dressing the deer, then he moved over to the driver's side of the pickup. The window was down and he reached in and removed the ignition key and put it in his pocket.

It didn't take the two long to clean the deer and they were now dragging it back to the pickup. It was going to be difficult to surprise them and not have one run off. He decided Bourne being more likely the runner, because he was local and probably more familiar with the woods, and more afraid of being caught.

They were about ten feet in front of the pickup when Ian stepped into the illumination of the lights. They were looking into the lights and would be blinded. Ian decided to scare the hell out of them. This sometimes would take the fight out of a night hunter. Ian stepped in front of one headlight and hollered, "Hey! Game Warden. You are under arrest for night hunting." At the same time he reached out and took Bourne by the left arm and put his handcuffs on and then pulled him to the pickup and snapped the other cuff to the pickup door. Vince took off running towards the road.

Ian snapped the cuff locked and took off after Vince. He had a flashlight and Vince didn't. He had the upper hand, because Vince was already scared. If Ian had used his flashlight, then Vince would have seen the beam and know that Ian was running after him. In time, as long as he didn't know Ian was closing in on him, he would stop to see if he was in the clear. That's when

Ian figured to tackle him. But Vince wasn't as agile as Ian and he kept stumbling on the uneven ground and careened into a dead-furrow in the middle of the field.

Ian was on him before Vince knew what had happened to him. Ian grabbed his left arm and yanked it around behind his back. Hard enough so Vince started letting the screeches out of him. "I said before, you're under arrest for night hunting. Now, we can fight it out right…now, if you a mind to. But one way or another, you are going to jail. Do you understand that?"

Vince mumbled something, "I didn't hear you. Try it again," Ian said.

"Okay! Okay, I give up."

"Smart boy." Ian helped him to his feet and then let go of his arm. "Let's walk back to your pickup. What's your name?"

"Vincent Frenette."

"Well, Mr. Frenette, other than the camp you have in Oxbow, where are you from?"

"Fall River, Massachusetts."

"Are you paying Bourne to take you night hunting?"

"No, he just looks after the camp when we aren't around," Vince replied.

Back at the pickup Ian had Vince help him lift the deer into the back of the pickup, before unlocking the handcuffs from Bourne. "What are you going to do with that deer?" Bourne asked.

"I'm going to take it home. Take pictures of it for evidence against you two for night hunting. Then I'm going to cut and wrap the meat and put it in my freezer. This buck should taste darn right good this winter."

"You can't charge us for night hunting!" Bourne said. "We didn't shoot it. We drove out here and found it already dead. Just check the rifle there. You'll see it hasn't been fired."

"I know. It's clean as a whistle. You cleaned it right after you" and Ian pointed to Bourne, "shot it."

Bourne didn't have much more to say.

"Hey, Mr. Warden, if you know Bourne shot it, why am I under arrest for night hunting?"

"Because you held the jack-light, Mr. Frenette."

"We don't have a jack-light, or even a flashlight for that matter."

"You were driving the pickup and you used the headlights to illuminate the deer under the apple trees.

"Mr. Frenette, you'll be riding with me to jail. Bourne, you drive Mr. Frenette's pickup and follow us. I don't believe you'll run off with his pickup. Not unless you want his associates after you. We'll walk out, you follow behind us."

Bourne slid in on the driver's side and hollered out, "Hey, Vince I need the keys." Ian took them out of his pocket and handed them to Bourne. Both Bourne and Vince looked strangely at Ian, with a renewed sense of fear and respect.

Ian and Vince were in Ian's pickup and on their way to jail in Houlton. Vince's attitude had changed completely. "You were alone tonight weren't you, Warden?"

"Yeah."

"And somehow you knew Bourne and I were coming to kill a deer and you knew we'd have a rifle. You're out here in the middle of nowhere at night, in the dark after two people you don't know, and who you do know have a rifle. And you're all alone?"

"Yeah, what's your point?"

"You didn't even draw your gun when you confronted us. That I don't understand. Where I'm from, the cops draw their gun for the slightest reason. I wonder what they would do out here. I know one thing, there isn't any one of them that would be out here alone."

Vince looked at Ian and he could see how worn out and tired he was. "When was the last time you had any sleep?"

"Oh, I don't know…going on forty-eight hours, I guess."

"How many nights in a row have you been out here after us?"

"A week."

"What does your wife think of all this?"

"She left me."

"I don't blame her."

"Me neither."

"I have to ask, why? Why do you do it?"

Ian was silent for a moment trying to think of an answer he would understand. "This is how I make my living. And I enjoy it."

* * * *

At the jail, the deer was loaded into Ian's pickup and then the three went inside. "Two night hunters for you, Leroy."

As Ian was leaving, Vince said, "Warden, tomorrow morning we'll both plead guilty." He looked at Bourne who showed surprise. "And you won't have any more trouble from me."

Ian had to drive slow on his way home…with his side window down, so the cold air would keep him awake. Once at home, he parked his pickup behind his house, out of sight from the road. Then he took the phone off the receiver and went to bed. And the open-firearm season on deer had yet to open.

* * * *

Three days later on a warm sunny Sunday morning, Ian decided to drive up to Lougee's camp in the Oakfield Hills. Leave his pickup at Lougee's camp and walk out the old woods roads there that go over the hills to the South Oakfield Road and another old road that goes over the hills in a different direction to the South Oakfield Gulch. The Gulch was infamous for its night hunters, only they usually did it while on foot. Not from a warm pickup.

There was very little traffic on the road this morning, as Ian drove through Oakfield to the Thompson Settlement Road. This road had, at an earlier period, been all farm land. Now, the old fields were growing back with scrub bushes and all except for a few old buildings, the farm houses had long since disappeared.

He turned left onto the Nelson Road, a narrow graveled road that only serviced a single house. This house was unique. It was built underground and literally covered with dirt and planted to grass. Looking from the upper end of the field, no one could know there was a house. A young couple from California had built this underground house three years ago—a David and Sandi Goodson. During the winters, David would return to California to work, while Sandi stayed home. Sometimes during the winter, especially after a heavy snowstorm or extremely cold weather, Ian would stop and check on Sandi, to make sure she was okay.

Ian had all intentions of stopping this morning to say hello, but there were two other vehicles in the driveway. "I guess they don't need any more company this morning."

The house had been built in a field, and at the upper end the town-maintained road stopped and then turned into a four wheel drive road. Not muddy, just rough in places and wet. As he was driving downhill towards Moose Brook, Ian noticed a well used path on the left going up through an old field. Now growing back to nature, with an abundance of apple trees.

This path looked as if someone had dragged a bear or deer out of the field. Ian was curious, so he shut his pickup off and started following the path. He followed the path up hill to many holes in the ground. At first, it looked as if someone had been digging up small trees to transplant. But there were so many. And some were a year or two old.

It was quite obvious the path wasn't created by dragging a deer or bear out of the field. But what was going on here? Ian walked back to the road and started walking down hill. He hadn't gone far when he found another path on the other side of the road, going down a steep slope away from the road.

This path wound in and around old apple trees and bushes, and at the bottom of the steep slope, next to the tree line, planted in black soil were several marijuana plants. He actually could smell the sticky-sweet scent of the plants before he recognized them.

Some of the plants had already been harvested. There were sixteen plants still standing and those were about seven feet tall. If Ian remembered his D.E.A. training correctly, these plants looked like what is called *sensimilia*, a very hearty plant in colder climates.

From the foot prints in the soil, Ian guessed there maybe had been three people here harvesting the crop. Up to this point, Ian was not suspecting his friends at the underground house.

At the lower end of this garden patch, the path continued. Maybe to more plants. In places along the path there was bare soil. And from a closer examination, Ian discovered that this soil had been sifted in place. Perhaps the person was watching for foot prints of intruders. Ian kept to the side of the path from this point, not wanting to disturb the soil and warn those who were involved.

A short distance beyond the sifted soil, Ian found a single strand of black thread strung across the path, about a foot above the ground. *These people are very cautious*. He was glad he was staying off the path.

The path led him directly behind the Goodson's barn which was adjacent to their house. The path continued across the pasture to the barn door. Just then, someone was opening a loft door in the gable part of thc barn. Ian backed up quickly, so he wouldn't be seen. He wanted to see who was in the barn. But he was unable to see past the opened door. He had seen all he needed to see and he decided to leave before he was seen.

Not wanting to drive past the Goodson's house again, Ian drove up to the Lougee camp and out through the back trail to the South Oakfield Road.

He drove back to Oakfield to talk with a State Police Sergeant, Bob Scolnik. Ian knocked on the side door of Bob's house. "Hello Ian, come in. Coffee?"

"Coffee would be fine."

"What brings you out of the woods on a Sunday morning?" Bob asked.

"I was on my way to the old Lougee camp in the Oakfield Hills, when I found a marijuana patch. And I followed a path a blind man could follow back to a barn on the Goodson property."

"Do you have enough for a search warrant?"

"Yes. The only thing that I'm not sure of is whether the Goodsons are actually residing at their house now or if there is someone else staying there. I haven't seen either of the Goodsons around this summer."

"Well, you state in your affidavit, to search the Goodson house and all out buildings and premises, and you should be covered.

"I'll telephone our D.E.A. officer and have him meet you at the barracks and the two of you can write out the request for a warrant. There probably won't be enough time to execute the warrant in the remaining daylight today, so request a daytime search for tomorrow. Let me know when you have the warrant signed and I'll get a crew together for first thing tomorrow morning."

* * * *

Ian drove to Houlton and met the D.E.A. detective at the State Police Barracks. He had to wait twenty minutes for Detective Martin to arrive. Martin wanted Ian to take him to the marijuana patch and show him the path back to the barn. But Ian was adamant that that wasn't necessary and he explained about finding the sifted soil and black thread across the trail. "These people are not neophytes. They know what they are doing and they are super cautious. If they were to see me drive past their place again, they might begin to wonder why."

"Okay, maybe you're right. You go ahead and write the affidavit and I'll write the request for the warrant."

Before Ian could begin, he had to give Martin an exact description of the property to be searched and its exact location and who the property was deeded to. Ian couldn't operate a typewriter, so he printed the affidavit and later Martin could type it, all nice and neat.

Two hours later, the affidavit and request were typed clearly and signed by Ian and Detective Martin. Now they had to find a magistrate on Sunday to sign the warrant. Julian Werner in Presque Isle was the closest magistrate, but he would probably be the presiding judge and signing this warrant would disqualify him from hearing the case. So Detective Martin and Ian drove to Fort Fairfield to have Judge Griffen sign the warrant. The only question he asked Ian, "Is all this information in the affidavit true?"

"Yes, Your Honor, it is," Ian replied.

The warrant was signed and Ian telephoned Sergeant Bob Scolnik from his home that the warrant was signed and they could execute the warrant anytime tomorrow during daylight hours.

"Meet me at the barracks at 7 a.m. tomorrow. I'll have a team already to go on this."

*　*　*　*

This was all very interesting for Ian, but he was not experiencing the same kind of adrenaline high that he would experience when chasing a night hunter. He never had to pee.

Ian rode with Bob Scolnik from the barracks in Houlton to the Goodson house. Just as they were approaching the mouth of the Nelson Road, one of the vehicles that had been parked in the Goodson's driveway the day before, was now just exiting the Nelson Road onto the Thompson Settlement Road, heading towards Oakfield.

"Stop them!" Ian said. "Those are the people staying at the house."

Bob turned his blue light on, to stop the vehicle, a dirty brown older Buick. He advised them that he had a search warrant to search their premises and they would have to follow him back to their house. Detective Martin pulled in behind their car so they could not escape.

"They didn't look any too happy," Ian said.

"No, I guess I wouldn't either, if I were sitting where they are."

Once everyone was at the house, Kevin and Karen Tubman were escorted inside and told to sit at the kitchen table and not to get up. One of the troopers would stay with them while the premise was being searched.

The barn was not used for housing animals. In fact, there were no longer any animals there. The barn was now a processing shed for their marijuana. Some of the plants were on drying racks and a goodly portion was already processed in one pound plastic packages and there was found eleven five gallon plastic pails of processed marijuana. They were also making hashish. Ian took one trooper with him who had a camera and followed the path from the barn to the marijuana that was still growing. Ian had the trooper take photos of the black thread across the path and of the sifted soil in the path and of the standing plants before Ian cut them down.

All of the marijuana was brought up to the barn where the D.E.A. detectives were processing everything. "What would you say the street value of all of this is, Detective?" Ian asked.

"About $250,000."

Ian began to wonder if Roscoe might be involved in the marijuana business. That surely could explain his sudden appearance of wealth. Maybe he should search the woods around his cabin more thoroughly.

Ian was getting a headache from inhaling so much of the marijuana fumes. He left the barn and walked over to the house to talk with Sergeant Scolnik.

"Excuse me Sergeant," Karen said, "I need to go to the bathroom. May I go to the outhouse?"

The young trooper escorted her over to the outhouse and he waited outside for her.

Ian got up and walked across the room. "That's strange. There is a working bathroom in that room over there," and he pointed to it and then opened the door.

Sergeant Scolnik stepped inside and flushed the toilet. "This is working just fine. Why did she have to use the outhouse?"

Just then, Karen was being escorted back to the house. "You take your seat at the table Mrs. Tubman and you make sure she doesn't move," talking to the young trooper.

Sergeant Scolnik and Ian went over to the outhouse to see what she had been doing. Underneath the seat, lying on top of human waste, were five sealed and stamped envelopes. They were progress reports to five other marijuana farms scattered across the United States. This was a corporation and not a simple user case.

It took hours to process and document all of the marijuana and apparatus found in the barn and the gardens found out back.

By the middle of the afternoon, the D.E.A. detectives had finally finished. Everyone was tired, hungry and thirsty. Even Kevin and Karen. Those who had been processing the contents of the barn, now all had headaches from inhaling the fumes from the marijuana.

Detective Martin put Kevin and Karen in handcuffs and transported them to the county jail in Houlton. "I would like to see everyone else return to the barracks so we can critique this search."

Ian rode back with Sergeant Scolnik. "This is going to be quite a feather in your cap, Ian. You did a good job. The news media people are going to want to interview you."

"Aye, I'd rather you kept my name out of it. Just say you were assisted by the Warden Service."

"You don't want any credit for this?"

* * * *

Ian had planned to work all night, the night before the regular firearm season on deer opened. He had done so every year, ever since putting on the uniform. This year, other than a few would-bes riding around looking, there wasn't much happening. He didn't even hear any far off shooting. This was proving to be the quietest opening he had ever experienced.

The next day, Saturday, there were hunters crawling out of the woodwork everywhere he went. Some were dressed like huge walking pumpkins, they were wearing so much hunter orange. While some only wore the blaze orange hat, which was the only requirement.

The temperature was unseasonably warm and the deer, instead of moving, had laid down. Not many hunters were successful that opening day. Ian was tired and decided to call it a day, early. But after supper when he was about to relax in his reclining chair for the evening, the telephone rang. He knew what it would be, before answering. He was right. There was a lost hunter in the Duck Pond region in Smyrna. He enlisted Jerry Collier to help. Jerry knew the person who was lost and was familiar with the camp and was as familiar with the area.

They walked the woods and wetland for most of the night before the lost hunter responded to a signal-shot fired. He had used up all of his bullets early and Ian and Jerry were not able to hear him hollering until they were practically standing on top of him, when Jerry fired his last bullet from his .30 60 rifle. If they hadn't gotten a response from him, it was agreed they would quit for the night and start up again in the morning. But as luck would have it, Jim Houser, the lost hunter was at the East Branch of the Mattawamkeag River, just west of Emerson Ridge. Ian and Jerry were not that far above him on the ridge, when Jerry fired his rifle.

Once they had Houser, they still had a long walk back to the camp, north of Duck Pond. Ian got home at 8 a.m. and after eating breakfast, trappers and coon hunters started arriving to tag their fur. Apparently a fur buyer was coming to town that evening. This went on until 4 p.m. when the last trapper left. Ian was exhausted. But he also wanted to work night hunters that night on the Moro Townline Road. He parked his pickup behind his house, took the phone off the receiver, pulled the blinds and lay down. He only needed a couple of hours sleep and he would be good to go again.

The Moro Townline Road was farming country. Most of the old farms now were run-down, or not being farmed at all, but the fields were still enticing to deer. There were green clover fields this year on the Mill Brook Road, that circled around and came out at Kilgore Corner at Route 11. The Moose Run Lodge was at Kilgore Corner and the owner never paid too much attention to what his sports did at night. Just up the road was Bear Mountain Lodge and down the road was the Katahdin Lodge and Ian had never had any night problems from the hunters staying at these two lodges.

Eight o'clock passed and Ian was still asleep. Ten o'clock, midnight and at two in the morning, Ian finally awoke and realized he had way overslept. He pulled on his uniform, boots and gun belt. He'd shave later.

He left his driveway and headed for Route 11, at Knowles Corner. He had his headlights off, of course. No sense in giving the poachers any unnecessary advantage. Everything was quiet as he drove by the three lodges along Route 11 and he turned onto the Townline Road at Halls Corner. All was quiet. There was no moon out which made driving without headlights a little more difficult, but he wouldn't be as easily seen either.

As he drove by the Mill Brook Road, he saw red tail lights just as they disappeared over the top of the hill by the old Irving Bates farm. The adrenaline was already beginning to surge in Ian's body. He knew, by some sixth sense, that those in the vehicle up ahead were out there for one purpose only. To kill a deer at night. Ian looked at his watch—3 o'clock.

As he approached the top of the hill, he slowed just a bit. Perhaps the vehicle had stopped. He surely didn't want to spook them now. But as he reached the top, he could see a very bright beam of light being shined into the field on the right. Earlier this field had been all clover. Just prime feed for deer. The light was coming from a very powerful spotlight, from the passenger side of the vehicle. From the glow of their own headlights, Ian could see there were only two people. That made the odds a little bit better.

Ian pulled right up behind them without the two realizing they were being followed. Ian snapped on his siren, then the blue light and then his headlights. The vehicle started to bolt, then it stopped and then just kept idling forward, slowly, but wouldn't come to a full stop. Ian set his emergency brake and jumped out with his steel flashlight. As he ran along side of the vehicle, he began beating on the fender of the pickup with his steel flashlight; starting at the rear and working up to the cab. The driver's window was down, so he hollered, "Game Warden! Stop!" And much to his surprise it did stop.

Ian opened the driver's door and pulled the driver outside. Ian stood five feet, eleven inches, no shrimp. But when he had the driver outside and standing erect, Ian had to look up to see his face. He stood about six feet, five inches and weighed probably somewhere in the neighborhood of two hundred and forty. Ian was about one eighty-five. Ian looked up at him and said, "You are under arrest for night hunting." He had already seen the lever action rifle between the passenger's legs and a box of shells on the dash in front of the passenger.

The passenger—shooter—was busy trying to throw things out of his window. This guy was quite a bit shorter and very rotund and probably weighed about the same. "Roll your window up and do not throw anything else out." Ian demanded. The little fat guy did as he was told.

Ian frisked the driver and removed a hunting knife and asked "What's your name?"

The driver replied "Euclid, Herman Euclid."

"What's your name?" Ian indicated the passenger.

"Cormier, Carl Cormier."

"Carl, hand me your rifle. Butt first."

"It's empty. There is no clip in it."

"Yeah, you threw that. Hand it to me butt first." When Carl had complied Ian said, "Now hand me that box of shells." Ian also took possession of the spotlight and put everything in his own pickup. After checking to see if the rifle was loaded or not. It wasn't. Ian walked back to the two and said, "Carl slide over and get out on this side." Carl did as he was told.

"I'll want your driver's license, Mr. Euclid." Herman gave it to Ian. "I'm going to take you to jail in Houlton. Carl, you'll ride with me. You'll need transportation after you make bail. So Mr. Euclid, I'll let you drive your own pickup and follow me. But I wouldn't recommend trying to run."

"Why are you arresting us for night hunting when the rifle was empty and we don't even have the clip for it?"

"Because, while you were just idling forward you removed the clip and the shell from the chamber and threw them out your window. But you forgot to throw the box of shells in front of you."

* * * *

On the way to Houlton, Ian tried many times, unsuccessfully, to engage Mr. Cormier in conversation. But Carl would not respond even to more amiable questions. Euclid kept dragging his feet, never quite driving the speed limit.

As they entered Houlton, Ian said, "I'll need your hunting license, Carl. So you can get that out for me now." He did and handed it to Ian. Ian glanced at it under the glow of the street lights. Just as he figured. These two were from Fall River, Massachusetts and probably part of the group that have the camp in Oxbow.

As they turned into the jail house parking lot, Cormier finally broke down and spoke. "We'll need money for bail. All we have is a family check."

Ian knew what Carl was inferring to, as the family. The boys back home that would probably punish him for getting arrested here. "There's nothing I can do about that for you. Once

I turn you over to the sheriff's department, you are out of my control. Perhaps one of them can help you."

Ian locked his pickup with the evidence lying on the seat and the three walked into the jail house. Ian still needed a shave, his hair looked like a rag mop and he had put on his old dirty uniform.

The deputy looked at Ian and asked, "You look like you have had a hard night, Ian. Did these two give you any trouble?"

"No, quite the opposite. They were quite meek."

The deputy looked at Euclid and Cormier and commented, "It was a good thing for you, you didn't try to give the warden any trouble."

"Are you two going to be able to make bail tonight?" Ian asked.

"I don't believe so," Carl answered.

"That means you'll be arraigned first thing in the morning. I'll see you two in court." Ian said and he left the jail. As he drove to the Elm Tree Diner for breakfast, he was thinking to himself about the night's events. It had never occurred to him to put the two in handcuffs.

*　*　*　*

After breakfast, there was still about thirty minutes before arraignments started. So Ian parked in the courthouse parking lot and tried to take a nap. It was to no avail, as the event of the night kept running through his head.

As he walked up the steps into the courthouse Ian looked back over at the jailhouse across the street. A deputy sheriff was escorting his two night hunters over for arraignment. Ian signed the complaints in the clerk's office and then found a seat in the District Court room. Euclid and Cormier were already seated.

The room was rapidly filling. This was going to be a busy morning for the judge. A few of the defendants Ian knew. Some, he had had before the judge for one reason or another. The courtroom was full. No one else was coming. The door to the judge's chamber opened and Judge Julian Werner, dressed in his black robe seated himself behind the bench. The courtroom was called to order and the judge said, "We have a night hunting case where the defendants couldn't make bail, so we'll proceed with this case first." Judge Werner looked at Ian and asked, "I presume these cases are yours, Warden Randall?"

Ian stood before answering, "Yes sir, they are companion cases."

"Herman Euclid and Carl Cormier." The two stood up. "Come forward please." Judge Julian Werner said. He looked at Euclid and said, "I guess you come by your name rightfully.

"The case against you two is night hunting. What do either of you have to say about it?"

They both answered at the same time, "Guilty your honor."

Then Cormier added, "Your honor, we were looking for deer and we did have a spotlight out the window. But the rifle wasn't loaded and we didn't have the clip for it."

Julian Werner looked at Ian and asked, "Did they have bullets?"

"Yes your Honor. The passenger, Mr. Cormier had a .22 mag. lever action rifle between his legs and a box of shells on the dash in front of him. He was also using a 150,000 watt spotlight, illuminating a clover field. The clip was thrown and I was not able to look for it."

"Why not?" Judge Werner asked.

"I was alone, your Honor."

"You were illuminating a clover field which is a grand place to find deer. And by your own admission, you were looking for deer. You had a rifle and it was between your legs and you may or may not have had the clip, but there was a box of shells on the dash. That fulfills all the requirements of night hunting. If Warden Randall arrested you for night hunting, then in all likelihood you were. I find you both guilty. The fine is five hundred dollars each and three days in jail, each. And…I'm going to also tack on twenty dollars a day for room and board. If you two think you can come up here from Massachusetts and expect to stay for three days with free room and board, I guess you can afford to pay for it.

"Warden Randall, will you escort these two back across the road?"

Euclid said, "Your Honor, we'll go over on our own. I don't want to be escorted by him."

"You'll be escorted by whomever I direct. Is that understood?" Judge Werner looked at Ian and winked.

*　*　*　*

Three days later as Ian was fixing supper after a long day, there was a knock on his kitchen door. When he opened it, there stood Euclid and Cormier. "We did our time in jail and we're leaving Maine and going home. We would like to have the rifle, shells, the spotlight and knife back." Euclid said.

"Those have been forfeited to the state by statutory law. Those items now are the property of the state. The only way you can get them back is to attend the state auction and bid for them."

They both left without saying anything and got into Euclid's pickup and was backing out of the driveway, back on to Route 212. But they forgot there was a turn at the end of the driveway and they backed into a four foot deep drainage ditch. The headlights of the vehicle pointing almost straight up. Ian had seen what they had done. Instead of rushing right out to offer to pull them out of the ditch, he waited for one of them to come and ask for his help.

It was Herman Euclid who came to the door. "Will you pull us out of the ditch, please?" Euclid asked.

"Why, sure I will. No problem." Ian backed up to their front bumper and let one of them hook the chain to their vehicle and he hooked the other end to his. It took very little effort to pull them out of the ditch.

When the chain was unhooked Mr. Euclid said, "We can't get out of this fucking state fast enough." They left and that was the last time that Ian ever saw either one of them again. He had heard years later that neither of the two were allowed to use the camp in Oxbow again.

* * * *

This run in with Euclid and Cormier in conjunction with Lincare and Frenette, made Ian wonder just what was going on at the Fall River camp in Oxbow. So one day the following week, Ian hid his pickup a mile in on the Smith Brook Road, on the south side of the Oxbow Road. He was going to sit in the bushes and watch the camp and see for himself what was happening there. He dressed entirely in dark clothing and took a compass course through the woods to a small field just below the camp and across the road from it. Since he was dressed entirely in dark clothing he had to be extremely careful about being mistaken for a deer or bear, and shot. There was a one article florescent orange law. The only thing he carried with him was his binoculars.

It took a while, but he finally found what he wanted. He crawled on his stomach up under a fir tree, whose branches extended to the ground. This would make for excellent cover. He was there for about thirty minutes when a station wagon car coming in from Route 11, pulled into the driveway and stopped and the driver went inside.

About fifteen minutes later, someone wearing an orange vest got into the car and backed out onto the road and drove east towards Route 11, out of sight. Then in maybe five minutes the same car returned and drove into the low end of the field next to Ian. The driver was alone and he got out wearing an orange vest and started working his way up along the treeline of the field, towards Ian's position. Ian watched him with great interest. He was sneaking, not hunting, and through his binoculars Ian could see that this person was carrying an automatic pistol and not a rifle or shotgun.

It looked as if this guy was after Ian, but how in hell had they known he was there. He had been so careful. Perhaps this guy wasn't after him after all, he just hunted with a handgun. "But not with a 9 mm or .45 automatic." He whispered to himself. He watched as the guy kept coming closer and closer, always staying next to the tree line. Ian glanced over his shoulder at the camp. Nothing happening there. But he guessed by now, he was probably being watched through a pair of binoculars.

Ian had to do something pretty soon. The guy with the handgun was getting closer and closer. Ian waited until he was about twelve feet away and thought, *Better to surprise him, than to be surprised.* So Ian jumped out, right in front of this guy and said, "Game Warden—freeze!" At the same time this guy was bringing his handgun up to bear on Ian in a combat position. Ian said very sternly without raising his voice, "If you point that gun at me, I'll shove the fucking thing down your throat." Ian seldom found it necessary to curse or swear, but under the circumstances here, he felt it was appropriate.

This guy dropped his gun to his side. He was several years younger than Ian. "I want to see your hunting license," Ian said. That was about the only appropriate thing he could think of to say. He had been caught red handed watching the camp.

Arrogantly the guy replied, "I'm not hunting, I don't need one."

Ian cleared his throat and said matter of factly, "You are in the fields and woods of Maine, during the open firearm season on deer, with a loaded firearm and dressed in hunter orange. If you do not have a license or refuse to provide one, I will arrest you now and take you to jail. Your choice."

The guy produced a valid hunting license. And wouldn't you know it. From Fall River, Massachusetts. Robert Charles, age twenty-seven.

"What are you doing here?" Charles asked.

"I'm watching your camp," Ian said flatly.

"Why?"

"I want to know what's going on over there. Your guests are running a little wild this year."

There was no sense at all to stay any longer. The jig was up. Ian disappeared into the woods. He still couldn't understand how Robert Charles had known he was there. He had been so careful crawling in under the fir tree.

CHAPTER 6

Roscoe Patch had almost given up entirely with trapping. The bounty on bear had been terminated. Some animal activist group had petitioned the legislature to intervene and coerced the Commission of Inland Fish and Game to stop the practice. Saying it was inhuman and no longer needed. And so too, followed the bobcat bounty. So Roscoe hung his traps in the shed. During the winter beaver trapping season, he was never around and this fall, he had lost all interest with fall trapping. In fact, he was spending more time in Woodstock, New Brunswick than he was at his own log home on Umcolcus lake.

At first, Roscoe would only drive to Woodstock when he needed to sell some of the gems and gold he had found near West Hastings Brook. He didn't dare risk selling the uncut gems and gold bullion in the states. Too many questions would be asked for which he would have far too few answers. So he had gone to Woodstock in hopes of finding a buyer who would know how to exercise discretion.

When he found a buyer with this quality, the only question asked was, "Are these gems and the gold, yours legally?"

"Yes, but don't ask how." Since then, Roscoe and Albert St. Pierre had formed a unique partnership.

At first the Canadian custom's officials would only ask him, "What is your destination Mr. Patch?"

"Woodstock."

"Your business there?"

"Just visiting."

After several trips of just visiting, the Canadian officials began to look at Roscoe's pickup more closely. Sometimes he would be asked to step out while they looked under the seat, and it was becoming routine to look under the hood and inside of the wheelcovers. They never once searched Roscoe. Good thing too, his pockets were always full. They overlooked the obvious.

It had been agreed between Roscoe and Mr. St. Pierre that neither one would disclose anything about the other. So he couldn't very well tell the custom's officials he was visiting Albert St. Pierre. What he needed, to create the ruse was a girlfriend living in Woodstock.

Roscoe did find a girlfriend after several more visits and it happened quite by accident. He had left Mr. St. Pierre's place late after concluding business and had stopped at a small café on the outskirts of Woodstock.

Renée Sirois, a black haired, Mic Mac Indian beauty was waiting tables at the Tribal Café. She was bringing Roscoe's order of soup, salad and a cheeseburger when she slipped on the wet floor. She, the soup, salad and burger landed in Roscoe's lap. She picked herself up out of his lap, apologizing four ways to Sunday, while trying to pick the food out of his shirt and lap. She was embarrassed, to say the least. But Roscoe was the only patron there in the café. It was closing time. "I'm terribly sorry. It was clumsy of me."

The more she tried to clean the food off Roscoe, the more of a mess she was making. "Here, you better let me do that."

"I feel just awful. The grill is off now and all the food has been taken care of for the night, and your clothes are a mess." She went over and locked the front door and then came back to Roscoe's table. "Look, I live upstairs. Why don't you come up, so you can clean up and I'll wash your clothes and cook you a supper."

That was the beginning to the end for Roscoe's border crossing problems and his life was about to take a completely unnatural turn. He discovered he would rather spend time with Renée than his hermitic lifestyle at Umcolcus. His interest in trapping had disappeared along with the bounties that used to be paid for black bear and bobcat. But he had not told her about the treasure he had found or anything about Albert St. Pierre.

Now when the Canadian Custom Officials asked where he was going, he replied, "To see Renée Sirois in Woodstock." That placated the officials and they soon stopped inspecting his pickup and asking other questions. They knew of the Tribal Café and Renée, the black haired Indian beauty. They fully understood Roscoe's frequent visits. As time progressed and whenever they saw Roscoe, they would simply motion him through without stopping.

CHAPTER 7

Ian had not seen Roscoe Patch around at all during the fall. He had stopped in to see him at his log house, but he was never there. Bushes were growing up around the buildings and Roscoe's canoe had not been removed from the woodshed at all during the summer. He couldn't trap bear and bobcat for the bounty any longer. He didn't fall trap at all. In fact, Ian could see all of his traps hanging from pegs in the woodshed, all rust covered and not used. He didn't winter trap for beaver either. And it had been two years since Ian had tagged any fur for Roscoe. Whatever he was involved in, he was as elusive as someone working for the CIA.

Ian had had a busy deer season, between chasing poachers and looking for lost hunters. Towards the end of the season he had taken a couple of days for himself and had stayed at the warden's camp on St. Croix Lake. He had shot a nice buck deer and had stumbled upon Parnell Purchase. He would have liked to have spent more time working Parnell, but time and work load would not allow for it. Parnell was a real enigma. As much of a poacher as Parnell was, he was as equally that interesting and righteous. John Corriveau had died and he really missed him. He was…intriguing.

* * * *

It was the last day of the deer season. The week had been quiet. Probably because most of the locals had already tagged a deer and the non-resident hunters had returned home for turkey dinner. The nice buck Ian had shot next to Beaver Brook was hanging in the garage and tomorrow he would pull the hide off. There had been no lost hunters during the week and Ian's enthusiasm was gone. He was tired of chasing night hunters and looking for lost hunters. For some odd reason, no hunter ever got himself lost on a clear, dry, starlit night. It usually was raining, or at best, threatening to storm.

After eating a hardy supper Ian sat down in his recliner to watch the evening news with a brandy. Just as he sat down the phone rang. He set his drink down and the phone rang again. Ian just sat there. It rang again. He had all intentions of not answering it. The temperature would stay above freezing and it wasn't raining. One night out wasn't going to hurt anyone. The phone rang a fifth time and Ian found himself saying, "Hello."

"Is this Ian Randall, the game warden?"

"Speaking."

"Mr. Randall, this is Gary Stillwell from Caribou. I'm a school teacher here and today my son and I were hunting in T8-R7 west of Grand Lake Sebois. At 9 o'clock this morning we had finished hunting and were back at my pickup eating a lunch and watching this huge bull moose on the side hill about one hundred and fifty feet in front of us. When we left, the moose was still there. We were on a side road that branches off the main road on that side of the lake. We met two men, and two women and a kid hunting together. Only one of them did the talking and his speech was heavy with French. I told him all we had seen were tracks and one moose and maybe later in the afternoon we might ride around some. He said they had shot an eight pointer in there two days earlier.

"This guy also said that they were staying with friends in Fort Kent but lived in Lowell, Massachusetts.

"When my son and I returned later in the afternoon we found the remains of the bull moose we had been watching this morning. The four legs and the loins were gone.

"It has to be those hunters from Lowell."

"Can you meet me tomorrow morning at the Oxbow gate and I'll follow you in. I want to look the scene over."

"I can do that. What time?"

"Can you be at the gate at six?"

"I'll be there. I would like to have the antlers if I could."

"No problem. I'll bring a permit with me. Thank you for calling, Mr. Stillwell." Ian sat down relieved the call wasn't about a lost hunter.

*   *   *   *

The next morning at five thirty Ian was parked at the entrance of the Oxbow Gate on Fournier's Road; which went west and intersected with the Pinkham Road, out of Ashland, in T8-R9. Ian was early. He hated to have to wait, but he never wanted anyone to have to wait for him. Mr. Stillwell arrived at exactly 6 o'clock.

There was six inches of new snow on the ground and Ian doubted if he would be able to find anything. But he would try. Fournier had not graded the road yet. He was waiting until after the deer season when all the sports would be home. The road consequently was rough.

Ian followed Mr. Stillwell to the end of a branch road in T8-R7 near the south end of the township. "You can see their tire tracks here," and Gary pointed to impressions made in the mud, and now under six inches of new snow.

Ian started kicking through the snow and soon came up with two empty shell casings. One .357 mag., and one .223 caliber. He and Gary both kicked around more snow and those were the only empty shells they could find.

"Where is the moose…the remains?"

"Right behind that blow-down up there. They must have made several trips back and forth because they left quite a good path."

Ian followed Gary up to the remains and he gasped when

he saw how huge the antlers were. He would have liked to have had them also. But he had already promised them to Gary for showing him where the moose was shot.

Next to the remains, Ian found several cigarette butts. He picked those up carefully and put them into a plastic baggie. "You said last night that one of them had shot a buck up here earlier in the week?"

"Yes. The one who didn't do any talking."

"What did they have for a vehicle?"

"It was a Ford Bronco. Dark blue with two truck air horns mounted on the roof, on the passenger side; it also had Massachusetts plates."

"I have an idea and if it pans out, I'll give you a call later and tell you about it. While you're cutting those antlers off, I'm going to drive back to Oxbow. Thanks Gary. Something may come of this yet."

Ian drove to Oxbow like a mad man over that rough road. He wanted to check the tagging station there, to see if they had tagged this hunter's deer. Ian walked in and asked if he could look at this week's tagging book.

June reached under the counter and handed Ian all of the tagging books. "Are you looking for anything in particular, Ian?"

"Yes, an eight point buck that was shot three days ago."

"It should be there in the last book. That was the only deer tag on Thursday and only two since then."

Ian found the tag slip. Brad Newman from Lowell, Massachusetts. "Do you remember what this guy Newman had for a vehicle?"

"Sure do. It was a blue Bronco with chrome air horns on the roof," June said. "He said they were staying in Fort Kent, but had to go back to Massachusetts this afternoon."

"Can I use your telephone June to call the dispatcher at the state police barracks in Houlton?"

*   *   *   *

"Hello Bert? Ian Randall."

"What can I do for you Ian?"

"There are five people staying in Fort Kent who are traveling back to Lowell, Massachusetts today. The vehicle is a blue Bronco with two chrome air horns mounted on the passenger side of the roof. I do not have a plate number, but the owner, operator, should be a Eugene Levesque. Another passenger, Bud Newman, two women and a young boy. They'll have an eight point buck registered by Mr. Newman.

"If any officer sees this vehicle, have it stopped. I want to talk with the occupants about a dead moose in T8-R7. If the vehicle is spotted, have it stopped and one occupant will have a .357 magnum handgun. Hold the vehicle until I can get there."

"I'll put this out on the teletype and I'll broadcast it to all officers north of Bangor to be on the lookout for this vehicle."

"Thanks Bert."

"Thank you, Ian. I have to run. If I come up with anything, I'll let you know."

Ian knew he didn't have enough for probable cause to search the Bronco, if found, for the moose meat. But he knew that any officer would keep searching for the .357 magnum handgun until they found it. Since handguns are prohibited in Massachusetts without a permit, this handgun would be well hidden. And there was no doubt that while searching for the handgun, the moose meat would probably be inadvertently discovered. Then the vehicle and occupants could be legally detained until he could get there.

He had only driven a short distance from the tagging station towards Route 11 when the dispatcher called Ian.

"Go ahead, Bert."

"Ian, I ran a check on Mr. Levesque. The Bronco is registered to him. He is under suspension for failure to appear in the Portland District Court, for O.U.I. He is also an illegal alien, originally from Sherbrook, Quebec."

"Thanks Bert. I'm going to wait at the intersection of the Oxbow Road and Route 11."

"Okay Ian. Do you want me to advise your supervisor?"

"Not necessary, Bert. He is off this weekend."

"Okay, good luck."

Ten minutes later…

"Houlton, this is Ashland P.D. I have that Bronco stopped on Main Street in Ashland."

"Hold the vehicle, Ashland; one occupant has a .357 magnum handgun. I should be there in travel time from the Oxbow Road," Ian said.

Twelve minutes later Ian arrived. All five occupants were in the Bronco and the Ashland Police Officer handed Ian a .357 magnum handgun.

"Where did you find it, Dale?"

"In one of the boxes in back. There's also something in there, you might want to look at. I haven't said anything yet to the occupants about what I found."

"Maybe it'll be best if we take them down to warden headquarters and get off the street."

Just then, Jim Dumont, the warden from Portage stopped and offered his help. "Jim, the guy I want to talk with, Eugene Levesque, can't speak English. I'll need you to translate."

"Sure thing."

"Tell Mr. Levesque that I want him to follow me to the warden service headquarters. I want to talk with him about a dead moose in T8-R7."

Jim translated and Mr. Levesque followed Ian to the warden service headquarters about a half of a mile away. Jim followed the Bronco.

"Jim, I'm going to want to talk to each of them separately. We are going to have to sequester them in separate rooms. Keep Mr. Levesque downstairs here and I'll talk with him last."

Ian went upstairs and isolated the other four in separate rooms. He started first with Bud Newman. "I didn't look at your deer, how many points did it have?"

"Eight."

"What did you use for a rifle?"

"A .30-06," Newman replied.

Ian advised him of his Miranda Rights before questioning him about the moose. Ian knew the Miranda Rights, and he didn't have to read them from a cheat card.

"What can you tell me about the dead moose I found where you people were hunting yesterday?"

"I don't know nothing about no moose."

"Oh, then what kind of meat is that in the back of the Bronco, divided up equally in five trash bags?"

"That ain't moose. We've been cutting up a beef critter."

"Well maybe you were cutting up a beef critter earlier, but the meat you have in the Bronco is moose."

"It's beef."

"Okay. You stay right here. I'm going to talk with the others."

Ian talked with Ruth next. Eugene's wife. She wasn't any more help than Newman had been. As far as she knew the meat was beef.

Ian talked with Charlene next. She was a girlfriend to Newman. She was the only one who did not have a hunting license and she was very petite and wore casual clothes. Where the others were wearing more woodsy looking clothes. Probably she had not been hunting at all. She was a smoker though and she smoked the same brand of cigarettes that Ian had found near the moose.

Charlene was scared and was crying. It was obvious she was too scared to say anything or know anything about the moose meat. When Ian left her alone, he took the four cigarette butts that were in her ash tray and he put them in his pocket.

The young boy Charlie was a minor and Ian decided not to question him. He then went downstairs to talk with Eugene Levesque.

Downstairs, "Jim would you advise Mr. Levesque of his Miranda Rights so he understands?"

Jim was in deep conversation with Eugene. Ian couldn't understand a word of French, and he was glad Jim happened by. "He understands, Ian," Jim said.

"Okay, you tell him I know the meat in the five separate trash bags is moose. I want to know who shot it."

Jim translated that and replied, "Eugene says that is only cow meat."

"You tell him I know the difference between beef and moose and what he has is moose."

"He still says it is cow."

"Okay, you tell him, he and all his friends are under arrest for illegal possession of moose. That I am going to confiscate all the meat and take them all to jail in Presque Isle, where they'll stay until they can make bail."

Ian put all five bags of meat into the back of his pickup. Then he went upstairs to get the others. Once they were all together downstairs, "You all are under arrest for illegal possession of moose. There are five of you and five separate bags of meat. I am going to take you to jail in Presque Isle. As soon as you can make bail, you'll be released. Eugene and Bud will ride with me. Ruth, you, Charlene and Charlie follow me in the Bronco.

"Thank you, Jim, for your help."

* * * *

Neither Eugene nor Bud would say anything during the ride to Presque Isle. After a while Ian stopped trying. There was an empty parking lot at the jail, so it wasn't difficult to find an empty spot. Ruth pulled in behind him.

Inside the jail Ian asked, "Ruth, are you and Eugene Charlie's parents?"

"Yes. Is he going to have to be locked up, too?" she pleaded.

"He is under arrest the same as you. But we are not going to lock up a juvenile. He'll be kept in the visitor's room."

After all five had been booked for illegal possession of

160

moose, Ian escorted the four adults downstairs to the holding cells. Charlene was the last to the locked up. Each one had a separate cell.

As Ian was walking away he heard, "Siss, siss." He turned to look at Charlene. She was motioning for him to come closer. "Come here," she whispered.

Ian stood up against the iron bars. Charlene was pressing her body against the bars and whispered, "I'll give you anything, anything, if you let me out of here."

She was indeed pretty and as much as Ian would have liked to oblige her, he turned and went upstairs, shaking his head.

*   *   *   *

Deer season was over and now Ian could get some well deserved rest. Two days later he advised the District Attorney that he was going to dismiss the charge against the juvenile. At the arraignment a month later all four adults pleaded guilty to illegal possession of moose, with the understanding that the two women did not have to do three days in jail as did Eugene and Bud.

*   *   *   *

Ian stayed at home for two days lounging around and writing reports. On the third day, he was tired of doing nothing, so he hiked into see Roscoe Patch. He wasn't home and the cabin had been closed up, as if for all winter. Roscoe had built shutters for all of the windows and they were bolted closed across the windows. The door window also had a blind across it from the inside. *Well, it doesn't look as if Roscoe will be back this winter.*

There wasn't enough ice yet to hold the beaver trappers and Ian needed something to do. So he went on vacation for two weeks and went to work in the woods at the Fournier Lumber Camps in T8-R8 at Isthmus Brook. He would be felling trees for the skidder operator John Bean.

Ian knew John; he was from Oakfield. Most of the crew were from Canada; very French. There was one crew from Caribou; also very French.

The first week went well. They were cleaning up two other lots and they had good wood. And the scale was good too. Every time John returned to the woods, Ian would have a twitch down and limbed and ready to be hauled to the yard. The weather was warm, actually too warm, and Ian worked in his shirt sleeves.

In the evenings after each day, Ian was tired. But it was a different tiredness than chasing after poachers. Here it was more physical. The uniform created mental stress. The food was good and he didn't have any problems sleeping at night. He was enjoying himself. But he knew he wouldn't want to have to work in the woods forever.

The rest of the crews went home that weekend, but John and Ian stayed and worked through it. The foreman, Paul LaRoche had put them on another lot that had been harvested about fifteen years earlier and the crew had left a lot of spruce trees. They were about two feet diameter chest high now.

Paul LaRoche would visit with John and Ian each evening after supper. Not to be mean, but the two decided to play a trick on Paul. During the day on Sunday, Ian had found where a deer had died; probably by coyotes, and he put a hand full of deer hair in his pocket. That evening while Ian was talking with Paul, John put some of the hair on Paul's shoulder. Then sometime later while Paul was talking with John, Ian walked in behind Paul and picked up some of the hair from Paul's shoulder, making sure Paul could feel him touching his shoulder.

When Paul turned to look at Ian, Ian was examining the hair in his hands and looking up at Paul and then back at the hair. He did this until Paul started to get real nervous. Ian said, "Paul, have you got something you'd like to tell me?" Everyone at the camps knew by now that Ian was a game warden.

"No, why?"

"Well, Paul, this is deer hair and it ain't that old," Ian said.

"It's just dog hair," Paul replied.

"No...I know what deer hair looks like, Paul."

Paul left the camp without saying anything else. John and Ian started laughing. "Hope we didn't string him along too much."

They would know just how too much, come the next morning. Paul pulled them off the good lot with the big spruce trees and made them walk the skidder eight miles up the road to a new lot. The trees were thick and nothing more than pecker poles. And that's all they had to cut for that second week.

As John and Ian were packing up to leave on Friday, John said, "I guess Paul got the last laugh, after all."

"Yeah, he sure did," Ian added.

For two weeks Ian forgot about chasing people, lost hunters and Augusta. The mental stress was gone. He had worked hard during the two weeks at Fournier's Camps, but he had also found the work and the life there relaxing, in a strange sort of way. Now he was ready to put the uniform on again and go back to work.

* * * *

That fall Ian had been issued a Bombardier Snowmobile with a twelve horse power engine. Light enough so he could lift it, when he was stuck and light enough to stay on top of even light powdery snow. It didn't have enough power to spin the track, but Ian didn't care about the power. This machine would allow him to cover much more country during the winter and he wouldn't be wearing out as many snowshoes.

When it was cold and not many people ice fishing, Ian would enjoy exploring the woods with his new Ski-Doo. The woods were vacant of people and everything was covered with a beautiful blanket of white. Some days he would use two gas tanks full of gasoline.

It was New Year's Day and Ian had been out on Grand

Lake Sebois. The Spoon Mountain watch tower had been dismantled and the fire warden's camp sold. Ian didn't know what had become of Fred and Lucille. He was on his way back, coming out the Camp Violett Road in T8-R6, when he came across more snowmobile tracks, that had turned off the road into a smaller access road that led to a new log cabin. There were several snowmobiles parked around the cabin.

He recognized Ansel Snow as Ansel stepped out onto the porch and invited Ian to come in. "Come in Ian. It's too cold to stay out here and talk."

Ian shut his machine off and went inside. He took his heavy refrigerator suit off and left it by the door. Some of the people he knew and those he didn't Ansel introduced them to him. "I know you are on duty, but would you like a drink?" Ansel asked.

Ian took his gun belt off and put that with his refrigerator suit on the floor. Then he removed his shirt and badge and put that on the back of his chair, sat down and said, "I just went off duty. I'd like a beer. Thank you." Ansel laughed and laughed and handed Ian a cold beer.

"How are you and Mr. Purchase getting along?" Ansel asked and chuckled. He knew all too well.

"Like a cat and mouse. Only I'm not sure who's the cat. It's too bad he never became a warden. He would have made a good one," Ian said.

"I don't think there is any right or wrong with what Parnell does; it's all causation," Ansel added.

* * * *

Ian had heard a rumor that Roscoe had a lady friend in Woodstock, New Brunswick, and that would explain his periods of absence from his cabin on Umcolcus Lake. He checked Roscoe's cabin many times throughout the winter and it was obvious that no one had been there at all. The snow was dangerously deep on the roof and needed to be shoveled. So one weekend when he didn't have anything better to do, he found a wooden ladder hanging on the side of the woodshed and he shoveled the snow off the roof. In places the snow was four feet deep.

Spring came early that year. The snow pack was deep and the water content high. April was unusually warm and it seemed to rain off and on all month. And when May came along, the snow and ice were gone and it had stopped raining. Farmers had their crops in the ground early that year. Ian knew the stream fishing would be good until the water started to drop and then the trout would all school up in deep, cold, spring holes.

One day just before Memorial Weekend Ian decided to check Umcolcus Stream. But this time he would work it backwards from how he would usually approach it. He left the Oxbow Road and headed south on the Jack Aikens Brook Road. Gene Bates from Smyrna had logged in that area during the winter and because he kept the road plowed, frost had really wreaked havoc with the dirt road. There wasn't much for gravel in the road bed and the tire ruts were deep. But someone had been using the road.

He had to lock his front hubs in, and shift into four wheel drive. The road was that bad. Beaver had started to build a dam on Jack Aikens Brook below the road. Before driving through the water, Ian got out to inspect the depth. It wasn't as deep as he had thought. But on his way back to his truck, he noticed one set of fairly fresh tire tracks, either going into, or coming out of the road that followed down along the brook to where the brook joined Umculcus Stream. He knew there was a hunting-fishing camp there, owned by Aubrey Stevens.

Ian had to back his pickup back for quite a ways before he could find a place to conceal it off the road. He suspected that whoever might be fishing, would probably have way over their legal limit. He left his lunch and thermos in his pickup. He didn't figure on being too long. Not if the fishing was as good as he was thinking.

The tire tracks were fresh alright. The water was still stirred up and muddy. Probably whoever was here were only a few minutes ahead of him. Just before he could see the camp, he noticed the back end of a red and white Willis Jeep. *Good, they're still fishing.* Not knowing if they would be fishing the East or West Branch of Umcolcus Stream, he decided to sit where he could watch the Jeep and wait for their return. He found a somewhat comfortable spot and sat down to wait. The blackflies were terrible and he had left his fly dope in the pickup. He really didn't want to light a cigar, because the smell of cigar smoke would carry down along the stream. He unrolled his long sleeve shirt and that helped, but they kept up that incessant buzzing around his face.

When noon had come and gone and still no fishermen, he thought that maybe they had stopped to cook the fish they had caught this morning and were now catching, probably, a second limit. The only noise was the slow gurgling of the water, song birds, and the ever present buzzing of the hoards of blackflies.

To amuse himself while he waited, he started killing blackflies and putting the bodies on a yellow birch leaf, just to watch the black mass grow. When the leaf wouldn't hold any more flies, it dipped and the flies fell to the ground. It was now three in the afternoon. "They must have caught hundreds of brooktrout by now." He began to calculate in his head what the fine would be for a hundred fish over the limit.

As the afternoon worn on and the temperature began to drop, the blackflies and now the mosquitoes were worse than they had been previously. His stomach was growling from hunger and he was dying for a drink of water; or some of his coffee in the thermos he had left in his pickup. It would probably be cold by the time he got back to his pickup.

He started whittling to pass the time. But he soon lost interest in that. Finally at 6 o'clock in the evening, he decided to sneak through the trees to have a look at the jeep. When he could plainly see the camp, he looked through his binoculars at the door. There was a padlock on the door and it was locked. Well, whoever was here didn't necessarily have to be staying in the camp.

Keeping to the cover of the trees, he worked his way closer to the jeep. He looked at the tires and then at the tracks left on the ground by the tires. He looked again and blinked and scratched his head. "This jeep hasn't been moved since last fall." Ian came out of the bushes to have a closer look. Sure enough, the last tracks the jeep made were old. He turned around to look at what he had thought were fresh tracks and decided that someone probably had been here during the weekend and had left yesterday. He had a good laugh at himself. He had sat there enduring the hoards of blackflies for nearly ten hours and there was no one here. He guessed he wouldn't be telling Aubrey Stevens about this just yet. Someday perhaps.

He walked back to his pickup and drank cold coffee and went home.

*   *   *   *

Just before leaving his house the next morning, Ian received a telephone call from Emmett Brown in Oakfield. He was complaining about the beaver damming the stream and flooding his woods road and killing the trees around the pond. "I'll be down this morning, Mr. Brown, and set some conibear traps and remove the beaver for you."

Ian sharpened his axe and put it in his pack-basket, a coil of wire and his hip waders. He knew where this flowage was. He had worked the fields that were nearby for night hunters.

He had about a quarter of a mile to walk through the woods from his pickup. As he came down the embankment, one beaver, that had been working on the dam, slapped its tail on the water, as a warning for the other beaver, then it swam off. Ian broke a hole in the dam to let out some water. Just enough so he could see the beaver's runs through the alder bushes. He set three of the conibear traps and had two of them all staked off and was about to do the same to the last trap. He waded back to the dam to cut more alder poles and he placed his left foot on the dam to steady himself as he swung the axe. Well, the axe was sharp and it sliced through the alder bush very nicely and then in to the top of Ian's left foot. It hurt like hell.

He didn't need to take the boot off to see if the cut was serious or not. He could feel warm blood oozing out against his cool clammy skin. He was in a bad fix and he knew he had to get out of there in a hurry. He picked up his pack and hiked the quarter of a mile back to his pickup.

Once there, he climbed into the body of his pickup and sat on the fender to pull his boot off. His sock was so full of blood, that it looked like a moose liver. He was surprised to see how much blood ran out of the boot. He tied his handkerchief around his foot to stop the bleeding. Then he hopped down out of the body and started to go for help. There was one problem. The transmission was a standard and each time he went to push the clutch, blood would gush from the wound.

He turned the ignition key with the transmission in first gear while the clutch was engaged. The engine did start and the pickup jumped forward. He idled down the knoll to the main road. His closest help would be Whitey's Store in Oakfield, if Casey was working today. He was a physician's assistant. Casey and his wife Linda owned Whitey's Market. That was the only choice he had.

Ian had experience with driving big trucks, and he knew he could shift the transmission without the clutch by using high rpm's. This was working okay until he came to the store yard and had to stop. He had to coast to a stop in high gear and the truck bucked like a new driver was behind the wheel.

Linda came out to see what the problem was. "Linda, is Casey here?"

"No, he won't be around all day. Can I help you." She looked in the passenger window then and saw all the blood on the floor. "You need to get to the hospital. I'll drive you. I'll just go tell one of the girls first."

Ian slid over in the seat to let Linda drive. "How did you do that?"

"I was trapping nuisance beaver for Emmett Brown and cut my foot with the axe."

When the doctor washed the wound, it was more painful than when Ian had cut it with the axe.

"You'll have to stay off your foot and out of the mud and beaver swamps for three weeks." That was like hitting Ian in the stomach.

During the first two weeks Ian did as he promised. He stayed off his foot. Most of the time he sat on his porch with binoculars watching his friend John Bean cutting wood across the road and on the other side of the hay field. He also read a lot.

But by the third week he was tired of convalescing, and would run up and down the driveway, using his crutches. Then one morning a woman from Fort Kent stopped and said she had just run over a small bear, just north of Knowles Corner.

Ian didn't have anything else or better to do, so he drove up and found the bear. It was a yearling, and about eighty pounds. There wasn't a cut or mark on it. Then he had a devilish idea. He put the bear in the back of his pickup and drove home. He went back on his porch and began watching his friend again through the binoculars.

John was having skidder problems. He just walked out and retrieved some tools from his pickup and walked back into the woods. Ian put the bear on his three wheeler and drove down to John's wood yard. He shut the three wheeler off and listened. The skidder wasn't running. He put the bear in John's wooden tool box that was directly behind the cab of his pickup. He fixed the bear in a sitting position and found a bolt and propped the bear's mouth open. The bear was facing towards the open end of the box. The box was big enough, so Ian could close the cover without knocking the bear over. Then he rode the three wheeler back to his house and sat on the porch with his binoculars and waited for John to come after more tools.

He didn't have long to wait. John came walking up the skidder trail directly to the back of his pickup. He climbed in and knelt down directly in front of the box and lifted the cover. All he saw was a bear staring him in the face with its mouth open. John hollered and then flew off the back of his pickup onto the ground. Ian was rolling with laughter. If John had taken just a moment to collect his wits, he could have heard Ian laughing. Instead, John picked up a large open ended wrench and walked around on the driver's side of his pickup and without any hesitation, he lifted the box cover and threw the wrench in at the bear. Then he jumped back. Not knowing what to expect or what the bear was doing in his tool box.

Ian though was having a grand time laughing. Now, John could hear laughter and he suspected something was afoul. He eased the cover back on the box and the bear had tipped over sidewise and wasn't moving. John reached in and shook the bear. Then he fully understood why Ian was laughing so hard.

John got into his pickup and drove up to see Ian. Ian was still laughing and his eyes were full of tears. John started laughing also. The two enjoyed a cold bear. No hard feelings.

* * * *

While Ian sat on his porch convalescing, he saw Roscoe Patch drive by. Roscoe even sounded the horn and waved. There were two people in the truck and the passenger looked like a woman. "I guess there was something to those rumors last fall."

CHAPTER 8

Before the fall trapping had started, Roscoe decided to take another trip to see Renée and sell more of his gold and gem stones.

"How much do you have this trip Roscoe?" St. Pierre asked.

Roscoe emptied a shoe box full of gold and gemstones on St. Pierre's counter top. St. Pierre whistled. "I can tell you right now, I don't have this much money with me. It'll take a couple of days to get it together."

"How much?" Roscoe asked.

"I'll give you seventy five thousand for the lot. But this will have to be the last time."

"What's the matter? Aren't you making enough off this? You should be," Roscoe added.

"It isn't that. There has been someone around who is looking for this type of transaction, in gold and gemstones. I told him I didn't know anything about what he was talking about."

"Who is this guy, Al?"

"I don't know his name."

"Describe him to me."

"He stands under six feet, not much less. Blonde hair, maybe 175 pounds. Oh yeah, he wears fancy boots. Black."

"What did he say about the gold and gems?"

"He said his family, a long time ago, had been robbed.

"This is all legal stuff you've been selling me right? I don't deal in stolen stuff."

"It's all legal and I didn't steal it."

"You come back in two days and I'll have your money for you."

Roscoe left and drove over to Renée's apartment above the café. She had been wanting to get married for a month now. Roscoe was dragging his feet. That is until now. He surprised her when he suggested, "Why don't we get married this afternoon."

They located a justice of the peace and were married and on their way to a short honeymoon. "Let's go to Fredericton tonight, Roscoe."

It was a beautiful drive, following the St. John River south towards Fredericton. As they drove through the town of Prince William, there were signs indicating a King's Landing. "What is this place Renée?"

"It is settlements rebuilt to replicate the early settlements from 1790 to present day. There is a lot of history there and a nice museum. Maybe we could visit there tomorrow." She knew he would. "I was there once a long time ago. Did you know that many of the early settlers in New Brunswick were American Loyalists?"

Renée knew of an elegant motel in Fredericton, away from the busy section of the city that sat high on a hill overlooking the St. John River. There was a balcony outside their room which had a tremendous view of the river valley. There was an awning to keep the hot sun out and the rain.

Roscoe and Renée sat out on their balcony long into the evening, with a bottle of sparkling champagne. Even for an evening in late October, the air was unusually warm. The lights all along the river valley looked like stars in the night sky.

Standing together at the balcony railing, facing each other; not caring about the river valley or lights, Roscoe embraced his new wife and held her tenderly to him. He kissed her lips and inhaled her sweet breath. He could feel life pulsating through her body.

Renée moved her head to one side, inviting her husband to kiss her neck, exciting her passions. She breathed faster and stronger. She kissed him hard and passionately on his lips, as his hand slid down her back and held her butt firmly.

He picked her up and carried her into their room and laid her on the bed. She bagan to hungrily take her clothes off. Not caring if she tore a button. Roscoe's clothes were already off.

* * * *

They lay in each other's arms long into the next morning. Not much caring about the events in the world or what was just outside their door. For now, their only concerns were of each other.

"Renée, we need to give this lovemaking a rest. My back is killing me. Let's get up and eat breakfast, if it isn't too late, and then go visit the museum at King's Landing." There was also an emergency why they should go. He couldn't understand why, so he forgot about the hurry to get there.

"I'm sorry to say, sir, but we finished serving breakfast an hour ago. We are now serving lunch, if you would care to order?" the waiter said.

They had a light meal of soup and a sandwich and topped it off with coffee.

As they entered the historic site, Roscoe was surprised with the immense setting. There were probably a hundred different buildings, situated on over a thousand acres. There was so much to see. "Roscoe, let's take a wagon ride through the settlement."

This was part of Renée's heritage and she wanted to share it with him. Then he thought, *Is it really her heritage at all? She is a tribal member of the Mic Mac Indian Tribe. There wouldn't be any heritage here for her. Maybe she was simply interested.* But Roscoe had a peculiar feeling that there was something here in particular that he was supposed to see. So he would let Renée guide him.

The wagon tour took them through most of the settlement. With the driver also being tour guide. The trip ended at the museum, where they each would be on their own to explore the many artifacts and historical information.

Roscoe and Renée found one exhibit particularly interesting—more so for Roscoe.

The original settler at King's Landing—which today was flooded by the Macnaquac Dam in 1965 but the original buildings were moved back away from the rising river—was Andrew and Priscilla Joslin from Exter, Rhode Island. The Joslin family were wealthy and originally from Hyde Hall, England. The Joslins living in Exter at the time of the American Revoluation were very loyal to their British patriots. Andrew enlisted in the Loyal New Englanders to fight with the British and against America's independence. After the war, Andrew emigrated to New Brunswick, to Prince William, and obtained twenty-one lots of land, or 1832 acres. Many of the settlers already in the region were also British Loyalists who had been run out of the Colonies.

At another exhibit which was titled "Legend of Captain Horace Holigard's Treasure,". Roscoe's skin felt like pins and needles. He could feel the hair on the back of his neck curling and twisting. A shiver went through his body.

He started to read about the legend when he could feel the presence of someone standing behind them. He turned to see who was there, because up until now this person had been silent.

When Roscoe's vision focused on this person, he held his breath for a few moments. This person was of the same description as the man that Albert St. Pierre had told him about. The one who wanted to know about the sale of any gemstones or gold.

"Excuse me," this stranger said with a little bit of an English accent. "I observed your interest with this legend of Horace Holigard. May I inquire if there is any particular interest? You'll have to excuse me again. I don't know what has happened to my manners. Let me introduce myself, I am Horace Holigard V. Captain Holigard was my fifth great-grandfather. The Captain sailed for His Majesty during the little tiff the Colonies forced on England, and then later in the War of 1812."

"Hello," Roscoe didn't want to give Holigard his name unless he had to. He wasn't sure what all of this was coming to. But that peculiar feeling he had had just moments ago was telling him to be cautious.

"What is this legend?" Roscoe asked.

"Captain Holigard was a great British Naval Officer. He ran a tight ship, but his men respected him and would have followed him anywhere. He engaged French and Spanish war ships many times before the outbreak with the Colonies. He never lost a battle and he brought back to England unbelievable spoils and riches from those battles. His crews always received equal shares.

"During the tiff with the Colonies, he was well known for running their blockades. Once off the Boston port, the Colonial war ships thought they had him pinned in. But he fought his way out of the harbor and almost died from his wound. He lost many good men in that battle, but so too did the Colonial Navy. He almost lost this battle, but he escaped and lived to attack again, when he and his ship were repaired. That was the closest he ever came to losing a ship."

Somehow Roscoe doubted if the exhibit held all of this information in its legend.

"When the war ended in 1783, Captain Holigard returned to England. The Colonies little tiff had cost England dearly in capital funds. The Captain vowed to fill His Majesty's coffers, by attacking French and Spanish merchant vessels that would be transporting gold, silver, gems and other riches from the Caribbean and South America.

"This isn't in the recorded history in front of you. The Captain returned to England twice with his ship loaded with rich spoils. There was another chest of riches that he and some of his crew had buried on a deserted island, off Eastport, but still in waters controlled by the British Empire.

"His Majesty had spies working near the new colonies and rumors came out of these new United States that they were going to declare war on England. So according to family history, this single chest of wealth was left on Grand Manan Island to help England buy information from the colonists; for bribery and for financial assistance in this undertaking.

"After burying the chest, according to the ship's log, most of the crew died of malaria, while on her way back to England. The bodies were of course buried at sea.

"At the beginning of the war in 1812, the Captain was commissioned to recover that chest and use its contents to purchase information and supplies, to outfit the war effort. But when he returned to the island, the chest was gone.

"The admiralty in London then accused the Captain of piracy. But because of his outstanding service to His Majesty, he was retired from service and given a generous stipend.

"He was disgraced and he and his family moved to Saint John, New Brunswick. There, he could still live like an Englishman and being retired, he spent the rest of his life looking for that treasure. He had a schooner of his own and he would sail back and forth along the New Brunswick coast and Maine—then it was part of Massachusetts, though.

"He sailed up and down the St. John River looking for anyone who suddenly had become independently wealthy. I think this must have finally driven him mad. He was obsessed with finding that chest.

"He died in bitter hatred for whoever found it and dug it up. The one thing he could never understand, how anyone could have simply stumbled on to it. Whoever stole it, had to have known it was there on Grand Manan Island.

"After his death in 1840, every Horace Holigard after him has taken up the search."

Not wanting to be too curious, Roscoe asked, "Did anyone ever find it?" The obvious question.

"No, but I have learned that someone from the Province

has been selling uncut gemstones to Mexico."

"How much was this treasure worth?" Roscoe asked. Another obvious question.

"According to the Captain's papers, which our family still has, today the gold and gemstones would be worth about $4.7 million."

"And if you should find it, you'll return it to England?"

"Not on your life."

Right then Roscoe fully understood that this Horace Holigard would probably kill to get that chest of riches. He would have to be very careful. And above all else, terminate his business and friendship with Mr. St. Pierre.

"Where are you people from?" Horace asked politely.

"Woodstock. We are the proprietors of the Tribal Café there." Roscoe wanted to answer before Renée had a chance to say that he was actually from Maine.

"This is certainly an interesting bit of information. I wonder though, if it might only be a legend," Roscoe said.

"I have just told you the true story sir. And what's more, I have Captain Holigard's ship log. No, it certainly is not merely a nice story. And some day I will find this treasure and reclaim it."

* * * *

That evening, back at their motel room Renée said, "You told Mr. Holigard that we are the proprietors of the café."

"Well, maybe we should spend the winter in Woodstock and in the spring move to my cabin on Umcolcus Lake. This will give you enough time to file for a permanent visa to the states. I don't think it would be wise to move there in the middle of the winter."

That night he lay awake for a long time thinking about this Horace Holigard and what he might do if he discovered Roscoe had the chest full of treasure. He didn't dare tell Renée about it yet. He didn't want to worry her. He wondered if Holigard suspected him already, and that was why he had told them the story behind the legend. If he did suspect him, there was no doubt in Roscoe's mind that Mr. Holigard would be stopping at the Tribal Café, to see if Roscoe and Renée had been telling him the truth.

With the cash he had now, from this last sale, and what he had locked away under his cabin at Umcolcus, he and Renée could live a very comfortable life there in the woods. As he was finally drifting off to sleep, he wished he knew the entire story of Captain Holigard and his treasure.

* * * *

Roscoe moved into the upstairs apartment with Renée. It was small but comfortable. His pickup, with Maine plates on it, he parked in the old barn behind the café. They would use Renée's car with New Brunswick plates until they left in the spring. This way, if or when Holigard came snooping around, he wouldn't discover that Roscoe was actually from Maine.

Roscoe forgot about trapping and learned how to wait on tables for the rest of the winter.

Holigard made an appearance about a month after Roscoe moved in with Renée. He recognized him immediately when he walked through the door. But he pretended not to recognize him. As if he had not left much of an impression on him a month ago.

Holigard sat at the counter, "Hello, Mr. Patch, right?"

"Yes sir. And you—I'm terrible with names," Roscoe alleged.

Holigard extended his hand to shake Roscoe's, "I'm Horace Holigard. We met at King's Landing a while back."

"Oh yes, I remember now. You're the chap who told that mystery about some treasure. Would you like to order?"

"A cup of tea and a ham and cheese sandwich please."

Roscoe hoped he was convincing.

Holigard ate his sandwich and as soon as his tea was gone, he left.

178

He didn't make another appearance at the café until late March. This time Roscoe thought it wise to at least remember his name. He ordered tea and a sandwich again and left.

They never saw him again at the café, but Renée did say that one day she had seen him in town.

CHAPTER 9

Renée had her permanent visa and she and Roscoe left the café and didn't tell anyone where they were going. No goodbyes.

It was a surprise to Renée when Roscoe stopped the pickup near the shore of the lake, but there was no cabin in sight. "Where is it, Roscoe?"

"From here we have to go by canoe. This is as close as we can drive to it." They unloaded their gear and a few food supplies and then Roscoe dragged out his canoe he had hidden in the bushes. They were loaded heavy. But that was okay, for they didn't have far to go.

Renée loved the cabin and its natural setting. This brought out her Indian nature and she glowed with happiness. Roscoe… well, he was glad to be home and he was happy, just watching Renée .

That evening was cool, but he and Renée sat out on the porch watching the sun set. *Life was good,* he figured. There on the porch that night, he told Renée his story about the treasure. "Where is it now, Roscoe?"

"It's buried under this cabin. There is a trap door in the bedroom that opens up to the crawlspace underneath and there's a padlocked side entry from outside.

"Tomorrow, we'll have to go into town for more supplies and I have an awful lot of cash here that should be in a bank. I never opened an account because I didn't want to have to explain how I came by the money. We can set up an account in your name. That way, no questions will be asked. You could simply say this is your dowry. It came along with you."

"Just how much cash do you have here, Roscoe?"

"Oh, in the neighborhood of a $120,000."

They both laughed. "And what about Horace Holigard? Do you think he suspects you?"

"No, I don't. But there's nothing to say that he won't ever discover who has been selling gemstones and gold from New Brunswick. But I believe St. Pierre's business cohorts will close that door for us."

* * * *

A week after Roscoe and Renée had driven by Ian while he was still convalescing, Ian's doctor had given him the okay to go back to work. "But stay out of beaver swamps and no long hikes."

The first order of business was to see what Roscoe was up to. He left his pickup next to Roscoe's and hiked through the woods to his cabin. Renée was planting flowers along the rocked-up wall under the cabin and Roscoe was working up firewood.

Roscoe looked up from his wood pile just as Ian stepped into the opening. "Hello, Ian, I've been looking for an excuse to take a break." Renée was a little shy around people she didn't know and she quickly went inside the cabin.

"Hello, Roscoe, you have been away for a long time this time. I thought you might have been involved in something illegal."

"No, not illegal. I got married. Come on in and we'll have a cup of coffee." Ian followed Roscoe inside. It was already obvious that a woman had taken up residence here. Roscoe didn't live like a messy pig, but now everything was so tidy.

"Ian, I want you to meet my wife, Renée. Renée, this is our local game warden, Ian Randall."

"How do you do, ma'am." He looked at Roscoe, "I guess this answers a few questions."

"Some fellas in town said you cleaned the roof off this winter. Thank you. When I left, I didn't think I'd be gone all winter."

"Are you planning to live in here year round?" Ian inquired.

"Yes, we'll go back to New Brunswick occasionally, but we're here for the duration. I probably will start trapping again this fall. Renée wants to go with me tending traps."

Ian was beginning to understand Roscoe's frequent absences, but not his sudden and seemingly affluent living. He knew there was no way that Roscoe could afford his lifestyle on what he had made from trapping and bounty hunting bear. He supposed that this was a question that would go unanswered forever.

He sipped his coffee and enjoyed the conversations with Roscoe and his new wife.

* * * *

As he walked back to his pickup, he couldn't help thinking and comparing Roscoe and Parnell. They both were very mysterious, but completely different. Both, he concluded, were educated men; although he knew little of Parnell's background. But one thing was for sure, Parnell was not stupid.

Where Parnell was a cunning and an unaware participant in the game. Roscoe didn't participate at all. He simply was an enigma. He would like to spend more time watching him, to discover the secret behind Roscoe Patch.

His left foot started to hurt before he got back to his pickup. He sat down for a minute to rest it. "Guess I won't be taking any long hikes for a few days," he said aloud.

* * * *

For the rest of that summer Ian stayed away from long walks or on difficult terrain. He wanted his foot to heal, so he wouldn't have to miss hunting season. Oddly enough, this was his busiest time of year and when he felt more stress, but he welcomed each new season and then he was glad when it was over.

One rainy Thursday in September, Ian didn't have anything better to do, so he thought he might take a ride into Pleasant Lake in T6-R6. The old road was full of truck ruts and insatiably rough. This was extremely good moose country. Better than deer, because of the mature forests. And through the years a few moose had been illegally shot in this wooded country.

Some of the wood crews usually quit early on Thursday afternoons for the weekend. Maybe one of them might decide to try his luck this afternoon in the rain.

When Ian came to the first mud hole, he stopped and checked for tire tracks. Sure enough, there was a vehicle that had come in ahead of him. And it was still in, unless it had turned at Grassy Pond and went back out to Route 11 by Rockabema Lake.

He enjoyed this ride even though the road was rough. The trees had been harvested, but many years ago. The trees were tall and meaty. He'd enjoy working on a crew in this piece of woods.

When he came to the turn near Grassy Pond, he stopped again and checked the tracks. Nothing had turned towards Rockabema. That meant the vehicle was still ahead of him. The next mud hole proclaimed this quite clearly. There was mud splashed out of the ruts on both sides of the road. The hunt was on.

The rain was beginning to let up. There was only a steady drizzle now. Ian hadn't driven only about a mile beyond the Rockabema turn, and as he was going around a tight corner, suddenly there was a brown pickup in front of him. They both stopped and Ian recognized Jack Craig immediately.

Jack had worked in the woods all of his life, and it was repted that he might take a deer now and then. He was sort of a Robinhood when it came to poaching. "Hello, Jack."

"Hi, boy. You're the warden who lives up at Knowles Corner aren't you?" Jack opened his door and stepped out. Ian did also. Jack walked to the back of his pickup at the tailgate. Ian noticed there was a lever action savage rifle lying on the seat, partly covered over with a rain coat. It was empty though.

"What you looking for in here warden?"

"These woods is great moose country. I thought I might find someone with a dead moose," he replied.

"What brings you way in here ,Jack? The road is rough and it's awfully wet today."

"Oh, I didn't know but what I might try fishing where Spring Brook puts into the lake. It can be awful good fishing at times. It weren't today. I couldn't get a bite."

Ian looked at his fish pole laying in the body. The worm on the hook was so old, it had hardened like rock. Ian laughed to himself. *He plays the game pretty well.*

"Maybe you should have used something else for bait."

"Well, if'n I had had anything else to use, I might have tried it.

"I grew up in here. It was a good place for a young man to be. My father, Mel, was woods boss for Emerson in here for years. The first camp was back, the other side of Pickett Mountain Stream. Did you ever do any fishing in Pickett Mountain Lake? I have. When I was a boy, me and old Homer T, that was some grand fishing. Especially off the point at the far end. The brook used to be good too. Until the damn beaver started building dams. Then the trout couldn't get up the stream from Mud Lake and those caught behind the dams after the beaver left usually died off. No sir, beaver killed that brook.

"Yes sir, beaver is the worse plague that ever came into these woods. They dam up the inlets to the lake, then the trout can't get to their spawning beds, so the trout can spawn, and the old breeders die a useless life. I would think your biologists ought to be out here dynamiting these dams, so the trout can get to their spawning beds.

"When the wood was all cut off around Pickett Mountain and the brook, Mel moved the camp in further, to the next brook. Mel had twenty-nine men working in the woods then. Most of them were French, from Quebec, or French speaking Irishmen, from Allagash."

"Emerson wouldn't let Dad cut any softwood. Only hardwood veneer used for aircraft plywood, for the airplanes in WWII."

They talked for two hours before Jack said, "Well, it's time I was heading for home. I was supposed to be there at noon. See ya, warden."

"Maybe you'll have better luck next time, Jack."

"I plan to."

Ian couldn't simply turn around and drive out of there without knowing for sure what Jack had been up to. And it surely wasn't fishing. That worm hadn't been used for years. He continued following his tire tracks all the way to Spring Brook. He found where Jack had turned around, but that was all. "I guess this was your lucky day after all Jack." Ian laughed as he got into his pickup and began the rough drive out.

* * * *

Quite often during that fall, Ian would park his pickup either next to Roscoe's, or out on the old Umcolcus Road and hike in to see Roscoe and Renée and drink a cup of coffee. For some odd reason, now that Roscoe had a wife, Ian was more comfortable stopping by and talking over a cup of coffee. There was still a point or two about Roscoe that was vague and maybe a bit suspicious, and he wasn't sure where he stood with him. Unlike Parnell, Ian knew exactly where each of them stood. Although Parnell did at times ardently surprise him.

As Ian was approaching the cabin, he noticed that Roscoe had boiled his traps and they were now hanging up to dry. "I see you are going to trap this year, Roscoe."

"Yeah, Renée wants to learn. It'll be fun having her along. We're not too sure yet about beaver trapping. If this winter turns into an old fashioned snowy winter, we'll probably hold up right here. Or go south for the winter." They all laughed. But somehow Ian thought there might be more truth to that than simple humor.

"What you need, Ian, is a good woman." Renée surprised Roscoe as much as she did Ian. "Roscoe tells me you have been single for a long time now."

"I have had two wives. One at a time though. Because of my job, I can't say I was ever home much. That has to be hard on any woman. I'm not sure if I want to go through it again."

"Maybe it's time for you to retire, Ian. That way you could have a life of your own," Roscoe said.

"I have been thinking about it. But I'm having fun being a warden."

"I know someone who'd make you a good woman, Ian." This time Roscoe was more surprised. She continued. "I have a cousin in Kedgwick, New Brunswick, Maria. She has Mic Mac blood in her like me and some French. We look alike and she is a year older. She is a nurse. And she was divorced this spring."

Ian certainly wasn't expecting this, when he decided to walk in for a cup of coffee. Renée could see the doubtful look in Ian's face and added, "I'll invite her here and you can stop in to see how trapping is going. I won't tell her about you, that way, in case you change your mind, she won't be hurt."

Before he could even think about it, Ian found himself saying, "Okay."

Roscoe choked on his coffee and spit it up. Then he looked at Ian in total shock. "Good, Roscoe and I have to go out to town this afternoon and I'll telephone her. As soon as I know for sure when she is coming, we'll let you know."

Again, Ian found himself saying, "Okay," almost as if he wasn't in control of his own voice. What was happening to him?

Renée was smiling to herself. Roscoe saw the smile and didn't quite understand it. She made another pot of coffee. While she was doing that, the two men kept talking.

"I found something odd the other day, Roscoe. I was walking around West Hastings Brook, above the I.P. Road and I found the remains of an old building. I started looking around and it appeared as though there had been a small farm there at some time. A few acres had been cleared across the brook from the main building. There are huge spruce trees growing there now. But it is pretty obvious that the land had been cleared and cultivated. There wasn't a rock anywhere.

"The brook was probably named after, whoever built there, Hastings. But the oddest thing I found was old bones of a bear in a hole." Roscoe dropped his coffee cup and it broke. There were pins and needles on the back of his neck. He didn't say anything and Ian continued.

"The entire skeleton was there. I pulled the eye-teeth out of the jaw and I was going to take the claws, but I think that bear had dug the hole because he had worn his claws down to nubs. As I was digging around for the claws, I dug up this," Ian reached into his pocket and pulled out a gold wafer two inches in diameter and tossed it to Roscoe. "Have you ever seen anything like that Roscoe? It's the damnedest thing too. There was just the one. I know, because I dug and dug looking for more."

Roscoe's face had turned white. He turned the wafer over and over in his fingers. It was just like all the others. With the distinguishing feature, Spain stamped on one side. "Have you said anything about this, to anyone?" He handed the wafer back to Ian. Renée brought the coffee in and she, too, was quiet.

"No, I haven't. I don't believe there is anything illegal about it. It would be an interesting story to learn how and why it happened to be there. Had the Hastings found some gold and smelted it into wafers like this. It would make it a lot easier to handle, if they had. But why would they stamp "Spain," on one side?

"With the price of gold today, that wafer is probably worth a couple of thousand dollars."

"It would be interesting to learn more about it," Renée said as she looked at Roscoe.

Renée wanted to change the subject, so she turned Ian's attention back to Maria. "Maria has an eleven year old son. I hope that won't make a difference. I didn't want you to walk in here to meet her not knowing about him."

"No, no that won't be a problem. The sooner you can set this up, the better; before I get too busy with the hunting season."

"Well, if I can reach her when I call today, I'll ask her here this weekend, how's that?"

"That would be fine." Ian finished his coffee and walked over and set the cup in the sink.

They left at the same time, in different directions. On his way to his pickup, Ian thought he had finally solved the riddle of Roscoe Patch. He knew the bear had been in a trap, by the broken bones on one hind foot. He knew Roscoe trapped bear for the bounty and he didn't know of another trapper that would be so close to Umcolcus Lake. *That has to be his secret.*

Then he started thinking about meeting Maria. He was actually looking forward to it. He had been alone long enough. But if he and Maria should hit it off, to keep her, Ian knew he would have to retire. He wouldn't put another wife through the hell that his first two had gone through. But was he ready to quit. This was gnawing at him.

* * * *

The following weekend, five days later, Ian put on a clean uniform, shaved and combed his hair and drove out where he usually left his pickup on the old Umcolcus Road, to walk in to the Patches' cabin. He wouldn't have admitted to anyone, but he was excited about meeting Maria. As far as retiring right away, well, he'd wait on that decision, until he was ready to make a commitment to Maria.

He was early and he knew it. But he just couldn't help

himself. He had walked in to Roscoe's cabin so many times from the Old Umcolcus Road, he now had a nice trail to follow. It actually zigzagged back and forth across the T7-R5 & T8-R5 Township line.

Maria and her son Eric were sitting on the porch when Ian walked around the corner. "Hello."

Maria and Eric both jumped from surprise. They had not heard Ian coming, and had not seen him until he said hello.

"Oh, excuse me sir. You startled me. I didn't know anyone was around. I didn't hear you coming."

"An occupational hazard, ma'am. Oh, excuse me, my name is Ian Randall." He walked across the porch to shake her hand.

"Mr. Randall, this is my son, Eric, and I'm Maria." She saw the uniform and asked, "What are you, a fire warden?"

Oh, how he hated being called a fire warden. "No, ma'am, I'm a game warden." To keep the charade going, at least until Roscoe and Renée returned to help him, he said, "Is Roscoe around? I came in to see him."

"No, he and my cousin Renée canoed up the lake earlier to tend to some traps. You're welcomed to sit here on the porch and wait until they come back."

"Thank you." He hoped they wouldn't be long. He wasn't liking this awkward moment.

"Would you like some coffee, Mr. Randall?"

"Yes, thank you, and it's Ian."

While Maria was busy with the coffee, Eric started bombarding Ian with questions. Ian didn't mind. Eric was just a typical curious eleven year old. Maria was back with the coffee and two cups. "Don't pester Ian, Eric."

"Oh, he's okay. He's just curious about the uniform."

With a cup of coffee in his hands, Ian relaxed. Maria saw the tension leave and she began telling him about herself and growing up in Kedgwick. "Are you married, Ian?"

That was a logical question, from someone who might have an interest in that other person. "I'm divorced. I have been now for several years. To be honest with you, I have been married twice." There was a little reaction from Maria, Ian thought, by the way she moved and the smile on her face was gone. "Both were good women. When I first took this job, I wasn't home much. I slept more often in the woods than I did at home. Times have reversed things now. I'm home every night."

"Do you regret losing either of them?"

"Well, everything happens for a purpose. I never look back with regret. It isn't part of my nature."

They had talked the afternoon away and now the sun was below the trees on the west side of the lake. "I wonder what is taking Roscoe and Renée so long."

"Look," Ian said and pointed up the lake. "You can just make out something breaking water, coming this way. That'll be them, I'm sure." Eric ran out onto the wharf to wait.

"Hello there!" Roscoe hollered from the canoe as Eric steadied it for them to step out.

"Sorry we're so late, Maria." Renée said. "We had to chase after a coyote in one of the last sets. I see you two have met."

"While the men are skinning, Maria, you can help me with supper."

Ian could pull the hides off as easily as Roscoe and they were finished only moments before supper was ready.

When supper was finished, Ian invited Maria out on the porch for a breath of fresh air. "I would enjoy that."

Eric started to follow and Renée got his attention and shook her head, no. "Let them have a few minutes alone, Eric. I would imagine Ian will have to be leaving soon."

"It'll be colder tonight than I had thought during the day," Maria said.

"It is cool, but nice."

As they talked, loons were carrying on a conversation of their own up at the head of the lake, and the full moon was beginning to make an appearance above the tree line along the eastern shore. Ian was enjoying Maria's company and he wished

190

he didn't have to leave. "I have truly enjoyed meeting you, Maria, and I have enjoyed your company. I wish I didn't have to leave tonight."

"I have enjoyed you also, Ian. I'm very glad you came in to visit Roscoe," she looked at Ian and grinned.

"How long will you be here, Maria?"

"Eric and I must leave tomorrow."

"I would like to see you again."

"I would like that, also."

"In two weeks, I'll have a four day weekend. Maybe I could come up to Kedgwick and visit you." This would be the first time in Ian's career as a game warden that he would take his regular days off during the deer season, instead of working. Maybe it is time for retirement, after all.

They turned in the moonlight, facing each other. Maria's eyes were sparkling in the moonlight like tiny diamonds. There was mutual attraction and Maria stepped closer to Ian and he cupped her cheek in his hand and kissed her. She didn't back away. As he held her close to him, she whispered, "Two weeks is going to seem like a lifetime."

They went back inside, "I must be leaving. Thank you, Renée and Roscoe, for inviting me for supper." He turned to Eric and said, "You take care of your Mom, okay? I'll see you in two weeks."

After Ian had left, Maria turned to Roscoe and asked, "How is he going to get out of here tonight? He doesn't even have a flashlight with him."

Roscoe started to laugh, "Don't worry about Ian, Maria. He knows these woods so well, he doesn't need a compass anymore and he can probably follow his path back to his pickup with his eyes closed. He'll be fine."

* * * *

Maria had been right. Those two weeks seem to stretch

on for months. Early Friday morning, Ian was on his way to see Maria in Kedgwick. For the first time in his career, he had found something, someone, who meant more to him that did being a game warden. And this was the first week of open firearms season on deer, and Ian was not only away from home, he was out of the country and no one knew where he had gone.

Maria knew Ian would be driving through Friday morning, so she had arranged with her supervisor at the hospital to have those four days off. She was as excited about seeing Ian again, as Ian was to see her.

Once he left the St. John River behind and was inland, the forest closed in around the highway. Much like the forests did just north of Patten, on Route 11. Ian was accustomed to this kind of driving and he found it relaxing. While he drove, he thought about the gold wafer he had found at the old settlement on West Hastings Brook. And because of that wafer, he had decided to talk with Roscoe and casually mention it, to see what his reaction would be.

He reacted like Ian had supposed he would. There was no doubt, now, to Ian, that this is where Roscoe had found his sudden wealth. It was all legal and he could understand why Roscoe had been so reticent. But if it had not been for the gold wafer, Ian would not have walked in to see Roscoe and Renée and would not have ever have met Maria.

He took the wafer out of his pocket and turned it through his fingers. "Yeah, thank this wafer, and who buried it there, who knows when. Thank you."

* * * *

Ian and Maria had four marvelous days together. Eric had fun also, when he could join them, when he wasn't in school. On the drive home, Ian knew he was in love. Neither of them had said anything about love. But Ian knew he was. His only question now was, could he or was he ready to give up being a game warden. 'Could he give up the game.'

The first thing Ian did Tuesday morning was to check who had registered a deer, during the first week of deer season, at Whitey's Market in Oakfield.

There were three names that stood out amongst all the others. These three were staying at Lucien Shaw's camp, on the west shore of Umcolcus Lake: Al Carr, aka Digger, Dale Brown, and Joe Young. All three had shot and tagged a deer the previous week.

Four inches of new snow had fallen during the night, and this would make for some excellent tracking conditions for a deer hunt. So good in fact, that most hunters with a full tag would have a difficult time to stay in camp, way back in the woods somewhere. So Ian left Whitey's Market and drove to the west side of Umcolcus Lake.

It was just as he figured, the three were not at camp, and fresh tire tracks indicated they had headed north. He decided to follow their vehicle tracks in hopes of catching up with them.

The tracks had gone by where Ian had supposed they would have been hunting. He continued on to the Camp Violett Road and the tracks turned east. He kept following. These were the only tracks in the snow that morning.

Just before reaching the turn off to Ansel Snow's camp, the vehicle turned right onto an abandoned road, near an old fuel truck tank. Ian followed the tracks and he found the vehicle just beyond the T8-R6 & T8-R5 Township line. He parked his pickup and locked it and looked for foot tracks of the three outlaws. Ian knew that if he could follow their tracks in the new snow, following deer tracks, whether or not they shot any deer, he would have a good case of hunting deer after having killed and registering one deer.

He picked up his pace trying to over take them. They had a couple of hour's head start. After about a half of a mile the three split up. So he chose one track.

It wasn't long before he found where this hunter had

jumped a deer out of its bed and now the hunter's foot tracks were following the deer's tracks. He quickened his pace. But still trying to snake his way through the bushes and be quiet.

The sun was coming out from behind the clouds and Ian knew the snow would soon be gone. He followed along even faster now and he could almost see the snow melting. It was getting warm. The tracks led him out into the opening of an old skidder trail, and the snow was gone out in the opening. He kept walking in the same general direction hoping to find the tracks again. He walked back and forth in the skidder trail, trying to pick up the hunter's tracks.

The snow was now completely gone and even if he found the same hunter he had been following, he would not have enough for a case. He had no alternative but to return to his pickup.

He sat down on a tree stump to rest and he reached into his pocket for his compass. It wasn't there. He checked every pocket he had. Still no compass. Boy, he was in a fix and he knew it. He drew a sketch in the dirt of his travels and figured he would have to go west to hit the road he had driven in on. But which way was west? The sun was behind a dark bank of clouds and he couldn't get his bearings from that.

Just then a B-52 flew over head on its way to Loring Air Force Base in Limestone. He knew that through here the B-52's usually flew south to north. He hoped that was so today. He started west, according to the direction the B-52 had been flying.

Ian walked for about an hour and came out to the same road, he had walked in on after leaving his pickup. Ten minutes later he was back to his pickup. The three hunters had come out ahead of him and had gone back to camp. "They'll have a laugh at camp tonight," and he laughed, too.

It was a quiet afternoon, so Ian decided to drive west on the Camp Violette Road to the junction of the Snowshoe Road and patrol around Wadleigh Brook Crossing and Batch Brook.

There was a hunting camp set up; a mobile RV camper

and two pickups, both Massachusetts registrations, where the old horse hovel was still standing, where Great Northern Paper Company had once had a lumber camp.

Ian knew who this camper belonged to Gene Dumont and Francis Carmell. Neither one was notorious, but they both warranted watching. He had had information in the past that these two would ride the woods roads at night, after the other hunters had left, looking for a deer to shoot.

He had wanted to come in before now, to work these two for night hunting, but had never had the opportunity to do so. He had met or run into these two before; they had always seemed amiable enough, but this time, Ian had that peculiar feeling in his gut. He didn't go any further. In fact, he turned around and drove home.

He parked his pickup out front where everyone driving by could see it and he signed off at home with the State Police Dispatcher. "Are you feeling okay, Ian?" the dispatcher asked.

"10-4, I am."

He had an early supper and relaxed in his recliner. Watching the clock as it finally moved beyond 6 P.M. He started his pickup and turned off his state radio. Tonight he had a particular job to look into and he was not going to be called away. Not even for a lost hunter. Tonight someone else would have to go in and find him. He was preoccupied. Besides, the air was unusually warm and the sky was clear, and no moon, which made driving in the woods without headlights challenging, to say the least. But Ian had taught himself to drive without lights, by practicing in the daylight, on wood roads, with his eyes closed. He learned well.

He found the hidey hole that he had in mind. There was a winter log landing, just up the road from the campsite, and there was a slick spot to hide his pickup. He took his binoculars and eased the door shut quietly and walked out to the road and then down it, until he could hear conversation at the Dumont camp. He could look through the alder bushes and see by the fire light and gas light.

He stood there in the road in the warm night air listening to their conversation; only it was all in French. But there was more than two people. An hour had passed and suddenly everything went quiet. Then the lights were turned off and a pickup started up. Ian ran back to his pickup and was ready to pull out behind them and follow without lights; if they turned his way. But they didn't. They turned north. North was a deadend and eventually they would have to come back this way. But there were many side roads. It could be a long wait.

He hadn't counted on this. They had turned the wrong way. Maybe they were only driving up to the Burmingham camp to visit John and Mimi. If that was the case, then it might be several hours before they returned.

He walked back to the gravel road to wait. If there was a shot, he wanted to be outside in the open and he wanted to watch for lights in the tree tops. Adrenaline was beginning to surge and he had to pee. Then he started pacing back and forth in the road.

As he turned to look north, he saw lights flickering in the tree tops. They were returning. Who else could it be? He knew it would be them. He raced back to his pickup and had it running by the time the lights went by him. He drove out and pulled in behind them without lights. He'd follow wherever they went and if they shot at anything, he would be there. Even though it was absolutely dark, it was easy to follow the red glow of the taillights, and they were ditch hunting and not driving in any particular hurry.

They turned east onto the Camp Violette Road. Still ditch hunting. They crossed the townline into T8-R6. Ian couldn't see the yellow post, he knew just by knowing how the road twisted and turned in the vicinity of the town line. Just beyond the town line they turned off the road; north. Ian was quite familiar with this road. Scott Nevers had harvested wood in here a few years ago. Mostly clearcuts that were growing back with some excellent moose habitat. Maybe they were after a moose instead of deer?

t was obvious now that they were not driving out to town. There could only be one purpose for turning onto this road. Ian turned also to follow and just as he did, the vehicle pulled a sharp left and put its headlights out across a clearcut. Then the vehicle jigged twice to illuminate more of the clearcut. Adrenline was really surging now and Ian had to pee again.

Then the driver of the vehicle did something totally unexpected. It backed up and turned to come back to the Camp Violette Road. Ian backup up as fast as he could and still try to make the corner and stay on the road, without being seen. There was no place to hide now. He waited in the road, hoping the vehicle would turn east and not towards him. If it did turn his way, he already had enough to prove night hunting, but he would like to have more. Like a dead deer.

The driver did the unexpected again and turned west towards Ian. There was nothing he could do now, except block their passage and overhaul them. He drove forward to take them off balance and he then jumped out and ran up to the driver's window. He saw four people inside. Both windows were down and the driver and front passenger both looked bewildered. Totally surprised by Ian's presence.

The front passenger was trying to conceal a .308 Browning lever action rifle. Ian turned his flashlight on and pointed it at the driver. "Game Warden, don't move." He flashed his light in back at the other two passengers. One had a shotgun and by the manner in which he was holding it, it too was probably loaded. "Don't you move either and don't try to unload your shotgun."

"Now you in front! Hand me your rifle. Butt first." The passenger did as he was told and handed Ian his rifle. Ian popped the clip out with four shells in it and opened the action and ejected a live round. He put the clip and shell in his pocket and he laid the rifle on the hood.

"Now you, pass out the shotgun! Butt first." The passenger did and Ian removed three double aught buck shells. And put those in his pocket. So far, none of the occupants had said a word.

He put the shotgun on the hood, also. The two rear occupants were only boys. Probably no more than 18 or 19.

Ian returned his attention to the driver as he opened the door, "Step out, please." And to the front passenger, he said, "You...roll up your window." He did. He frisked the driver and removed a hunting knife and laid that with the firearms.

To the driver, "What's your name?"

"Gene Dumont," heavily French accented.

"Okay, Gene, what were you looking at in that clearcut?"

"There was nothing there. We come back tonight to see if another deer would be there." This told Ian they had been here before and had seen a deer. Probably at night, also.

"What would you have done Gene, if there had been another deer?"

Gene didn't answer. There was a cap on the back of the pickup. Ian walked back to look inside. Gene followed. There was plywood on the floor of the body, with a red stain. Ian climbed into the back to have a closer look. "We shot partridge yesterday," Gene said.

Ian looked doubtfully at the blood, "This isn't from a partridge, Gene. There's too much blood."

"Francis shot rabbit."

"Gene, this isn't rabbit blood, either. And here is deer hair," he climbed back out of the body. Ian and Gene walked back to the opened driver's door. "You stand right here, Gene. You," and he indicated the passenger, Francis, "slide over here and get out." Francis did as he was told.

"What is your name?"

"Francis Carmell," with a heavier French accent. Ian frisked him and found four more .308 shells and a hunting knife.

"These two in back, I take it are your sons?"

"Yes," Gene said.

"Okay, Gene, Francis, this is what I am going to do. All four of you are under arrest for night hunting. Eventually I will take you to jail in Millinocket where you can post bail. But...

right now, we're going back to your camper. Gene is going to ride with me. Francis, you follow with this pickup."

Ian secured the firearms and knives in his vehicle. Gene got in and Ian closed his door and walked around to the driver's side.

* * * *

On the way to their camper Gene said, "You have me over de barrel, you know that?"

"Yes, I know that. Why don't you tell me about the blood on the floor of the body."

"You already know we have other deer."

"The one you shot here last night," not a question, but a statement.

"Yes, we come back tonight looking for another."

"I didn't see a deer at your camper. What did you do with it?" Ian had not been to the camper, but he wanted Gene to believe he had.

"You already know. It's a doe and no one has tag for doe. We hide it in trees behind camper."

It didn't take but a few minutes to drive to the camper. "Francis, you and the boys stay in your pickup."

Ian followed Gene out back and into a spruce thicket. There, way up in the tops of the spruce trees was a small doe deer. Gene untied the rope and let it down. There was no tag on it as Gene had said. Gene helped Ian carry the deer to the back of Ian's pickup.

"Okay, we go to jail now. Francis, you follow me. Anything here you want to lock up, Gene?"

"No, everything should be okay 'til we get back."

* * * *

At the temporary lockup at the East Millinocket Police

199

Department, Ian ushered the four inside to the conference room. "Have a seat. It'll take me a few minutes to write out all of these summons."

"What are you charging them with Ian?" Bill Brennan asked.

"Night hunting for all of them and for Francis Carmell, an additional charge of possession of a doe deer without a permit."

As Ian was writing the summons, Bill told Gene that the bail amount for all four would be $1,100 each and $25 for the bail-bondsman. Out of the corner of his eye Ian watched Gene pull out a roll of money and counted out the exact amount; for all four of them.

When Ian had finished writing the summons, he said to Gene and Francis, "The court date will be December 15th in Millinocket. Now, I'll make a deal with you. You two plead guilty and I'll dismiss the charge against your sons." They both said they would agree to plead guilty and that they would be in Millinocket on the 15th.

"Now, where we can find place to get drunk and good time with a woman?"

Ian and Bill both laughed. "This is your lucky night. Just up the road on the right at a place called Casa de Fiesta. There's a motel there and topless girls at the bar."

Both Gene and Francis were smiling now. Maybe this night wouldn't be a complete wash out after all.

Much to Ian's surprise, Gene extended his hand to shake Ian's and said, "No hard feelings. You did good job. We go now, but will be back for court."

That was the first time that someone Ian had arrested had shaken his hand and said, "good job." He almost hated having to prosecute these guys now.

* * * *

On his drive home Ian couldn't help but go over in his

mind, again and again, the events of that night. He was satisfied with the job he had done and apparently so too were Dumont and Carmell. This was what the job was all about. Could he give it up? Could he stop playing the game? Then he thought about Maria and how much he was missing her.

* * * *

On December 15th, Ian was at the courthouse in Millinocket early. Hell, he was always early, no matter what he was doing or where he was going. Dumont and Carmell and their sons were already there.

Gene came over to speak to Ian, "Where do we go? I have never been to court before."

Ian showed them to the courtroom and said, "You can all sit here. When the judge is ready for your case, she'll call you by name."

The courtroom slowly filled to capacity. Some of the invited had to stand in the hall. Ian expected the arraignments today to go into the afternoon because there were so many people here. But to his surprise, the judge pulled his night hunting cases off the top of the pile.

She read off "Eugene Dumont."

Ian stood and said, "Your honor, there are four companion cases to this same charge."

She looked through the pile and read off the other three names.

Ian spoke again, "Your honor, I told Mr. Dumont and Mr. Carmell that if they both pleaded guilty to night hunting, that I would dismiss the charges against their sons."

"Was the decoy deer used in the case Warden?"

"No, Your Honor," Ian replied.

"That is a very gratuitous recommendation. Are you willing to accept the warden's recommendation?"

They both said, "Yes."

"Then this court has no choice but to find you guilty. You understand that there is a three day jail penalty that goes with the $1,000 fine?"

"Yes, we understand."

"Are you prepared to start serving your time today?"

"Yes."

"You must also understand that you will lose your right to hunt for a period of one year in the State of Maine?"

"Yes."

"The court accepts your plea of guilty and the bailiff will escort you to the clerk's office where you'll pay your fines and you'll be in his custody until you are transported to the county jail in Bangor."

Ian's business in the courtroom was over, so he left. Gene Dumont and Francis Carmell were waiting for him in the hall. "We wanted to thank you for letting our sons go. And to let you know we have no hard feelings. You did good job. In two years we come back. But…every night after supper we handcuff ourselves to bumper." They laughed and so did Ian. They shook hands as if good friends were saying goodbye.

CHAPTER 10

For five generations the Horace Holigards had exhausted every avenue looking for clues to what had happened to Captain Holigard's treasure chest. Up until now the former Holigards had concentrated their search in New Brunswick and Nova Scotia. Since the Maine coast in the area of Grand Manan Island was so scarcely settled.

Horace Holigard had contacted the gemstone market center in London, the Netherlands, and South Africa looking for suspicious sales of uncut gems that might have had their origins in North America. Sometimes an answer to his request would take weeks. And then the answer was always the same. "Sorry, we can not help you."

The only information he could find was in Mexico City and then he wasn't all that sure about the information, that there had been shipments from Woodstock, New Brunswick. The informant himself was not known to be reliable and Horace was not able to corroborate any of the information with his own investigations. He didn't have a name or business, only rumors of gemstones coming from the Woodstock area.

So Mr. Holigard started to concentrate his efforts in his search for the gold. He had come up empty, as his predecessors had in New Brunswick, so he was now looking across the border into Maine, looking for claims that never existed, sales without claim registrations or the sale of a large quantity of high grade gold bullion.

He needed to search through old records and to find those he went to Augusta, the state capital. At the reception desk in the State House, he was told he would probably have to contact someone in the Department of Environmental Protection at 17 State House Station. "Where is that, ma'am?"

"It's across the river on Route 9. You can't miss it. There is a big sign right next to the road, that says Department of Environmental Protection."

"Thank you."

* * * *

At the DEP's office, Holigard was asked to wait and "Mr. Champley will be right with you."

Holigard waited 20 minutes before Mr. Champley ushered him into his office. "What can I do for you, Mr. Holigard?"

"I'm looking for gold transfers or sales that might have occurred after 1808. I was wondering if I could inspect your assay and claim reports."

"We used to keep that information here, but everything in the Northeast is now kept in the State Assayers Office in New York."

"Would you have an address, please?"

"That would be: 32 Old Slip, East River, New York. One block south of Wall St."

"Who would I ask for in that office?" Holigard asked.

Champley checked his files and said, "That would be Harry Baxter."

The next day, Holigard flew to Kennedy Airport and took a taxi to the Marriott Hotel on Broadway. After getting a room, he took another taxi to the Assay Office on the Old Slip on the East River.

"Can I help you, sir?" the receptionist asked.

"Yes, I'd like to speak with Mr. Baxter, Harry Baxter."

"Won't you have a seat. Mr. Baxter will only be a moment."

"Thank you."

Instead of sitting, Holigard walked around the waiting

room looking at the old mining photographs on the wall.

"Mr. Holigard, I'm Harry Baxter. How may I help you?"

"Could we go to your office, please?"

"Yes, of course. My apologies.

"Now, what can I do for you?"

Mr. Holigard started from the beginning with a partially fabricated story. "In 1808, my family lost a sizable fortune in uncut gemstones and gold bullion. I am trying to locate it, or find evidence where it was sold. The fortune was stolen you see, and my family has never been able to discover any information. We have investigated about as far as we can go with locating the uncut gemstones, and have found absolutely nothing. The gold might be more traceable. I am more interested about any gold, or bullion, that may have been sold from Maine. Any claims that may have been filed after 1808. And I'm sure that any large transaction with gold must have been recorded."

"That is a lot of documents and files to look through. I do not have the time for this undertaking, nor do I have the staff. I can provide you with our records for your perusal. But no material can leave this facility. We have a conference room you can use.

"It would help, if you knew what the 'hallmark' was on the bullion that you are looking for," Baxter inquired.

"According to family archives, there was the word SPAIN stamped into the gold on one side of gold discs about ten centimeters diameter and about one centimeter thick."

"What an unusual form for bullion," Baxter remarked.

"This may help me locate early sales or transfers," Holigard said.

"The conference room is down the main hall and second door on the right. I'll have all the information on claims that have been filed brought to you. When you have finished with this material, it'll be returned and the rest of the files will be brought to you. I must keep the claims information separate, you understand. I would not want to lose any of the documents."

Horace waited in the conference room while the claim information was being located and brought to the room. One easy way to dispose of the gold would have been to file a fraudulent claim and sell the gold under the auspices of a claim.

There was another alternative, that whoever had found the chest buried on Grand Manan Island had sold the contents wholly, to an entrepreneur who would have the means to dispose of it. But none of his earlier predecessors had ever located such an entrepreneur or a sale on the large scale that this would have had to have been.

There before him was a table full of mining claims on file. He started at the beginning which according to the earliest available information wasn't until the 1850's. Prior to that time, most of the information pertained to early geological surveys and explorations, mostly around the coastal area. But there was no information there about any discoveries or gold.

Most of what he was finding was claims to tourmaline and feldspar deposits. There was a gold mine registered in Strong which was of no consequence and another in the Dover area. Neither one of them providing much information.

In more recent years, recreational mining had taken place in areas such as Swift River in Byron, Alder Stream and Gold Brook in Alder Stream Township. But nothing substantial.

Horace wasn't discouraged. He really hadn't expected to find anything interesting in filed claims. What he was most interested in was gold sales and assay reports. But that would have to wait for another day, as he was being ushered out, before closing for the day.

The next day, Holigard reviewed the files regarding gold discoveries. It appeared that gold dust and rarely, nuggets, were sometimes used as a medium of exchange, instead of legal tender or the real coin. There was information of a Mr. Hastings who had discovered gold in Northern Maine, but he had never filed a claim and there was no description of the mine or where it was found.

There was a discovery in the Blue Hill area. Between 1879 and 1883, a William Stewart who reportedly may have discovered the Nevada's Comstock Lode and William Darling, a copper miner, got together and sold shares worth $25,000,000. Soon buildings and shafts were being erected everywhere. But the fever petered out and the mine was closed.

In 1917-1918, the American Smelting and Refining Company reopened the shafts and mined and smelted copper for the war effort, and then soon closed. Then in the 1960's and 1970's a Canadian firm had reopened the shafts for a brief time.

There was nothing there unusual that caught Holigard's attention. There was a small discovery found in Strong and a claim had been filed, but the ore was so low grade quality, that it was soon abandoned.

There were panning discoveries in the Rangeley area, Kibby Township and Gold Brook and Swift River in Byron, Maine. But there was no discovery that Holigard thought may have been for the auspices of selling pilfered gold bullion.

He did find that the gold dust and nuggets found by Mr. Hastings was of a higher quality than that of the other discoveries. In the Blue Hill mine the line of gold was in granite. The panned gold was often mixed with sand quartz and or pyrite. Where as Mr. Hastings pannings were almost pure gold. Almost too pure, unless Mr. Hastings was extremely meticulous.

He scribbled down Hastings name on a piece of paper. There was nothing else note-worthy in these files and records. He set those documents aside and started perusing through reports of gold transfers and exchange. He started at the beginning of the records and skimmed through the more earlier ones until he came to the year 1808.

A Mr. Hamilton of Bucksport had made several entries of settlers and traders exchanging gold dust and nuggets for goods, as well as for land and homes. And it seemed that Mr. Hastings had sold several hundred dollars worth of dust and nuggets; that he claimed he was paid in gold for a load of fish and his boat to a French fisherman. But what was more interesting was that when assayed, the gold was 100% gold, no impurities. This time Holigard put a star beside Hastings' name.

All of the rest of Hamilton's transactions with gold, was of the quality one might expect. Often times mixed with sand and quartz or a rock of granite or quartz with a line of gold in it. But nothing that assayed as pure as Mr. Hastings.

Holigard noted on the paper that Hastings had probably lived on the coast, or near to it, since he had been a fisherman. But why did he go to Northern Maine? "Maybe to escape from Captain Holigard," he said aloud.

But how did Hastings know about the chest buried on Grand Manan Island. He obviously wasn't a crew member, and the Captain had not mentioned it in his log, of sighting any vessels in that area during that time frame. "Then he had to have been on the island," he said aloud again.

Holigard continued his examination of the documents. Mr. Hamilton continued buying and selling gold, but never did any of it assay out to the purity of Hastings.

There was a trader at Benedicta, a Vining Gould, who bought and sold more gold than Mr. Hamilton in Bucksport. And Holigard wasn't surprised when Hastings name surfaced again.

It appeared that between 1808 and 1812, Bill and Gus Hastings had made several transactions of gold; dust and nuggets. Sometimes stating that a fur buyer had paid them in gold for their fur. This was it. This is what he had been looking for! Bill Hastings stating that he and his brother Gus had found some dust and a few nuggets while panning. But apparently he, nor his brother, had ever filed for a claim.

The assay report on this gold was the same as in the other transactions. Almost pure gold. Now if the two brothers had been panning as stated in the assay reports, then there would have been evidence of impurities, such as: sand, quartz, pyrite, iron ore and other minerals. But Hastings assays always was almost pure gold. "He knew enough not to ever sell the gold bullion in discs or wafers, that carried a hallmark of SPAIN. He knew this would have attracted attention."

Holigard knew now where the Captain's treasure had disappeared to. Or by whom. He still didn't know where Hastings had gone beyond Benedicta, or if they had traveled any further. He was sure Hastings would have chosen a well secluded place. But Northern Maine was a large piece of real estate.

The last transaction in gold made by either Hastings was in 1812. There was absolutely nothing beyond that date. Holigard checked the assay records again to see if by chance Hastings had sold a huge amount of gold.

The answer was no. He never sold more than two or three thousand dollars worth at a time.

His search wasn't over yet. If the Hastings no longer had the chest, then maybe someone else would be in the assay reports. He kept reading.

Two hours later he had found nothing that looked overtly suspicious. He decided that after five generations, he had finally discovered who had taken the Captain's treasure. The Hastings had only sold off a very small amount of gold, and then there were no more sales at all.

He would have to locate where the Hastings had settled and learn if he could, what had happened to them. Had they been killed for the gold and gemstones? Had they fled the country? He would have to return to North Maine and visit the county seat and try to find where the Hastings had settled and learn what had become of them. Perhaps the Hastings had buried it where they had settled, and maybe, just maybe, it might still be there. Holigard was closer to discovering what had happened to the Captain's treasure than any of his predecessors.

* * * *

Horace Holigard V booked passage to the Bangor nternational Airport where he leased a vehicle from Hertz Rental

Car Company. He drove to Houlton to the Registry of Deeds, only to be told that any land acquisitions or titles and deeds prior to 1820 would have been filed with the Commonwealth of Massachusetts.

So back to Bangor and he boarded another flight to Logan International Airport in Boston. Then to the Registry of Deeds. Not wanting to drive the streets of Boston, Holigard hailed a cab.

"Where to sir?"

"Registry of Deeds at 24 New Chardon St."

The receptionist at the front desk was very pleasant. "If you'll have a seat, Mr. Holigard, I'll find someone to help you sort through that material."

After a few minutes, a woman introduced herself, "Excuse me, are you Horace Holigard?"

Holigard stood up and replied, "Yes, ma'am."

"I'm Linda Ashbury. I have been asked to assist you. Usually when people come in to do research, they are on their own, unless they are looking for material that came from the District of Maine, before it became a state. That material is a little more difficult to locate."

"If you'll follow me, Mr. Holigard, those documents are kept in the basement level." Linda led Holigard to a large research room and it was empty, except for tables and chairs, paper and pencils.

"If you'll have a seat, Mr. Holigard, I'll bring the documents to you. Now, what are you looking for?"

"Information about Bill or William Hastings and a Gus Hastings."

"Do you know the town or county?"

"They settled in the wilderness. I don't know if it was ever a town. It was in Aroostook County, though."

"And the year, Mr. Holigard?"

"From 1808 to 1812 or 1813."

"I'll be a few minutes Mr. Holigard. I'll bring the documents back with me."

As Holigard nervously waited for Linda to return, his anxiety was getting worse. He began to pace along the row of tables. He was close now to finding the Captain's treasure.

"Sorry it took me so long, Mr. Holigard. But Bill Hastings' real name was Wilmot and not William. But this is all the material I could find." She set books on the table and said, "When you have finished, Mr. Holigard, ring that bell there by the door and I'll come back. There is paper and pencil, so please do not write on the pages."

"Thank you, Mrs. Ashbury."

He opened the first book and followed the alphabetical order of title grantees. And under the H's, there it was, two parcels of land granted to Wilmot Hastings in the Rockabema Township and a second parcel granted to his brother Gus Hastings also in the Rockabema Township. Wilmot's lot being situated on what was later named West Hastings Brook and Gus Hastings lot was situated nearer what was later named East Hastings Brook, just west of the old caribou migration trail. Each lot was forty three acres and granted as homestead lots. But the lots returned to the District of Maine in 1814 when both Hastings family abandoned the lots and moved back to Bucksport. Wilmot and Gus had left their families to fight in the War of 1812, and were killed. The families then left and the land was returned to the District.

Holigard copied the exact description of the two lots. "Oh, Mrs. Ashbury, would you have a surveyor's map of this lot or a copy of a tax map?"

"We have a rough lay-out sketch of that area, by Rusfus Greenleaf. In later years I understand he did a complete mapping of that area. That map we do not have."

Mrs. Ashbury gave Holigard an old oilcloth sketch of that area. East and West Hastings Brooks were on the sketch, but there was nothing to signify any buildings or settlements. This sketch would get him close. All he would have to do, would be to find the town office in Rockabema Plt., which according to Greenleaf's sketch was approximately 15 miles north of the town of Patten.

"Thank you, Mrs. Ashbury. You have been most helpful."
He stood up to leave.

* * * *

The next day Holigard was on the road again driving north
on I-95. Instead of flying, he rented a car. As he drove north, he
was feeling very pleased with himself. He had discovered who
had taken the Captain's treasure and he was close to finding it.
He pushed himself to drive. He only stopped for gasoline, never
to rest or have lunch.

By early afternoon he drove through the town of Patten.
When he saw the post office, he had a sudden idea: to stop
and ask for directions to the Rockabema Plt. Town Office. The
building was empty except for the one postal worker. "Excuse
me, ma'am. I was wondering if you could give me directions to
the Town Office in Rockabema Plt?"

The woman started to laugh and then said, "The name was
changed to Moro Plt. About 150 years ago. This is the first time
that I have ever heard Moro called the Rockabema Plt. The town
office is at the Bear Mountain Lodge right next to Route 11 on
the left, about 15 miles north of here. You'll want to talk with
Carroll and Deanna Gerow. They own the lodge and they both
are town officers."

"Thank you, ma'am," and he left. He was so obsessed with
finding the treasure he didn't see the big red log truck coming
down the road. It missed him only by inches. On the door of
the cab was the company's name 'Probert Trucking.' "You
barbarian! Watch where you're driving!" he hollered after the
truck. People stopped to look at who was hollering and making
such a fuss.

The further north he drove, the rougher the paved highway
became. *How could anyone live in this god-forsaken wilderness?*
He found the Bear Mountain Lodge without any difficulty. There
were vehicles parked in the driveway, but no one was outside.

He knocked on the door and a woman answered, "Yes, can I help you?" Deanna asked.

"I hope so, ma'am, my name is Horace Holigard and I am doing some research about an early settlement and I was hoping perhaps you might be able to assist me."

"Come in," Deanna said. "Sit down, I'll get my husband, Carroll, he's apt to be more help to you." She disappeared into the main part of the house and left him in what looked like a closed in porch, with dining tables. Perhaps this is where they serve their guests meals.

He sat down and waited. He didn't have long to wait. Carroll came through a doorway that looked like it led to the living room. "Can I help you?" Carroll asked.

Holigard stood up, "I hope so. My name is Horace Holigard and I'm doing some research on the Hastings families that settled near West Hastings Brook and East Hastings Brook. I'm hoping to find these and have a look around."

"My name is Carroll Gerow, and this is my wife, Deanna. The old building near East Hastings, actually isn't near at all to the brook. Route 11 goes right by it. It's on the left about three quarters of a mile beyond Harris Bog, which is on the right. Harris Bog is about a half of a mile beyond Knowles Corner. The old buildings…there ain't much left there now, is at the top of the knoll beyond the bog."

"Carroll," Deanna said, "why don't you drive up and show Mr. Holigard where it is. He'll never be able to find it on his own."

Carroll shook his head agreeably, "I can do that. But I never heard of the other settlement you were talking about. You said on West Hastings?"

"Yes. From the information I have, the main house was right next to the brook, and there were four cleared acres across the brook."

Carroll thought about this briefly and said, "If there ever was a settlement there, then it had to have been upstream from the I.P. Road. Downstream, all the way to the West Branch of Mattawamkeag River is too ledgey and steep for a house or cleared land. As I said, I have never heard about this settlement on the West Branch. I was raised at Knowles Corner, too, and I know most of these woods around here.

"If you drive two miles west on the I.P. road from the paved road, you'll come to West Hastings Brook. Just before you get to the brook, there is another road on the right that crosses a tributary of the brook. To the west of there, there is some flat ground. But I never knew of a farm or settlement there."

"Well, according to old homestead titles in Boston, there was once a farm there between 1808 and 1812."

"As I said, Mr. Holigard, we can't help you there. But if you want to follow us up to the first settlement that you mentioned, we can leave now," Carroll said.

"One more thing before we leave. Would it be possible to get a room here for the night or maybe two?"

"Yes you can," Deanna said. "The only thing though we don't serve meals during the off hunting season."

"That'll be fine."

"You can pick up a lunch at Lougee's Store. It's about a mile down the road from Knowles Corner on Route 212," Deanna added.

* * * *

Carroll and Deanna left Holigard at the top of the knoll and pointed to a clump of bushes. "This is where the house stood. Not much here any more. I hope you find what you are looking for," Carroll said as he and Deanna left.

"Me also." He stumbled through the bushes, kicking old rusty beer cans and broken beer bottles. There were metal pieces lying all over the ground. He didn't know if this was the remains of an old house or a local dump. The trees had been harvested behind the lot and were now overgrown with small trees that grew so thick and close together, that he couldn't walk through them. He didn't know where to start looking for the chest, if it was buried here. He would need a metal detector; a good one that would pick up on non-ferrous metal.

There was nothing more there to see. If the chest was buried there, he would have to clear the trees and bushes away and then use a metal detector. There was no way he would ever get permission from the land owner to clear the land. Maybe he would have better luck at West Hastings.

He turned his car around and drove down Route 212, to Lougee's Store. He saw a sign in a wide yard that said 'Lougee's Beer Store,' but it sure didn't look like a store. It looked more like a rundown wood shed. But Deanna had said he could get a lunch here.

There was one very narrow, short passageway that stopped at a crowded counter. And there sat an old grumpy man. Probably Mr. Lougee.

"Hello, I was told I could get a lunch here."

"Yeah, that's right. I have two sandwiches that I can warm up for you in an electric warmer in back. I have a ham and cheese and a cheese burger," Mr. Lougee said.

"Ham and cheese would be fine."

Lougee put the sandwich in the warmer and came back while it heated. "You from England? You have a British accent."

"Actually, I'm from St. John, New Brunswick. My family is English."

"What are you doing over here? You aren't dressed for fishing or bear hunting."

Holigard wanted to ask him about Hastings settlement on the West Branch, but he decided against it. *Perhaps the fewer people who knew what I'm looking for, the better.* "I'm doing some research."

"You with Chevron Resources?" Lougee asked.

"No, why—is Chevron looking around here for oil?"

"They have been after me to drill exploratory wells on my

property for years. One engineer said he knew there was oil, just by looking at the rocks he found in an old gravel pit on my property.

"I wouldn't sign the lease. I won't live long enough to see any royalties. I wanted to sell Chevron my 120 acres for a $1,000 an acre. But they wouldn't do that, either.

"They are up on the side of Mt. Chase now, exploratory drilling."

Holigard bought a bottle of soda with his sandwich, "Thank you, Mr. Lougee."

CHAPTER 11

Ian was spending more time in Kedgwick than he was at his own home. During that winter, he was using up a lot of extra vacation time that had accumulated. All through his career he had lost the extra time off, preferring to work. But now, since he had met Maria, he had found that life with her was more important than work. And because of this new interest, Ian knew it was time to retire. He hated having to give up the game, but if he didn't, he knew that life with Maria would not be any different than the other two marriages. No, it was time to give it up and let someone younger take over. His biggest regret, if you could call it that, would be...well, the game with Parnell Purchase would be over.

Ian began to laugh out loud at himself then, and wondering what John Henri Corriveau would have thought of him giving up the game for the love of a woman.

So, on August 15th, Ian signed his retirement papers. His retirement would be effective on September 16.

During that interim, Ian would awaken during the night and question if he was doing the right thing by retiring. And inevitably Maria would come to focus and then he would know the time was right for retirement.

He began counting the days and one evening two weeks before he retired, he had finished eating supper and was about to get ready for bed when the telephone rang. The caller was from A.L.E.R.T. U.S., and he was reporting there were three bear hunters from Baltimore, Maryland, who were riding the roads in beyond Shin Pond that were looking to kill whatever they saw. "Be careful warden, these three have had a lot to drink and had just picked up another six-pack of beer," the caller from A.L.E.R.T. U.S. said.

Ian put his uniform back on and fastened his gun belt. He drove like lightning towards the Crommet field, an old farm that once supported the early lumbering days. Now the fields were pretty much grown up with old apple trees, and apples attracted deer when they were ripe.

The three could be anywhere in an area of 300,000 acres that was accessible by roads beyond Shin Pond. He decided that rather than look for them, he would wait in a corner of the Crommet field and let them come to him. If the three were actually looking to kill something, he knew they could not drive by the Crommet field without checking it out. He backed his pickup into a sheltered corner of the field, where he would not be seen, if they were using a spotlight. He flicked all the toggle switches, shutting off all of the pickup lights. He even turned his radio off; the truck engine was shut off and both windows rolled down. It was a dark moonless night. His adrenaline was already flow in his veins and he had to pee.

He waited patiently; his total concentration on catching the night hunters.

There were headlights reflecting off the trees. By the shadows, Ian knew the approaching vehicle was coming in and not the one he wanted. It drove by the field and Ian could hear the vehicle, as it slowed and turned onto the Snowshoe Road a quarter of a mile up the road.

All was quiet again. He wished he had had time to put up a thermos of coffee. He could use a cup right now. But at that moment Ian heard a rifle shot, and it sounded like it came from the other end of the field. His first instinct was to get out and chase after the shot. But he knew better than to do that. He waited and it wasn't long before he could see headlights coming towards him. The vehicle was coming out. And not the same vehicle that had just turned onto the Snowshoe Road.

He waited. The vehicle was moving slow. As it approached the field road that Ian had driven into the field on, a flashlight beam was extended into the field from the front passenger seat. The vehicle drove by. But this was all Ian needed to prove a case of night hunting. He started his pickup and drove out to the road, without lights. The other vehicle was about 200 yards down the road and was attempting to turn around and come back. Probably to drive into the field this time. Ian was on the road by now and committed. He drove right up to the turning vehicle and snapped on the bluelight and then the headlights. There were three men in a station wagon.

Ian jumped out of his pickup with flashlight in hand. The three were looking at him and there was a lot of movement. He knew they had been drinking and were possibly intoxicated, so he used language he was sure they wouldn't mistake. He hollered, "Don't you fucking move!"

All three put their hands up over their head. This was the first time Ian had seen this. The passenger in back started crying and saying, "Don't shoot! Don't shoot!" The two in front were speechless. He wanted to laugh.

As Ian approached the vehicle he could smell the strong aroma of gun powder. He also noticed that the passenger in back had the rifle; the front passenger had a four cell flashlight. "You three are under arrest for night hunting. You," and he pointed to the guy holding the rifle, "pass me the rifle. Butt first."

He did and Ian removed a live round from the chamber and a clip holding three more shells. He also noticed an empty shell on the floor in front of the back passenger.

After securing the rifle, he frisked each of the three, one at a time and all he recovered was one hunting knife. "Okay, what did you shoot at just before you came around the corner of the road, back there?" No one answered. "Well, that doesn't really make any difference. You were driving," and he was now talking to the driver, "that makes you responsible for what goes on inside here. And you," now he was talking to the front seat passenger, "were using the light to illuminate the field looking for animals. And you," now he was talking to the passenger in the back seat, "had the rifle, and you shot at something. That makes all three of you culpable participants of night hunting. I'm going to take you to jail in East Millinocket. If you can't make bail, then I'll have to take you to the county jail in Bangor. And since all three of you have been drinking, I can not let you drive your car to East Millinocket. I'll call out another warden and he'll drive your car for you. Now, why don't you have a seat back inside of your car. We'll have to wait for a few minutes."

Ian radioed the dispatcher at the Houlton State Police Barracks and asked him to telephone Warden Alvin Theriault and ask him to come to the Crommet Field asap. While he waited for Alvin, he knew he should probably charge the driver with operating under the influence, but from his experience with the courts, the night hunting charge would be dropped in a plea agreement.

While they waited, the three in the station wagon were having a lot to say amongst themselves. Ian chuckled to himself. He had them over the proverbial barrel and he and they knew it.

After about twenty minutes, Alvin arrived. "What have you here, Ian? The dispatcher just said you needed help."

"These three are under arrest for night hunting and I can't let any one of them drive their car and follow me to East Millinocket, because they have all been drinking."

"Sure, who do you want me to take?"

"I'll take the driver and the one in back. He was the shooter."

"Did they kill anything?" Alvin asked.

"They fired one shot, but deny that. After we come back, I want to look around. I have enough already to prove night hunting without a dead deer. But that would be frosting on the cake."

* * * *

On their way to East Millinocket, the driver asked "What happens if we don't come back for court?"

"Your bail, which will be $1,000 each, will be forfeited and the judge will issue a warrant for your arrest, which will be good for seven years."

"What about the rifle? That belongs to my grandfather."

"That will become property of the State, whether you skip court or not."

"Then there ain't no way we're coming back. We'll stop at the Kittery Trading Post on the way back and buy a new rifle for my grandfather."

The three didn't have enough money for bail, so one of them called a relative and the $3,000 was wired up by Western Union.

Ian and Alvin returned to the Crommet field. "This is one hell of a way to end your career, Ian. Any regrets?"

"Yes, until I think about Maria, and then I know I'm doing the right thing."

* * * *

Back at the field, "Where were they when you heard the shot?"

"I was in that corner back there," and Ian pointed to an obscure corner in the field, "and the shot sounded like it came from around the corner in the road. He hit something. There was a bang and then immediately following, a *waup* sound. Like the bullet had hit something."

Ian parked his pickup at the corner and Alvin walked the right side of the road and Ian the left. "What exactly are we looking for? An empty casing?"

"I have the casing in my pocket. Look for tracks, blood, anything that might indicate what they shot at."

After walking both sides of the road back and forth several times, the only thing of interest that was found with a bullet hole was a yellow road sign. "I bet they shot at this sign. They were out raising hell and when they didn't find anything to kill, they shot this sign."

"Well, Ian, you got three night hunters out of it at least. That's a pretty good way to end your career."

"Thanks for your help, Alvin."

* * * *

It was too late to think about going to bed now. Ian fixed a pot of coffee and wrote up a report for the District Attorney. Ian had scheduled the arraignment the following week. That way, he would have all of his court work complete and finished when he retired.

When he had finished the paperwork, he sat out on the porch with a steaming cup of coffee, thinking about Maria. The stars were still bright over head. The air was cool and crisp and so quiet. Off to the east, he could just hear the B&A Train as the huge engines backed off, coming down through Dudley Siding. He was in his element there on the porch with a cup of coffee in his hands and listening to the night sounds. "I hope Maria won't be too upset if I sleep outside on an occasion."

CHAPTER 12

Horace Holigard didn't sleep much that night. He was obsessed with finding the Captain's treasure, now that he was so close. He firmly believed that it was still buried at one of the two Hastings settlements. And if it was there and if he could find it, there was no force strong enough to prevent him from reclaiming it. Finally, after five generations, the wealth would be his. The loss of the treasure in 1808 had finally left the Captain demented. He would not allow that to happen to himself. He had very methodically researched and investigated the theft of the treasure and its final location. No, no one, now, was going to stop him.

Horace had never spent much time in the woods or wilderness and he didn't now feel secure or comfortable being in the vast wilderness of northern Maine, alone. He donned casual attire for trekking in the woods and removed a small caliber handgun, a .25 automatic, from his valise and put it in his pocket.

He left everything else in his cabin. He would be returning later. He drove north on Route 11, beyond Knowles Corner and to the I.P. Road, just beyond the Harris Bog. There was no street sign at the mouth of the road, but he had followed Mr. Gerow's directions explicitly. Then he followed this road for two miles and came to a brook crossing. "This has to be West Hastings Brook."

Downstream the contour of the land was indeed too steep and ledgey to farm, but upstream the contour of the land appeared to be flat. He turned around to take the road that followed up along the brook. After about a mile, the road forked and he

223

took the left which crossed a smaller stream. *This must be the tributary that Mr. Gerow spoke about.*

He found a wide place next to the road and parked his car out of the way. He didn't have a compass and he wasn't sure he would know how to use it if he had one. He went west from the road and in a few minutes he came to the main branch of West Hastings Brook. He crossed the brook, because the walking was easier. The ground was flat and dry and more trees and fewer bushes.

On the extreme west side of this level area, he found a pile of rocks. He turned around with a renewed interest in this piece of flat ground he had just crossed and realized that this must have been the cleared area Hastings had made. *Then the buildings would be upstream somewhere, and across the brook.*

He began to walk in a zig-zag pattern across the old cleared ground back to the brook. When he had reached the brook, he turned around and took an objective look at the ground he had just traversed, trying to visualize how it would look without the trees. He knew he was in the right location.

The east side of the brook rose about five feet above the brook. A natural spot to build a house. He saw the squared-off area of green fir trees, but this didn't mean anything to him, until he stumbled over the remains of an old wood stove top. That's all that remained of the stove, just the top. The rest had rusted and disintegrated. He found old window screens and metal hinges. "This has to be where the house was!" He was jubilant now.

He walked back and forth through the small fir trees while kicking at the moss laying between the trees. "I'm going to need a metal detector."

He left the spot where he figured the house must have been and started looking at the ground contour on this side of the brook, more closely. He slowly walked around the wooded area and back and forth across it. When he found the bleached bones of the bear, he kicked at the bones without much interest. He saw the hole the bear had dug, not realizing that the treasure his family had sought after for so long had been buried in this hole.

He walked on and eventually found the remains of the root cellar Gus had made. This really sparked his curiosity. But he would need a spade or shovel to dig through the ruins. He walked around some more, but he couldn't find anything else that interested him. He had been at it for hours now and he was tired and hungry. But he was so close, he was sure of it, that he didn't want to stop. But without a spade and a metal detector there was nothing more he could do here.

*   *   *   *

As he drove along the I.P. Road towards Route 11, he decided to take a trip to Houlton to the registry of deeds and find out who owned this land and purchase a metal detector and a spade.

The registry of deeds wasn't difficult to locate. It was in the same building as the Superior Court and adjacent to the County Jail.

"Good morning, how may I help you?" Joyce Burns asked.

"Good morning Ms. Burns. My name is Horace Holigard and I am doing some research in the Knowles Corner area of the county and I am trying to find the ownership of land in T7-R5."

"If you will follow me, Mr. Holigard, that should be simple enough to find. How far back do you wish to go?"

"Oh, I'm only interested in the present ownership."

Ms. Burns pulled a large red cover book off the shelf and removed a folded map from inside the cover. She unfolded the map on the table top. "Now Mr. Holigard, which piece of property are you interested in? As you can see there are very few land owners."

Horace pointed to the West Branch area of Hastings Brook. "This piece here."

Ms. Burns wrote down the map and page number and the lot number and then removed another book from the shelf and turned to the correct listing. "That particular piece, Mr. Holigard, is owned by the International Paper Company, i.e., I.P. In fact, they own most of the entire township."

"Thank you, madam. And could you direct me to a local electronics store?"

"Sure where are you parked?"

"Right out front on Military Street."

"You drive past the jail and take the left. Follow that until you come to Main Street. Turn right and there is a Radio Shack Store on your left."

"Thank you Ms. Burns. Have a nice day. I surely will."

Ms. Burns gave excellent directions. He found the store and just by chance, "We have one super-dooper detector left. It'll detect non-ferrous metals also."

"That is exactly what I am looking for." Horace paid for the detector, but not until the sales rep agreed to assemble it.

He stopped at Horten's Building Supply on his way back and purchased a spade. It was too late in the day to continue searching, so he returned to his cabin at Bear Mountain Lodge in Moro Plt. and Deanna invited him to have supper with her and Carroll.

* * * *

Horace was up early the next morning and left quietly so not to awaken the Gerows. At first he thought about going to the settlement that was along side of Route 11, but decided against it, as he had found more interesting prospects at West Hastings.

He retraced his steps until he came to the main branch of the brook, then he went upstream where the buildings had been. He was most interested in the old root cellar, although he had no idea that that was what it was. He began digging and pulling out the old rotten logs. For a break, he would scan the area with the metal detector before more digging. He found several old rusted spikes and the bales to metal buckets.

He dug and dug, until he came to undisturbed ground on all

three sides and the floor. And the metal detector was no longer picking up any signals.

He wasn't discouraged though. Horace knew the treasure lay buried somewhere in this small area. He wiped the sweat from his face and started using the metal detector in a grid pattern over the entire area.

*   *   *   *

After breakfast that morning, Ian decided to take a drive in on the Old Umcolcus Road. And instead of following it towards Umcolcus Lake, the woods operator for I.P., Maurice Bugbee, had put in a new road that went south through T7-R5 and connected up to an already existing road that came north from the I.P. Road, crossing a tributary at West Hastings. Bugbee had some French cutters working off this new road and they just might be tempted at trying to take a moose home with them. Since this was the tail end of the work week.

There was some real nice wood in there for the crews. Tall, straight spruce and heavy on the trunk. Beautiful thick maple, only there wasn't a paying market yet for high quality hardwood. Ian hoped the hardwood would be left standing for now. As he drove along, not in any hurry, *This is surely some grand deer and moose habitat.*

Beaver were already starting to dam up and plug one culvert. *Oh well, next week that'll be another game warden's worry.* This trip seemed like a ride through nostalgia.

About a mile before this new road intersected with the I.P. Road, Ian found a rather unusual car parked alongside the road. It could have been only an early morning bear hunter. But, whatever the reason for being there, Ian's curiosity was ignited. He backed up, so his pickup would be off the road also, and he eased his door shut quietly.

Ian knew what lay west of the road. This is where he had found the bear skeleton and the gold disc. He had no idea this morning that the person who had parked the car by the road, would be a direct descendent of the person who had originally stolen the gold from the Spanish galleon in 1808. (Who had the Spanish stolen it from?)

Quietly, Ian went directly to where the square-off block of fir trees were growing, where the old building had once stood. He waited concealed behind the tree thicket. This was a lot like waiting for a night hunter to come hunt the field he was in. From this vantage point he could see the hole the bear had dug and he could look across the brook to the now grown up area.

He waited patiently. He could hear something moving across the brook in what had once been cleared land and he didn't think it was an animal. Once in a while he saw movement, but not enough to see what it was. He waited.

* * * *

Horace crossed the brook to the grown-up clearing and began scanning the ground using a grid pattern across this piece also. He found old rusting horse shoes and broken bits of chain. He was getting tired, but he was not discouraged. He crossed back onto the east side of the brook and stood and looked at the hole the bear had dug. As he stood there looking at the hole he began to wonder if the treasure had been buried here and someone, had by chance, stumbled onto it. He began to scan the hole with his metal detector.

Ian knew now what this person was looking for. He quietly worked his way over to Holigard standing in the hole. Holigard's attention was so fixed on the hole and what he hoped to find, he didn't see Ian standing above him.

"Whatever it is you're looking for, Mister, you won't find it in there," Ian said.

Holigard was shakened almost out of his shoes. He jumped back totally surprised and when he hit the bank, he sat down in the hole. When he could compose himself, he stood up and stepped up out of the hole. "What do you know about what I'm looking for," he said defiantly.

"Well, you see a couple of years ago, I had some bear problems, so I set a trap for that bear," he pointed to the bones. "That bear was so big and strong, it broke the chain the trap was tethered to and ran off. I followed his trail here. You see those two trees," he pointed towards two white maple trees, "he got the trap caught in between those trees and started clawing at the ground and dug this hole." He was hoping to keep Roscoe's name out of this.

"That old bear couldn't have dug in a more convenient place."

"Why is that?" Holigard asked.

Ian pulled out the gold disc from his left pants pocket and held it out to show Holigard. "Because he dug this up." Ian noticed the changed expression suddenly come over Holigard's face. "You don't have to worry. This is the only one. I know, because I dug and dug looking for more."

Without thinking about what he was doing, Holigard withdrew his small handgun from his pocket and pointed it at Ian. Ian was wearing his service revolver, but it wasn't visible. Often times while hiking in the woods, he would put the loose end of the holster into his back pants pocket to keep it from bouncing around. He never carried handcuffs on his gunbelt, unless he was working night hunters, and he never carried extra bullets, nor radio or any other attachment. So naturally, Holigard thought him unarmed.

"Now, warden," Holigard said, "give me that disc. It belongs to me."

"Why does it belong to you?" Ian asked defiantly.

"Because in 1808, Gus and Wilmot Hastings stole a chest of considerable wealth, that my fifth Great-Grandfather Captain Horace Holigard had buried on Grand Manan Island. And now I have finally located it."

"And who did Captain Holigard steal it from?" Ian asked.

"That doesn't matter now. Those were different times. Now give me that disc!" Holigard was almost shouting.

"And if I don't, are you going to shoot me over one piece of gold? I have already told you, there is no more in that hole. Maybe there hasn't been for more than 150 years. When the Hastings left here, maybe they took the chest with them and this one piece was left behind." Ian was stalling for time.

"No warden. I did my research. The treasure never left here. Now give me that gold!"

Ian tossed it at Holigard's feet. And when he bent down to retrieve it, Ian jumped him and grabbed his left arm, with the gun. This move surprised Holigard and he dropped his handgun and Ian twisted his arm behind his back.

"That was a very stupid thing to do, Mr. Holigard. Now, I'm arresting you for armed robbery and terrorizing with a firearm. These charges should keep you secure behind bars for a good long time." Now Ian wished he had his handcuffs with him. But he'd make do without them.

"Now Mr. Holigard, if I let go of your arm, are you going to act like a gentleman? Or do I deck you and carry you out of here over my shoulder?"

Holigard had no doubt that Ian meant every word he spoke. "I won't give you any trouble, warden."

"Good, you walk ahead of me, that way," and he pointed.

In a few minutes they were back on the gravel road, in sight of their vehicles. Ian radioed the state police dispatcher and requested a wrecker to tow Holigard's vehicle to the impound yard at the barracks.

While they waited for the wrecker, Holigard said, "Do you have any idea how many years and how much effort...well, how long my family has been looking for this treasure?"

"I have no idea," Ian said.

"All this work, and now, when I finally discover who stole it in 1808 and it was hidden, only to discover now, that it isn't here." Holigard was really beside himself with anguish.

"Maybe the two Hastings brothers discovered they couldn't farm these woods, they packed up and left," Ian commented.

"No. That's not it. The brothers left their families here and went to fight in the War of 1812 and were killed. From all of the research that I have done, I firmly believe that when the Hastings women and kids left, the treasure was also left, because they knew nothing about it. None of the gold or gemstones have ever turned up until recently." And Ian knew full well who had the treasure now and why Roscoe was so secretive about his sudden appearance of wealth.

"Well, Mr. Holigard, when I found that one gold disc, the rest of the treasure had apparently been removed many years earlier. I only found the one disc, because of that bear clawing at the ground. As I said, I dug and dug and didn't find anything else.

"But all of that now Mr. Holigard, is the least of your worries. You are facing serious charges."

Horace Holigard V didn't seem to mind the charges facing him. He was preoccupied with the disappearance of the treasure. Where was it now? Who had found it way out here in the middle of nowhere? Where would he begin his search now?

The wrecker finally arrived and after the driver had the car in tow, Ian took Mr. Holigard to the county jail in Houlton and charged him with Armed Robbery and Terrorizing with a firearm. Ian knew Holigard would be in prison for many years and Roscoe and Renée would be safe.

* * * *

Ian left Horace Holigard in the capable hands of the deputy sheriff at the county jail. It was the middle of the afternoon and he hadn't had anything to eat since breakfast; and that was ten hours ago. He ordered the meatloaf dinner at the Elm Tree Diner there in Houlton and a cup of hot coffee.

All while he ate his meal, he kept thinking about Holigard,

the Captain and his treasure and Roscoe and Renée. He began to laugh out loud and people were turning in their seats to see what he was laughing about. He wished he knew the whole story about the treasure and how it ended up buried at West Hastings Brook.

He finished his dinner and left a generous tip for the waitress. Instead of taking the interstate, I-95, back to Smyrna; the more direct route, he decided to take a leisurely drive along Route 2 for nostalgia. Even though this was not his district, until he came to the Smyrna Mills Townline, Ian was acquainted with most of the people along the way.

At Smyrna Mills he turned onto the Smyrna Center Road. This was old farm land that was growing back to nature. The road made a loop through this old farm land and came back to Route 2. Every mile along the drive held memories for Ian. He was as acquainted with each small woods road that left the paved road and the woods behind each old farm, as he was with the lines on the palm of his hand.

In Smyrna he turned north onto Route 212 and instead of driving home at Knowles Corner, he took a detour onto the Clark Settlement Road. This road went through some old farm land that had mostly grown back to nature also, and it came out onto the Moro Townline Road on top of Mitchell Hill. This was an infamous road for night hunters.

The old farms had not been very prosperous and as the old timers died, the younger heirs found new and better paying jobs, away. But these old farms were excellent habitat for deer. Particularly at night. There were few houses near these old farm lands and night hunters liked that.

Before gasoline prices rose to 45.9¢ a gallon, the local people would often make a loop around the Clark Road at night, simply to see the deer. On almost any evening, it wouldn't be unusual to see thirty or forty deer in the old fields.

Beyond the Lawlor farm, the Clark Road made a ninety degree turn to the left. There was a narrow dirt road that continued on, straight ahead, off the turn that eventually went close to the falls on East Hastings Brook in Moro Plt. "I'll have to take Maria and Eric into see the falls."

He drove slowly towards the Moro Townline Road, as the many memories of events that took place along this road, raced through his mind. Tears clouded his vision and he had to stop and wipe them with a handkerchief. Could he really give all this up? Well, he had already signed his retirement papers, so whether he was ready or not, his career as a game warden would come to an end in two days. But he would be starting a new life with Maria.

He continued on and at the Warden's Rock, Ian began laughing so hard, he had to pull over and stop, before he ran off the road. He shut his pickup off and got out to walk around and stretch his legs, as he recalled one night here at the Warden's Rock.

When he was hired as a game warden, he was put right to work without any training. That would come six months later. He was given a pair of binoculars, portable radio, a gun and a summons book, with the hopes he would use good common sense. To help him at night and to learn the tricks of the trade of catching night hunters, Ian's supervisor had asked a retired supervisor, Virgil Brown, to come out of retirement for that fall to work with him.

Ian knew how to hunt at night. One of the first questions asked of him at his first interview in Augusta, was if he had ever night hunted. The next question: had he ever been caught. He knew how to hunt at night; now he was being asked to put this knowledge to work, chasing after other night hunters.

Two weeks into his career, Virgil Brown had made arrangements to meet with Ian at 7 p.m. behind the old building at Hall's Corner. The west end of the Townline Road in Moro. Ian left his car there and got in with Virgil, and drove without headlights, out along the Townline Road, to the Clark Settlement Road in Merrill. The night was clear and cold and there was no moon.

Virgil stopped his car next to the Warden's Rock and got out. He hated to sit inside. He poured himself a cup of hot tea and Ian had a cup of hot coffee. There had been no traffic on the Clark Road at all, and only a very few vehicles using the Townline Road.

They stood next to Virgil's car on the Clark Road, listening and watching for lights. From the Warden's Rock they could see long distances across the tree tops to other fields along the Townline Road and the Clark Road. "This is an excellent place to sit and watch," Virgil said. "If anyone is out night hunting, they will eventually try this route before going home. Over the years, a lot of night hunters have been caught right here. Granted, many of them were out for their first experience at night hunting. But I have also caught a few notorious night hunters along this road."

Virgil and Ian both had just poured themselves another cup of tea and coffee, when they each saw lights shining into the trees next to them. A vehicle was coming up from behind them from the direction of the Lawlor farm. They threw their cups away and Virgil got into his car and started it up and took off towards the Townline Road, before Ian could get in. He stood there in the road dumb-founded.

He stood out like a sore thumb there on the road side. The only place to hide was behind the Warden's Rock. This rock was about four feet tall and sat on the shoulder of the road. The vehicle was still coming, slowly. Ian was excited and his breathing was heavy, not to say anything about his heart.

He had an idea: peek out around the corner of the rock with his binoculars so he could get the license plate number. This was a good idea he decided. Later he could call this number into the police dispatcher for an ownership identity.

When the vehicle came up over a little rise in the road the headlights blinded Ian and he pulled back behind the rock. The vehicle stopped and Ian's heart was beating like a sledge-hammer. He had stopped breathing. What Ian didn't know then, was that binoculars under headlights look exactly like deer eyes.

The vehicle started moving again. Ian had to change positions and put his weight on his other knee. *Where had Virgil gone?* Ian could walk faster than this vehicle was driving. Eventually, it pulled up beside the rock and stopped. The passenger window was opened and the passenger stuck out a rifle with a 2-cell flashlight clipped to the barrel. In that fraction of a second, Ian recognized the rifle as a model 742 Remington automatic, and probably a .30 06. The passenger fully extended the rifle to within six inches of Ian's nose.

The passenger was as surprised to see a game warden looking at him from the other end of his rifle as Ian was surprised to think that his career may end right here. The passenger hollered, "Holy shit! It's a fucking game warden! Get the hell out of here!"

The vehicle took off spraying Ian with rocks and gravel. Ian was new to the game and forgot he had a handgun strapped to his side. He picked up a rock the size of a softball and ran after the fleeing vehicle. After a quarter of a mile, he had to stop running. There was no way he was going to run that vehicle down. He stopped and was catching his breath, and for the first time noticed the rock he was still holding. He threw it off the road and started to laugh out loud at himself. This would be a story that he would not tell anyone for a good many years.

Ian walked back to the rock, and thinking about this experience. His adrenaline was still flowing, as he was filled with the excitement. He knew he was made for this line of work.

Virgil returned with the car, just as Ian got to the rock. Ian still had no idea where he had disappeared to, but he learned that Virgil had been close by, by his next question. "I wonder why they put that light down across the field?" This told Ian, he had to have been watching.

Ian replied, "They must have seen me behind the rock." He wasn't about to tell a retired supervisor that the two night hunters had seen the reflections in the binocular eye pieces and had mistaken those for deer eyes. He wasn't about to embarrass himself.

"Did you recognize the vehicle, Ian?" Virgil asked.

"No, it was a car and not a pickup. I did get the license plate number."

"Well, we'll call that into the police dispatch and have them run a check."

After about an hour the dispatcher came back with the information. The vehicle was registered to Paley McMann of Mars Hill, Maine. "The other one will be his brother, Grath. Paley would be driving and Grath would be the shooter. Damn good with a rifle too. Just ask your supervisor, Charles Vernon. He was chasing them one night for night hunting and Grath leaned out the back window and shot at Charles. He hit the driver's door handle. In court, he said he was shooting at the headlight. He did some hard time for that."

"In the morning, I'll call Charles and let him know the two brothers were here. He'll want to come down and work them with you if they come back."

The next week the two brothers showed up with a camper that they parked in an old farm yard adjacent to the Moro Townline Road, between the Millbrook Road and the old Darling homestead.

When Supervisor Charles Vernon learned of this he brought in six more wardens to help out. Retired Supervisor Virgil Brown was on one side of Bates Hill, using a pair of binoculars as deer eyes at the edge of a clover field and Warden Dan Glidden was on the other side of Bates Hill using a set of hand held eyes at the edge of an old apple orchard. The eight wardens worked the deer eyes there every night for a week trying to get Grath and Paley to shine a light into the clover field or apple orchard, illuminating deer, but they would drive by, as if they had no interest. Ian had not said anything to the other wardens about being caught by these two brothers the previous week with binoculars under headlights. He was too embarrassed to say anything. Being brand new and all.

Ian began laughing again and tears streaked down his face. He had been leaning against the Warden's Rock, as he was happily remembering those early days. He got back into his pickup, still laughing. He started down the road towards the Townline Road. But a quarter of a mile from the Warden's Rock, there was another larger rock and this was named after him. Ian's Rock. Driving in the daylight, you wouldn't notice it so much. The rock, like the Warden's Rock sat on the shoulder of the road. Even closer to the driveable roadway. And there was just the slightest turn in the road.

A year later after the incident at the Warden's Rock with the McMann brothers, Ian was again confronted with these two night hunting in his district. This particular night, Ian was following behind them without headlights. If they shot anything that night, Ian was going to be there to catch them in the act.

It was another dark moonless night and as the brothers went by Warden's Rock, for some reason they accelerated and Ian was driving about 40 mph trying to catch up. The McMann brothers were now beyond Ian's Rock and by looking at their taillights, Ian thought the road was straight. But he hit the rock head-on at 40 mph. The rock stood five feet tall and didn't budge when he hit it.

Ian was momentarily stunned, as he sat there wondering what had happened and watching the flames under the hood. The hood was buckled. Not wanting to miss a chance at the McMann brothers, Ian grabbed his flashlight and binoculars and ran down across the field so he could watch them as they drove down Mitchell Hill on the Townline Road. The year before, they had shot a deer under an apple tree on this hill.

As Ian ran across the field, he watched for lights coming down the hill. He never saw any lights and as he stood now just uphill from Gary Mitchell's house, he could look out across the Townline Road all the way to the top of Bates Hill, about five miles away. There wasn't a light in sight. The McMann brothers had turned towards Route 2 and driven out the other way.

Ian walked back to his defunct vehicle. It sat peacefully with the hood smashed up against the rock. Ian's stomach turned over and he was sickened by the sight. It was totaled.

* * * *

Ian stepped out of his pickup and walked over to look at the rock. The scratches and brown paint were still there on the rock. "One hell of a way to get a rock named after you." He laughed some more. And again tears clouded his vision. He was giving all of this up. There would be no more chasing night hunters or outlaws. Only in his memories. But there were enough memories to fill a book.

Things were beginning to change within the department, in Augusta, and he wasn't so sure he could live with the new changes. Maybe Maria had come into his life for another reason, one that even she was not aware of.

Yes, he would miss the game, but he was excited by the prospects of starting life over with Maria.

* * * *

He didn't eat anything for supper that night. Instead, he sat out on his porch in the cool crisp September air. Sipping a brandy and smoking a cigar. Tomorrow would be his last official day as a game warden. Would he miss it? He knew damn well he would. But he would miss Maria more if he didn't retire. He didn't want to lose her, like he had his first two wives.

At 10 o'clock, he heard the train backing off at Dudley Siding. At midnight, he went inside and to bed.

* * * *

Ian awoke early the next morning, before daylight. The excitement of the previous day still sending surges of adrenaline through his body. He went for a walk while it was still just a misty daylight. Truckers that passed him waved and sounded their air horns. A final salute. Everyone knew this was Ian's last day.

After the walk, he put his uniform on and got into his pickup and drove out to the old Umcolcus Lake Road to visit Roscoe and Renée. Instead of taking the direct route past Bugbee's lumber camps, he took the road that crossed the tributary to West Hastings and followed that until it intersected with Bugbee's new road.

He saw a partridge, a ten-point buck and two bull moose fighting. Bugbee was loading a truck that was backed into the loader across the road. Ian would have to wait. He didn't mind.

When the trailer was fully loaded with spruce trees, the driver pulled the truck off the road so Ian could pass. He waved to say "Thank you."

He parked his pickup at the same spot near the T8-R5 andT7-R5 Township line. He followed his own trail from the road to Roscoe's cabin. Both Roscoe and Renée were sitting in the cool autumn air on the porch enjoying the view and a cup of hot coffee.

Renée saw Ian come around the corner of the cabin, "Good morning, Ian. What brings you way in here so early?"

"I woke up early and decided I'd come in for breakfast," he smiled.

"That sounds like a good idea. I'll go get started," Renée said.

Roscoe knew there was more to this visit than wanting breakfast, but he would let Ian bring it up himself, without asking.

Renée brought a cup of coffee out for Ian while she prepared bacon and eggs. The two men sat silently for awhile, sipping their coffee.

"Ian, don't take offense with what I'm about to say."

"No, go ahead."

"You have always suspected me of poaching, haven't you? I'm not offended."

"At first, yes. Then I started watching you more closely, more out of curiosity than anything. But I soon learned that you were a man of integrity. I tried to compare you with Parnell Purchase, but you two are so completely different."

"I had a suspicion I was being watched, when I started finding snowshoe tracks where there shouldn't have been any or a boot track in the mud, again where there shouldn't have been any. I thought maybe you were watching me, but I didn't care. I wasn't doing anything illegal."

The two talked and sipped coffee until Renée announced, "Breakfast is ready."

"Why does food always taste better when someone else does the cooking? These eggs and bacon are delicious Renée!"

"When will you and Maria get married?" she asked.

"Today is my last day as a game warden. The wedding will be in a few days."

Ian had noticed that Roscoe had been building a stone fireplace. "This is a beautiful fireplace, Roscoe."

"Thank you, it's a lot of heavy work."

Renée put the dishes in the sink and poured more coffee and made another pot and then all three sat in the living room, looking out of the huge picture window at the lake.

"I ran into someone rather peculiar yesterday. Actually, I arrested him and took him to jail in Houlton."

"Who was it?" Renée asked.

"He had an English accent, but was from St. John, New Brunswick," Ian was watching the expressions on their faces, "a Horace Holigard V. Quite an arrogant fellow."

Renée stopped breathing and held her breath and then she released it with a big sigh. Roscoe remained silent, but his face had lost all color.

"You said you arrested him?" Roscoe asked.

"Yes. Yesterday morning I was checking out one of Bugbee's new wood roads that eventually connects to the road by West Hastings Brook, that intersects with the I.P. Road. I found a car pulled over to the roadside, about a mile up from the I.P. Road. Right where I had parked when I found the bear skeleton and the gold disc. I had no idea what was going on. It might have been only an early morning bear hunter, but I didn't think so. I walked in and waited behind the fir thicket where the Hastings house had once stood. Eventually this Holigard came into view as he was criss-crossing the old cleared land across the brook. As if he was looking for something." Ian looked first at Roscoe and then at Renée; they both looked worried.

Ian continued. "After a while he crossed the brook and found the hole the bear had dug. That's when I stepped out and showed him the gold disc that I had found and told him there was no more. He became quite belligerent and pulled a handgun out and threatened to shoot me, if I didn't give him the gold disc. We talked for a short while and he kept getting angrier and angrier.

"I finally caught him off guard and got his gun away from him and arrested him for armed robbery and terrorizing. Once he is convicted, he'll spend about ten years in prison and then with a felony record, he won't be allowed in the United States ever again. I told him the treasure is gone and he had better forget about it.

"At least, whoever did find it, can now rest peacefully." He looked at Renée and Roscoe and smiled. Never asking if they were the ones who had the treasure. There really wasn't any need of asking.

"We met him once at King's Landing, at the museum there. He told us the story about the Captain's treasure being stolen in 1808. He said, that today it would be valued at about $4.7 million. He told us quite a story, how dedicated the Captain was and how he was going to use it for the war effort in 1812 and all that. But I'd like to know who the Captain stole it from," Roscoe said.

Roscoe got up then and went into the bedroom and in a brief moment he was back again. "The other day, Renée and I were walking along the shore when we found these pretty stones. We didn't know but you and Maria would like to have them for a wedding gift." Roscoe gave him six uncut diamonds and four uncut sapphire stones.

Ian held them in his hand and said, "These sure are pretty rocks," and he put them in his pocket.

"That sure is a nice looking fireplace, Roscoe."

"It should be, the material is really expensive. About four million dollars worth." Ian choked on this coffee and spit it up on the floor. They all laughed.

Ian got up to go. "Where to now, Ian? You can't do much in only hours left before you retire," Roscoe asked.

"I think I'll drive into St. Croix Lake and visit Parnell Purchase and tell him it's been a great game."

The End

EPILOGUE

In 1987, while exploring around West Hastings Brook and Tributaries—I wasn't looking for anything in particular, except maybe a good place to hunt that fall—I found myself standing in a rather unusual forest setting.

Up until this point I had been hiking through rough and rocky terrain. The ground littered with knolls and hummocks. This new setting was flat level ground and no rocks. There were tall straight spruce trees. As I wandered around, I came to a pile of rocks that were mostly moss covered at the west edge of this level area. I decided that this piece of ground had probably been cultivated at an earlier time. But why, way out there from nowhere?

I wandered around this area; it had been picked clean of rocks. I estimated that about four acres had been cleared. I found this intriguing, but not comprehending at all, why here?

I kept exploring and crossed the main branch of the brook. The brook bank rose about five feet above the brook and I found a squared off section where a very dense thicket of fir trees were growing. I know from experience that when a building is burned, the fire will burn away all nutrients in the soil, leaving it barren for many years. Until one day when seeds start to germinate and the whole area is overgrown with a thicket of small trees. In this case, fir trees.

All this was corroborated when I found old rusted pieces to a stove, metal hinges and other rusting pieces. At first, I thought that this must have been an elaborate trapper's camp. But a trapper would not have cleared the land nor built such a large camp. I had also found old remains of a log bridge crossing the brook.

Two days later, I was visiting Hubert and Emma Furrow at their camp on Rockabema Lake in Moro Plantation. And over a cup of coffee, Hubert told me a story about two Hastings brothers who had traveled up from the coastal area around 1808 and built two settlements in T7-R5. One next to the present day Route 11, about a mile and a half north of Knowles Corner and the other one on West Hastings Brook. Mr. Furrow, through his research, believed the two brothers may have taken some treasure (pirates) and moved away from the coast, far inland to T7-R5, in fear of being discovered by whomever they had taken the treasure from.

In 1812, the two brothers left their families in the wilderness to fight against the British and were killed. If they had homesteaded in the wilderness in T7-R5 to evade the law, then it wouldn't be reasonable to think that they would leave their sanctuary to fight in the war. When the war was over and the two brothers failed to come home, the two families packed up and left.

* * * *

If there ever was any treasure, in those times, it would be reasonable to believe that the men would not have told their women or children about it, or where it was buried—for safekeeping, as well as for their own safety.

Therefore, it is reasonable to believe that when the women and children left, they carried with them what they could of household items and probably closed the doors and not set fire to the buildings. Perhaps one of the large land owners had found the buildings and fearing a homestead claim had had the buildings burned.

Was there ever any treasure? I can't say for sure, one way or the other. But I do speculate, why in 1808 two families left the coastal region and traveled so far inland, beyond any roads or people and hacked out two farms in the wilderness. The hardships they would have had to endure to reach Knowles Corner, using only primitive trails, would be staggering to comprehend. They journeyed to Knowles Corner for a particular reason, and away from the law was not it.

This will forever remain a mystery:

A QUANDRY AT KNOWLES CORNER

* * * *

I would like to thank Hubert Furrow for the research he had done concerning the two Hastings settlements. At the time, I doubt if he ever figured that this information would some day be used in a book.

Gerald Mitchell is a real character and I would like to thank him for his stories and history that helped to make writing this book possible. And for his permission to use his stories. Gerald did have a small log camp tucked away in a cedar thicket on the west shore of Batch Pond, from which he trapped beaver and chased bobcats with his dog. He was caught once for trapping beaver during the closed season, but not at Batch Pond or by me. He was near Bear Brook in Dyer Brook behind his dairy farm, and Amos Steen from Patten was the warden.

Fred and Lucille Smith were fictional as was the story told about them, although a similar event had occurred.

Roscoe Patch and Renée were also fictional and their cabin was situated where Frank McMannus had had his camp.

All of Ian Randall's stories are true. They are some of my many encounters with those who had stepped on to the other side of the fish and game laws. The individuals in these capers are real; I just changed their names.

There are many more stories to be told. Perhaps in another book.

Author, Randall Probert

Randall Probert lived and was raised in Strong,Maine; a small town in the western mountains of Maine. Six months after graduating from high school, he left the small town behind for Baltimore, Maryland and a Marine Engineering School, situated downtown near what was then called "The Block". Because of bad weather, the flight from Portland to New York was canceled and this made him late for the connecting flight to Baltimore. A young kid and alone from the backwoods of Maine finally found his way to Washington DC and boarded a bus from there to Baltimore. After leaving the Merchant Marines, he went to an aviation school in Lexington, Massachusetts.

During his interview for Maine Game Warden he was asked, "You have gone from the high seas to the air. . .are you sure you want to be a Game Warden?" Mr. Probert retired from Warden Service in 1997 and started writing historical novels about the history in the areas where he patrolled as a game warden, with his own experiences as a game warden as those of the wardens in his books. Mr. Probert has since expanded his purview and has written 2 science fiction books, *PARADIGM* and *PARADIGM II,* and has written a mystical adventure, *AN ESOTERIC JOURNEY.* Mr. Probert is also currently working on another historical novel, which should be available in the spring, 2015.

Other Books by Randall Probert

A Forgotten Legacy

An Eloquent Caper

Courier de Bois

Katrina's Valley

Mysteries at Matagamon Lake

A Warden's Worry

Paradigm

Trial at Norway Dam

A Grafton Tale

Paradigm II

Train to Barnjum

A Trapper's Legacy

An Esoteric Journey

The Three Day Club

Eben McNinch